ARROYO

Some other books
by Donald R. Burleson:

NOVEL

Flute Song / *The Roswell Crewman*
(Black Mesa Press, 1996 / 1997)

SHORT STORY COLLECTIONS

Beyond the Lamplight
(Jack O'Lantern Press, 1996)
Four Shadowings
(Necronomicon Press, 1994)
Lemon Drops and Other Horrors
(Hobgoblin Press, 1993)

LITERARY CRITICISM

Begging to Differ: Deconstructionist Readings
(Hobgoblin Press, 1992)
Lovecraft: Disturbing the Universe
(University Press of Kentucky, 1990)
H.P. Lovecraft: A Critical Study
(Greenwood Press, 1983)

ARROYO

DONALD R. BURLESON

BLACKMESAPRESS

ROSWELL, NEW MEXICO
1999

Published by
BLACK MESA PRESS
P.O. Box 583
Roswell, NM 88202-0583 USA

PUBLISHER'S NOTE: This is a work of fiction. All characters in this novel are fictional, and any resemblance between them and real persons, living or dead, human or alien, is entirely coincidental and unintended. (Francisco Vásquez de Coronado was of course real, but his mention here is for fictional purposes.) Though its locale is real, the town of Chasco, New Mexico does not exist and is not intended to resemble any real town; all real geographical locales mentioned in the novel are employed fictionally. So far as the author or publishers know, NOPAL (a fanciful choice along the lines of the well-known Top Secret MAJIC) is not really a government security classification codeword, past or present, and neither this nor any other expression in the novel is intended to reflect any trademark or other registered name.

Library of Congress Catalog Card Number: 98-093529

ISBN: 0-9649580-2-3

Printed in the USA by

MORRIS PUBLISHING

3212 East Highway 30 • Kearney, NE 68847 • 1-800-650-7888

For

Glenn Dennis

This whole day have I followed in the rocks,
And you have changed and flowed from shape to shape,
First as a raven on whose ancient wings
Scarcely a feather lingered, then you seemed
A weasel moving on from stone to stone,
And now at last you wear a human shape,
A thin grey man half lost in gathering night.

——William Butler Yeats,
"To the Rose Upon the Rood of Time"

1

She stirred, shifted in her resting place, stretched her long sinewy legs, blinked her ancient eyes once, twice. Across the desert plain, the sun was setting beyond the Capitan Mountains in a watercolor frenzy of red and orange and gold, painting the New Mexico sky with dream, and Araña, getting slowly to her feet, cast a bizarre jumble of shadows out over the warm sand.

To an observer it would have been abundantly clear why people called her Araña, "spider," for her spasmodic yet oddly controlled movements reminded one of the scuttering of a great angular arachnid, furtive and somehow appalling. Her very act now of rising, from where she had been squatting in the ragged shadow of a large mesquite, would have been unsettling to watch. At first she was a nondescript cluster of rags huddled in the sand. A closer look would have revealed two dark eyes embedded in a saurian nest of folds and wrinkles that only a certain amount of scrutiny could have resolved into a face. When she began to move, it was initially

7

only a directionless kind of shudder. She scissored herself halfway up on her bony arms, bringing her legs up and out at incomprehensible angles, and when, still at a crouch, she shifted her weight from her arms to her legs, the meager mass of her body had a disconcerting way of swiveling off in unexpected directions from one moment to the next, until she stood, thin and withered but strangely regal, stood at her full height and cast a wraithlike shadow out among the yucca and sagebrush, a desert presence among desert presences.

Night was gathering over the land, and night was her time.

She walked through the moon-washed stillness of the chaparral, taking long, slow strides, the tatters of her garments swishing about her as she went. Later tonight she would sleep, but first she had things to do.

Obscure herbs to gather, words to say over them, sorcery to make.

For she was a *bruja*, a maker of magic, one of those rare, lone figures who wander the desert, outcast and apparently content to be so, feared by their own people, adrift among the spirits of earth and sky, made truly one with Coyote Trickster and Brother Crow and Snake.

The Spanish word *bruja* suited her tolerably well, though there were other words in Tewa, her native tongue, that more nearly captured her essence. The Anglos had sometimes simply called her "witch," reflecting their own pitiable limitations of viewpoint. None of them knew her real name, certainly, or had any clear idea how old she was. In truth, she wasn't sure about her age herself, though she thought she might be somewhere around 85. It mattered little, anyway. At whatever age, by whatever name, she was what she was.

When she went into town, to Roswell or Chasco or Corona or Vaughn, people would sometimes just look at her and say: there's that crazy old Indian woman. And sometimes they would look at her and not say anything, because they didn't see her, didn't know that they were looking at her, didn't even know she was there.

She didn't always look the same.

Even many years ago, in her childhood home of Nambé Pueblo, where there had been a long tradition of witchcraft kept sternly at bay by the tribal priests, she had been thought to be a shapeshifter. The clan priests had taken a dim view of these matters, in her case, because with such a person, especially a *bruja* of extraordinary and dangerous powers, one could never be sure whether her magic was for good or ill, and at an early age she had found herself driven out, loathed by her own people, exiled and alone, a wanderer. It was just as well—here, under the vast open sky, with her feet in the timeless sand and her animal brothers and sisters around her, she was closer to the spirit world.

Walking in the light of the rising moon, she came to a spot at the base of a rocky ridge where there would be certain plants that she knew. Plants that knew her. Squatting among them, she spoke softly to them, stirring them with long, cadaverous fingers, crooning a magic song that had been old when her people lived in Chaco Canyon a thousand years ago. Few people, even few sorcerers, knew *this* song. She gestured with a withered arm, and a whisper of wind rose on the desert, moaning among the rocks, rustling the dry mesquite, crooning with her.

Reaching beneath the rags that covered her chest, she fingered out a leather pouch suspended there on a thong, and clasped the pouch as she sang. It contained an accumulated lifetime of desert magic, personal medicine. Some enchantments would come out of the bag tonight. Some would go in.

By the time she had communed with her spirits, gathering her plants, taking her sustenance, intoning her ancient song—by the time she had made her world real again—the moon had risen high above her to paint the fathomless turquoise sky with bone-white radiance, and she was

9

tired. Curling up where she lay in the sand, she felt herself descend into the sable caverns of dream.

An observer, had one walked past in such a remote and lonely place, would have seen nothing in the moon-drawn shadow of the ridge. Nothing but a scraggly few clumps of mesquite and sagebrush, and perhaps a half-hidden tarantula hole in the sand. But seen or unseen, someone dreamed there.

And her dream-vision was of a time long past, long before her memory but well within her dream-time, a time four centuries gone and more, when under the star-frosted skies of what would one day be New Mexico, the Pueblo Indians found themselves visited by strangers from faraway lands.

Very far away.

2

The year was 1541.

It was spring, but even this usually inspiring rebirth of the sun was hard put to dispel the ravages of the long, bitter winter that had fallen like a cold and pitiless shroud over the desert highlands. The great rivers of the Tiguex region and Cicuyé had frozen like stone, and now that the weather had turned and the sun had reasserted itself, the thaw was so precipitous that the Río Cicuyé had overflowed its banks, running down country in a wild flood and presenting fresh problems to the newcomers who watched its tumultuous torrent from close by.

With the fall of night, the party of explorers, edging some considerable distance down the west bank of the Río Cicuyé and keeping as close to the river as the flooded banks would permit, had encamped in a long band along the nearest dry ground, waiting to see if they would be able to cross the river with their horses and supplies. Somewhere in the confusion of campfires and shadowy human forms huddled against the night, the figure of Francisco Vásquez de Coronado sat among his cohorts, but even in his distinctive attire, his plumed and gilded headpiece which he had not yet quitted, and his glistening armor which reflected the light of a million stars, he would have been difficult to find, in the dark among hundreds of others gathered here: Spanish captains, soldiers, Indian servants and guides and interpreters, eating their simple meal and drawing blankets over their shoulders, blankets hard won in the recent trouble among the Tigua pueblos.

But Captain General Coronado was indeed present, somewhere in the surreal flicker of firelight, and he had already decided that to cross the swollen river the party would have to delay its eastward progress toward the great buffalo plains—and, it was to be hoped, toward the gold and silver paradise of Quivira—would have to stop and build a bridge. The golden streets and jewel-encrusted houses of fabled Quivira would have to wait a few days longer.

Somewhere, also, in the encamped string of explorers along the river, sat the noble form of Don Carlos de Moya. A captain under Coronado, Moya had distinguished himself in the battles at Tiguex, though his piety taught him that this experience should occasion no lofty thoughts of himself. If one came through such travails only slightly wounded—and indeed his wounded arm was less serious than the wounds suffered by Coronado himself at Cíbola—if one survived, it was through the grace of Almighty God; and it was proof that one's cause was just. Had not Pope Alexander VI declared that it was the will of God that Spain should lay claim to these lands, treating all who resisted these rightful annexations as traitors to the Crown, enemies of Christ? It was a holy work, this exploration, and, Moya reflected, cradling his bandaged left arm, one must expect it to be a protracted and sometimes painful trial.

It would all be worth it, he told himself, when the golden splendor of Gran Quivira came into view at last.

But a persistent and disturbing thought nagged at the back of his mind.

Was Quivira real?

Earlier, to the west, the promise of the Seven Golden Cities of Cíbola had turned out to be a bitter disappointment:

12

mud huts instead of palaces, scattered fragments of turquoise instead of gold. Now the new Indian guide, the one they called El Turco, had explained that it was all mere confusion; the true golden land of which legend spoke was Quivira, far to the east across the great buffalo plains, but possibly within reach.

Sighing, and removing his heavy bullhide headpiece, Moya wondered. They had all been misled by the extravagant stories of Fray Marcos de Niza, concerning Cíbola. Could these further promises, these even more fantastic tales of El Turco, not be destined to lead to more disappointment?

Moya, troubled by these thoughts, sat in the wavering glow of his campfire and glanced at the ghostly visages around him, the weary faces of footsoldiers, for only the Spanish sat near the fire. Behind these nodding heads, one could just discern a dimmer multitude of Indian faces, spectral and indistinct in the farther reaches of the firelight. A low murmur of voices, some in Spanish and some in other languages, played among the silhouetted forms like phantom-sounds, and somewhere in the dark, the waters of the Río Cicuyé rushed and babbled, seeking their way, whispering their own watery thoughts.

General Coronado's staff had advised that the bridge across the river would take at least four days to build, so the whole party would be encamped here for a while. Even though it meant some rest for weary feet and backs, the delay was a depressing prospect, when everyone wanted to press onward. Off in the dark, the gurgling of the unseen river seemed faintly mocking, as if it said: your quest will not be easy, my friends, not if I have anything to say about it.

Gradually a deeper hush came over the scene as fatigue overcame the forms huddled along the river beside dying fires. Until now, the men had been without any real sleep for days. No doubt the Captain General, who had been visibly worn out by the day's trek, was already asleep, and Moya himself felt wearier than he had been for a long time. It was going to be good to stretch out in the cool sand—

But someone was approaching.

From out of the dark, a dim group of people, Indians evidently, appeared at the edge of the firelight. These newcomers stood in silence for a while, until at length one of them stepped closer to Captain Moya and spoke. The words were incomprehensible, and Moya leaned around to one side and shook one of his soldiers awake.

"Go and bring me an interpreter."

The soldier gathered his blanket around him and went among the Indians lying nearby, and returned with one of the interpreters on whom the explorers had often had to rely, a young Indian man with an expressionless face.

The newly arrived spokesman repeated his speech, and the young Indian rendered it into broken but adequate Spanish.

"He says that his name is Owl. Among his people he is a medicine man. He has heard of the quest for the golden realm of Quivira, and he has come with news. He wishes to speak to the leader."

Moya shook his head. "Tell him the Captain General is no doubt asleep. It would be folly to wake him for any but an extraordinary reason." He looked toward the visitor, whose face was half hidden in shadow. "Anyway, what news do you bring that is so important?" Beneath his words, the interpreter was murmuring to the newcomer, who then replied at length. The interpreter repeated the speech in Spanish:

"You seek a golden realm far to the east, and whether there is such a place in truth, I cannot say. But much closer by, only fifteen leagues south of where we stand, a more magnificent discovery than Quivira awaits you."

Moya stirred the fire with a stick, to try to dispel the shadows and see the man's face more clearly. The newcomer who called himself Owl was apparently rather aged, and was dressed in buckskin, and was painted brightly about the face. "What marvels can you be talking about," Moya asked him, "to rival what we have heard of Quivira? More gold? More silver?"

"Precious metals," Owl replied through the interpreter, "precious metals beyond your imagining, and much more."

Moya sat and pondered this for a moment, reflecting that if it turned out to be more nonsense like Fray Marcos' description of Cíbola, and if he bothered the Captain General with it now, he might well find himself a bit out of favor with that illustrious figure, and might impair the mission of the whole exploration besides, delaying their discovery of the true wonders they all hoped awaited them.

On the other hand, if what the visitor said held even any residuum of truth—a modest amount of gold or gems, say—the matter might well be worth pursuing, as a side trip. But not at the risk of Coronado's displeasure. He felt certain, in any event, that the Captain General would not object if Moya let him sleep but left word of Moya's own departure, gathering a few men about him and taking a quick trip to the south. The time would otherwise have been wasted anyway, waiting for the bridge across the river to be completed—work that could certainly go forward without Moya's supervision—and assuming no unusually rough country to the south, a fifteen-league march should take less than a day, not much longer even if they stopped to rest, which they most probably would have to do. He could still get there and back in three days, with time to spare before the Captain General's whole party moved on eastward.

There might be a real element of discovery waiting on the other end of this little southward march, and it did not escape his notice that a certain amount of official approval might well then attach itself to one Don Carlos de Moya in the bargain. He turned to face the old Indian again.

"I will take a small party of my men and follow you to the place you describe," Moya said. "We will leave immediately. But I warn you, old one, if your report is false and if you are wasting my time, things are not going to go well for you."

Within the hour, Moya's party, though grumbling and weary, was on the march through the southward desert: Moya himself on horseback, with five Spanish footsoldiers and five Indians (including the young interpreter) following and leading two extra packhorses. Ahead in the darkness, Owl and his small party of perhaps a dozen Indians, on foot, moved like ghosts in the starlight, flanking the shadowy and burbling waters of the river. Both groups moved forward in silence.

At some point, just before dawn, Owl's party turned southwestward across the desert plain, angling away from the river, and Moya and his men followed, trudging through chaparral country dotted with the dusky shapes of sagebrush and low mesquite bushes.

A young Indian came back to mumble to Moya's interpreter that there remained ten leagues' march to the place in question. A general groan went up from the men, and Moya realized that they must all rest before going on, even if it meant a ten-hour march in the coming day. At least they had covered one-third of the distance by night; they could sleep for five or six hours and then go on. He called a halt, and his party bedded down, with Owl's party doing likewise a short distance away.

In the starlit night the scene looked like the one back where they had started, at the camp beside the Río Cicuyé, except that the bubbling murmur of the swollen river was now far beyond hearing, and was replaced by a dry soughing wind through the mesquite and chamisa and sage. Here and there, obscure heads nodded in the dark, seeking sleep.

Curling up in the sand at the base of a ragged-looking mesquite, Moya himself slept. And dreamed.

Strange, fitful dreams. Dreams shifting and unclear, but seemingly—did one really want to recall them?—dreams of spiders.

3

In the east, where a sable depthlessness of night had cast a bewilderment of stars over the New Mexico desert like a magic dust, the faint glimmer of golden sunlight crept into the fabric of the night, infusing the darkness with a pastel blur that slowly, slowly broadened, brightened, ripened into the crimson riot of oncoming day. Long, somber shadows edged out from the hunkered forms of mesquite and cholla and spiky-headed yucca, shadows that played over the sand like the impalpable touch of ghostly fingers, played quietly over the sand and edged slowly back to the source, contracting in the shifting light, ebbing away like a dusky tide as the sunrise, regal and undeniable, filled the whole turquoise sky with blinding brilliance.

In the shade of a mesquite, the dark within a tarantula hole shifted, sending the subtle fibers that stretched across the hole jittering with anticipation. The spider emerged, its sinewy legs spanning the hole and pushing its body out into the dawning sun. The spider ventured a few paces, stopped, angled inself to one side upon half its legs, left the remaining legs suspended a little off the sandy earth, stood motionless, cast its multifaceted gaze upon the rising sun.

The gaze shifted upward, tottered at its new height, focused itself differently.

Now an aged Indian woman raised her arms to welcome the sunrise, letting an ancient song emerge from the dusty depths of her throat to greet the day. It was both a song and a prayer, a prayer that had been old when, across unthinkable seas, the Romans had marched in legions upon neighboring lands and spread their strident dominion to what they thought was the entire world. Araña's song, her prayer, had indeed been old when the pyramids had risen new and majestic above the sands of Egypt, old when Sanskrit was not yet spoken in India.

Araña's song, in its crooning simplicity, stretched back farther into the mists of time than anyone, even Araña, could say. It was a weaving-together of the cosmos, a gesture of interconnectedness, a making-real-again of the world. The ancient woman raised thin angular arms to the rising sun, and thanked the sky-spirits that walked upon the wind, thanked Kokopelli and Brother Crow and Earth Mother for yet another day.

She walked, then, out into the dusty chaparral, gathering plants for her simple meal, and thinking her thoughts.

This was a barren, beautiful land, ringed with distant gray-blue mountains under a fiercely bright sky. This remote prairie, dotted by ranches at great distances apart, lay only perhaps forty miles northwest of Roswell, and perhaps a like distance southeast of Corona, yet it might have been a landscape on the moon, silent and eternal. Araña angled her face to peer into the sky. Far overhead, too high for any but a faint trace of sound to filter down, an airplane left a silvery vapor trail, but even this so quickly dispersed, so quickly melted into a gossamer thread, that it might as well have been a dream.

The ancient woman walked on, toward the little town of Chasco, fifteen or twenty miles to the northeast. She was a shapeshifter, and she would have had other ways to go there, but today the way was to walk, to walk and think.

She remembered her dream, of the tall strangers, Spanish explorers plunging in dust-choked bands across the New Mexico desert, searching eternally for fabled cities of gold. She recalled the figure in her dream, the one who had been enticed down country by the Indian *brujo* who seemed to have been called Owl. This questing Spaniard had been about to make a profound discovery, she felt, one for which he was but ill-prepared to make. But the dawn had gathered her dream-threads to itself, had wakened her before she could see what it was that the helmeted searcher was supposed to encounter.

Perhaps tonight the threads of dream would weave themselves back together, would show her what they had fallen short of showing her before.

Meanwhile, her thoughts spread themselves among a number of other things. Dark things, strange things.

The town of Chasco, for instance, situated upon the very ground, Araña somehow felt sure, to which the inquisitive Spaniard was being led in her dream. For her dream was not merely a dream. This she knew. It was a speaking, a story-telling from the past, every bit as real as the stories that her elders had spoken to her in the days of her youth at Nambé Pueblo, in the years before her powers had made her an outcast, an object of fear even among her own people, who were happy for her to live elsewhere, in the open desert under the open sky and far away from the adobe walls of the pueblo. She was happy to live as a wanderer, too; it gave her time to think her long, long thoughts, such as these thoughts about Chasco.

Ah, the town of Chasco. How many of the Anglos living there, how many Hispanics even, knew some of the things she knew about the place? They were blind, most of them, blind to everything around them. Mountains rose on the horizon but they did not see. Life sprouted and bloomed under their noses but they did not see. The wind howled in a husky flute-chorus in their very ears but they did not hear. The desert could have told them many things. Their dreams could have told them many things, showed them countless things. They chose not to listen, not to see.

But she heard. She saw. Most of them called her "that crazy old Indian woman." But she knew the things she knew.

She walked on, stopping from time to time to rest in the shadow of some outcropping of rock, or the shade of some lonely heat-blasted tree. She wouldn't go all the way into town tonight, preferring to sleep, as always, under the stars. But she was drawn to the town because of things that she knew, and would spend some time there.

In particular, she would visit Arroyo Encantado, that sprawling dry wash that started on the northwest edge of town and reached great probing fingers far, far out into the desert. She knew this arroyo, knew it well. Knew things about it.

Resting in the shelter of a lone tree, she felt for her medicine bag, the leather pouch that hung always around her neck by a thong and contained magic things, power objects gathered over countless years of wandering these desertlands and communing with its spirits. She fingered the bag a little open at the top, rooted in it with a bony finger, and pulled out a tiny strip of dull metal foil.

She held this object for a moment in her hand, murmuring some words over it, feeling its smoothness, remembering that other *brujo*, who had given the object to her many years ago.

It was not of this world.

She thought of what had happened in the desert near here, half a century ago, thought of a fiery silver object screaming to earth, crashing, spilling its innards upon the sand. Its innards and—

Pushing the little piece of foil back into her medicine bag, she walked on, toward Chasco.

Just a few miles outside of the town, she bedded down again for the night, and sought her dreams. Again, when the chalky face of the moon drew itself over the desert plain and illumined only a forlorn tarantula hole in the sand, something stirred once in the depths of the hole and then was still, and dreamed.

4

Curled upon the sand, Carlos de Moya still slept as the sun crept toward its highest point for the day. Moya's fellow travelers slept as well, huddled here and there in the chaparral like some odd herd of animals too dust-laden, too weary to move.

It was something of a shock to Moya, when he slowly opened his eyes and squinted into the towering sun, to see that it was this late in the day. He had hoped for an earlier start on the day's planned march, which was going to be perhaps another ten leagues. But then the party had not bedded down until nearly dawn, and even rising at this hour, close to midday, they had had only a scant few hours' sleep.

Moya rose, dusted himself off, retrieved his helmet from under the sage bush where he had placed it, and looked about. Snores rose from the recumbent forms everywhere around him, dry sounds from dry throats, like the snorting of beasts. He stepped to one side and nudged one of his soldiers with a boot. The man moaned, blinked, and sat up.

"Get everyone up," Moya said, strapping his helmet on. "Right now. It's time to move out."

"Yes, *señor capitán*," the man said, getting to his feet and snapping to attention. "*Ahora mismo.*"

The soldier woke his compatriots, who in turn went among the Indians waking them, both the Indians of Coronado's original party and the party of strangers who were to lead Carlos de Moya down country. Before long, horses were saddled, supply bags were resettled upon the pack animals, and the entire group was trudging off across the prairie toward the southwest.

Moya rode at the head of his party, tall and dignified in the saddle, his helmet nodding as the horse picked its way among the sage bushes and yucca and thorny clusters of cactus. Other soldiers rode behind him, and the Indians walked alongside. Ahead, in the sun-hazy distance, the group of Indian guides, including the *brujo* who called himself Owl, plodded across the desert plain, leaving a wake of swirling dust. They would all march straight through, this time, Moya had decided. No more stops to rest, no stopping even to eat; they could eat on the move.

The landscape seemed scarcely to vary itself as they proceeded. Its vast empty reaches of desert plain, furred over with prairie grasses and broken only here and there by low rocky ridges or the tracings of long arid arroyos, seemed to go on forever, stretching off beyond the limits of vision as if the entire world were a plain of yellow sand. Gradually the sun, behind and to the left, swung over to a position in front and to the right, and sank lower in the blinding blue sky, soon grazing upon the ring of mountains in the distance like a great golden buffalo, nuzzling the horizon until it ate its way through, dropping gradually out of sight to leave the sky dazzled with a crimson halo that soon dimmed and vanished like the evanescence of a dream. Night was coming on, and the questing soldiers had still not reached their goal.

Was there really any goal? Moya could scarcely help wondering if there were, or if this were another form of deception, destined to lead to further disappointments. Was

23

this ragged little band of Indians really leading him anywhere he wished to go? But heaven help them if they were not, he reflected. His, Don Carlos de Moya's, was the holy cause, and heaven help their wretched souls if they were deflecting him, even momentarily, from his aim.

At length he began to have the feeling that the group of Indians in the lead might indeed be taking him somewhere after all, as they seemed to be pointing, talking among themselves with more than usual excitement, gesturing as if the place in question were soon to be at hand. Before long, a place of access to what seemed to be a huge arroyo appeared ahead in the gathering gloom. Arroyos—those odd land-features that people back in Spain could barely believe existed, great long dry rivercourses that ran for leagues through the desert, sandy riverbeds flanked by canyonlike walls of sand shallow in places, but so high in places that one could not see over them, could not see out into the surrounding desert plain. One could walk in these arroyos for days, following their labyrinthine twistings and turnings, could even get lost in them.

Was this arroyo, ahead, the place to which the Indian medicine man had promised to bring them? And was it going to prove to have been worth coming this far?

The party of Indians drew itself into a narrower band and entered the place of ingress to the arroyo, which started out flanked only by low sandy walls but soon, Moya could see now even in the near-darkness, came to be contained between walls taller than a man. An Indian at the rear of the leading party turned to gesture to Moya that he and his men follow the others into the dry wash, and soon all were within the root-twisted walls of sand, trudging through the dry riverbed and trying to keep the leading party in view as it proceeded ahead of them, making odd-angled turns in the maze of the arroyo. The night was growing dark, and it was getting to be difficult to follow the trail, but before long a nearly full moon drew its bony face up over the land and cast a wan but helpful radiance upon the scene, making the arroyo a place of ghostly shadows and ink-black corners. The group up ahead keep marching deeper into the wash, and Moya and his men followed, until after what seemed a long time the party ahead rounded a corner in the dry rivercourse and drew to a stop. Moya and his men came up behind them and stopped as well.

What Moya saw next was something that would make him wonder, for the rest of his life, whether he had lost his reason that night in the desert.

Even in the moonlight, which was pallid and diffuse at best, it was difficult to know exactly what one was seeing. What Moya's eyes seemed to register was that ahead of the party of Indians who had led him here, a larger group of Indians variously stood, sat, or squatted in a wide place in the arroyo just beyond the spot where the leading party had halted. But it wasn't the larger group of Indians that arrested Moya's attention.

It was, rather, the uncanny thing around which they were gathered.

The bright object that hovered birdlike over the sand near the center of the wide space in the riverbed.

The thing was of a silvery appearance, round like a dish, except that it was flat not only on top and bottom but flat also on one curved end, rather like the heel of a boot, and overall perhaps the size of eight or ten horses. It moved slightly, gliding a little this way and that, a handspan above the sandy bottom of the wash, and emitted a humming sound of a sort that Moya had never heard before, rather like some large swarm of insects. It was dimly luminescent, casting enough of its own light onto the surrounding scene for Moya to see the faces of the Indians who stood around the object, close to it. The expressions on their faces seemed to be a blend of wonder and pleasure.

Presently the silvery object settled like an egg into the sand, and the humming ceased.

Moya, his eyes fixed on the thing on the sand, got slowly off his horse and took a few steps forward among the soldiers and Indians who were gathered between him and the object.

"Almighty God," he murmured to no one but himself. "What in the name of all that is holy, is this?"

He looked around in the dark and found the young interpreter and pulled him closer. "What is this thing?" he asked the young man. The moon had risen now, and whether the silver thing shone with its own radiance or reflected the yellow moonlight or both, the light was enough, barely, to distinguish faces.

The interpreter cast a glance at the old *brujo* Owl, who stood nearby. The two Indians exchanged a few quiet words, and the interpreter turned back to look at Carlos de Moya, and spoke in halting Spanish.

"It is the sky-elders," he said. "The wise children from the stars."

Moya shook his head. "What are you saying? I don't understand."

The interpreter only shook his head and nodded toward the silver object, around which a number of Indians and Moya's own Spanish soldiers were gathered at a distance of some arm's-length. Presently a sort of crack opened up in the silver egg, and those standing nearest drew back. A murmur went through the little crowd.

And the opening in the egg enlarged, and a childlike figure stepped out onto the sand.

Moya swallowed hard, removed his helmet, and ran a rough hand through his hair. "Holy Mother of God."

The figure from the silver egg was barely half the height of a man. Its arms and legs were long and thin, but somehow, paradoxically, these limbs appeared both frail and oddly strong. Each hand had four fingers, and no thumb. The head was disproportionately large, pear-like, with dark almond-shaped eyes a little larger than a man's, eyes that now

26

blinked slowly as the little creature swiveled and nodded its head and looked about at the crowd. The face of the thing featured only a thin slit for a mouth, and indentations that might have been orifices suggestive of nostrils and rudimentary ears. The skin was a kind of pale yellowish gray, and contrasted oddly with what seemed to be the thing's tight-fitting clothing, seemingly a sort of light metallic mesh that clung to the creature's contours like skin. The creature raised a thin little arm in a gesture to the Indians and soldiers nearest it, and opened its mouth, emitting a short, mewling sound that might have been a kind of speech, or might not have been, it would have been difficult to say.

The being who stood before them was clearly not human.

Moya, still standing some distance back from the thing, tugged at the interpreter and leaned and whispered to him. "Do you mean to tell me that your people have seen this—this creature before? Is it a demon from hell?" He tried to address his question both to the interpreter and to Owl, who still stood close by.

The interpreter and the old medicine man exchanged quick words, and the interpreter gestured to Moya, speaking in a low voice. "He is no demon. We have seen him, and others like him, many times before. Look, the others are coming out now."

Moya snapped his gaze back to the silvery object, where indeed four more of the diminutive creatures were emerging to stand beside the first. Their large heads nodded in the moonlight in a way that suddenly made Don Carlos de Moya feel that he was immersed in a nightmare.

The aged *brujo* was muttering something to the interpreter, who passed the remark along to Moya. "He says that our people have for some time been learning from the sky-elders."

"Learning?" Moya responded, more sharply than he intended, for some of the soldiers and Indians turned for a moment to look at him, then turned back to gaze upon the creatures from the egg. Moya took the young interpreter by one arm and shook him. "Learning what? What sorts of things? Tell me."

The interpreter brushed Moya's hand off and stood a little back from him. "Things about the world," he said. "Things about the spirits."

"Spirits?" Moya asked. "What spirits?"

"The spirits that walk upon the wind," the interpreter said. "The spirits of Earth Mother and Brother Coyote and Spider Grandmother."

Moya spat into the sand. "Heathen nonsense," he said.

But something was happening, among the creatures from the silver egg.

One of them made a gesture as if to enjoin all to watch and listen closely. It drew one of the Indians—not one of Moya's but one of Owl's—close to it, and seemed to be asking the man to kneel in the sand. Moya, watching, felt something in his mind stir strangely, as if he somehow knew that the little creature was asking the Indian to kneel.

In any case, the Indian did drop to his hands and knees before the little creature, who proceeded to make signs in the air over the Indian with wiry little arms, flexing its eight long fingers and passing its arms above the Indian's back again and again. In Moya's head, there seemed to resonate a kind of chant or song, though whether it was really sound or something originating in his own brain he could not have said. Owl, the old Indian medicine man, had moved quietly up beside the kneeling Indian and was imitating the egg-creature's motions, making passes over the Indian with his arms. Moya was growing more agitated at the sight of what was happening before him, and started to turn to the interpreter to say something.

And that's when it happened.

Don Carlos de Moya, in a life filled with strange and sometimes trying adventures, had never experienced anything remotely like this.

It was as if a wash of—of something: of thought? of light? of sound? of heightened awareness?—rushed upon his mind like a tidal wave, jolting him, filling him with a painfully seering vision. He suddenly understood that the little creatures from the silver egg were speaking directly to his mind, speaking directly to all their minds.

Speaking without words, and without any need of them.

Telling the tale of what was happening, what was being taught here.

The Indian on the ground was learning to be something called, Moya thought, a shapeshifter.

In the half-circle surrounding the kneeling Indian and the little creatures from the sky, the other Indians began to chant and sing in low voices, spontaneously. Or perhaps not spontaneously, perhaps in response to whatever tugging influence their minds were undergoing. Led by Owl, they sang and chanted, and the chant rose on the gentle wind, possibly in chorus with chanting or singing from the sky-children themselves And something truly appalling, to Moya's mind, began to take place.

A kind of cloud or mist gathered about the kneeling Indian, whose sun-bronzed face seemed to be elongating into a kind of furry snout, as if pulled into that shape by invisible fingers, while his limbs seemed to atrophy or curl into problematical shapes. Moya, thinking that his vision was failing, rubbed his eyes, but the cloud did not go away, and it was gathered only about the Indian on the ground, who with his now undeniably bestial face seemed to grow indistinct, grainy-looking, in the swirling cloud, until the vision cleared, knitting itself back into a coherence of light.

And in that light, really the pallid light of the moon, or the light of the moon reflected in the silver egg, or the cold radiance of the egg itself—in that light, there crouched at the little creatures' feet not an Indian but a coyote. Moya could actually smell the animal, a musky, funky odor that hung heavy on the air. The creature yipped once, curled its body and whipped its head around as if seeking a route of escape, and ran off across the sand as the Indians and soldiers scattered to make way for it. In a moment it was gone from sight, farther down the dark arroyo, leaving only a dismal but somehow suggestive howl in its wake, a howl which itself seemed to speak directly to Moya's mind, planting, there, a thought something like: *I am free.*

A silence fell upon the group. Amidst the watching Indians and soldiers, the little creatures simply stood quietly, their heads nodding. The Indian *brujo* Owl made a circular motion in the air with his hand as much as to say that the thing was done. All were silent still, as if what had happened was too striking to be marred by speech.

It was Moya who broke the silence.

"Do I understand you to say," he asked the young interpreter, "that this is what your people learn from the creatures from the silver egg? This pagan sorcery?"

"It is not new to us," the interpreter replied. "We have known of these things four countless years. The sky-children merely teach us more about how to do it. Shapeshifting is a part of our world."

"A demonic part," Moya cried, shaking his head violently. "A Satanic part. It is not part of God's plan for the world, that a man should change into a beast. This is the work of the devil, not the work of God."

"You have your gods," the interpreter said, "and we have ours." All the while, the frail little creatures from the silver egg stood quietly among the Indians, nodding their large heads, shifting slightly on their feet.

"You are guilty of an error of faith, for there is but one true God," Moya exclaimed. "Mary was His mother. Jesus, His son, rose from the dead."

Owl, who came back to stand beside Moya and listened to the translation, said something to the interpreter, who turned to Moya and translated: "Owl says he has risen people from the dead."

"He most certainly has not," Moya replied.

"Yes," the interpreter said, "yes, I am sure he has."

"Blasphemy!" Moya hissed. "The shame of it all, that a pack of heathen dogs would claim to have done what the one son of the one eternal God—!" The interpreter was repeating all this to Owl, who spoke quickly to the interpreter, who in turn said to Moya:

"Your son-of-God was no doubt a *brujo*, a worker of desert magic. There are others. There is magic in all things. A few special people are able to use it. The sky-elders have come to us from time to time over the years to show us—"

"You mean the demons have come to you from the glowing pits of hell to show you the way to perdition," Moya said, snorting so loudly that even the wispy-limbed creatures from the silver egg turned to stare at him, as did all the Indians and soldiers. "And anyway, I thought you brought me here to find precious metals."

Gesturing toward the silver craft upon the sand a short distance away, and toward the lithe creatures who stood around it, the interpreter said, "Is this not better than gold? These beings are from another world, here to bring us wisdom, the wisdom of the spirits."

"Christ is the source of all wisdom," Moya bellowed, practically frothing at the mouth. He reached across and pulled a cudgel from the belt of one of his soldiers and wielded it aloft. "I'll show you your wisdom-bearing gods from another world," he said, striding among the scattering Indians and soldiers and taking up a position beside the nearest of the sky-beings. "If this is a god, then this"—Moya swung the cudgel and struck the little creature a mighty clubbing blow to the head—"this will not harm him. I defy you to say now that he is in fact a god."

The stricken creature brought thin arms up to its head, where the blow of the cudgel had opened a large gash, from which a thin yellow fluid was seeping profusely. The creature cried out in its thin little voice, collapsed to the ground, and was still.

A shock seemed to go through the entire group. The remaining four sky-creatures turned as if by one will and began squeezing themselves through the opening in the silver egg, but in doing so they directed their collective gaze upon Moya for a moment, and it was again as if a mighty wave of thought had crashed upon his brain like the tide upon a shore, shaking him profoundly, filling his head with one wordless thought that seemed to mean: *so it is, with you who do not understand.*

Recovering, however, Moya turned to face the soldiers and Indians. Owl was down upon his knees, his hands upon the fallen sky-creature, his withered face a rictus of sadness. Moya pushed him aside and said, to all: "I rebuke this demonic presence in the name of God, and in the name of the Holy Mother Church, by whose divine authority, through Pope Alexander, we are come to this land to rid it of just such blasphemous outrages and Satanic temptations as this." But these words were nearly drowned out by the humming of the silvery egg, which, closing its portal now, rose above the sand like an unthinkable insect, hovered for a moment, then ascended in a blink of the eye to an astonishing height, fired itself off across the desert sky, and vanished.

Owl, pushing himself slowly to his feet, drew himself up tall in front of Carlos de Moya. The old *brujo*, his rags flapping in the dry breeze that had suddenly come up in the arroyo, looked somehow almost royal, and sounded so when he spoke, though Moya had to wait for the interpreter to repeat the words.

"It is you, unwanted stranger from another land, who are possessed by demons. I could kill you now, in retribution for the life of this noble little creature whom you have slain,

32

but to do so would be a wronging of the spirits. It would suggest that your wretched soul in some way makes amends for that which you have destroyed, when it clearly does not make amends. No, I curse you not to die, but to live—with your ignorance and with the evil that dwells in your heart. And I curse this place, because it has seen the evil done by your hand. Here will dwell something, forever, that is not to be looked upon. I bring it into the world, from the land of the Dark Kachinas who walk in the Silence."

Moya started to run at the *brujo*, but the old man raised his arms in the air and shouted something that seemed, to Moya's disturbed senses anyway, to make the wind rise to a howling tempest in the arroyo, sending a maelstrom of sand churning in the night air. Moya, at the same time, found that he could not move his arms or legs. The flying sand blinded him for a moment, and when his vision cleared and the wind diminished, a great black crow hovered where the medicine man had stood. It cawed once, wheeled, and flew off across the watching moon and was gone.

After a moment Moya found that he could once again move his limbs, and he turned and started to say something to his soldiers to the effect that they prepare to leave, but they and all the Indians were already running back the way they had come, toward the mouth of the arroyo a league or so away. "Wait—" Moya said, but an impression in the corner of his eye made him turn and look farther down into the nighted reaches of the arroyo, beyond where the silver egg had lain upon the sandy bottom.

Something was moving in there, in the shadows, something large and dark.

Moya had only a fleeting glimpse of it, but that was enough to send him sprinting through the arroyo after his soldiers, shouting for them to wait for him.

As he ran, he tried to look back over his shoulder, but had only the jumbled impression of something following, a shapeless thing that blotted out the moonlight in the arroyo and pressed so close behind him that he could almost feel it. Moya, his heart pounding, ran and ran, and finally emerged from the arroyo. Far ahead, the soldiers and Indians were fast disappearing into the night.

Moya caught up with them, and in time he and his men made it back to the main camp beside the roaring Río Cicuyé. When Captain General Francisco Vásquez de Coronado questioned him about the trek, Moya explained that his party had again been misled with promises of precious metals, but that nonetheless it had proven not to be a pointless journey, as it had provided the opportunity for him to correct some errors of religion, to the greater glory of God and the Spanish crown.

With completion of their bridge across the river, Coronado's party pushed onward across the great buffalo plains, seeking their jeweled paradise of Quivira.

Afterward, Don Carlos de Moya would return to Spain, where his life, through various kinds of political disfavor, would undergo deteriorations that made him wish for death. But he would not die until the age of eighty-five, many years after his existence had ceased to be marked by the presence of friends or prosperity. When the end did come, he died penniless and stark staring mad in the streets, and was shoveled into an unmarked grave, like a dog.

Four and a half centuries later he would be, in part, the subject of a dream, a curious nocturnal vision entertained by a curious mind out under the myriad stars of a New Mexico sky. In the dream, he was not the chief player on the scene. Rather, he was one who should have understood, but did not in fact understand, who the chief players were.

5

It was a rotten shame, old Miguel "Jefe" Sandoval told himself, shuffling his feet and stirring up the sandy soil at the side of the road to such heights that to an observer from a distance it might have looked as if someone were driving a tractor along the shoulder of the road and leaving a wake of dust. Yessir, it was a shame when a bar in Corona, New Mexico where you'd visited a thousand times would refuse you credit for a drink, for Christ's sake. Just because he was dressed in rags that some people wouldn't clean a shithouse with. What did he ever wear, anyway? Weren't they used to him by now? Would a cold bottle of Mexican beer have busted their damn budget?

He'd walked this way many times before, into the desert, south out of Corona to the road that turned east toward Chasco, and he'd walked it in hotter weather for sure—at least now in late October it was a little cooler—but he never remembered a thirstier walk than this. The sun was already westering, so if he didn't get a ride pretty soon he might well end up sleeping in a field again down the road somewhere, and even as many times as he'd done that before, he didn't think it would enhance his life at this particular juncture, *mil gracias*, thank you ever so much, especially when his throat was so dry it felt as if it wanted to fold up and close like a strip of beef jerky baking in the sun. Speaking of beef jerky, he'd brought some along ("Take it and get out," the bartender had said) so at least he wouldn't starve, but when he did get around to eating it, it was just going to make him thirstier. He could use a cigarette too, actually, but he didn't have any smokes. Hadn't had any for some time. ¡Carajo! He was getting too old for this shit.

He'd already been walking for at least two hours, he thought. He couldn't remember the last time he'd had a watch that worked, so there was no way to be sure how long he'd been on the road, but maybe it was better not to worry so much about time, especially when one hour was pretty much like the next, and one day pretty much like the day before. Unlike some people, he didn't need a watch to tell him when to be hungry; he was hungry all the time, just about. Sad but true.

Anyhow, it must have been at least a couple of hours now since he'd left the bar in Corona. For a while the road had been flanked by low, gently rolling hills lined in outcroppings of dark stone and peppered with clumps of cedar, but gradually the land had levelled out, and by now there was nothing on either side of the road but endless yellow expanses of range grass dotted by spiky upthrustings of yucca and great armies of cholla cactus standing sentry over the prairie like gaunt soldiers with sausagelike limbs and no discernible heads. It was strange—creepy, even—walking these roads at night, but it was a way of life when you didn't live anywhere in particular. He hoped he'd be off the road, one way or the other, by nightfall. He'd be in Chasco soon enough, tonight or tomorrow, and in Chasco a man who had a friend of two just might be able to get a drink there, you never could tell. It wasn't much of a town, but he did know some folks there. Knew them sort of.

A rumbling sound rose to disturb his thoughts, and for a moment he thought it was the wheezing of his lungs or the grumbling of his stomach, but when he turned to look back down the road behind him he saw that an old pickup truck was laboring toward him, creaking and smoking, one of the local sheep ranchers probably. Sandoval drew aside and raised an arm, and the truck stopped in a cloud of dust.

The driver peered through the cloud and shook his head. "Jefe? That you? Hell, you got so much dust on you I almost didn't know you."

It was, sure enough, one of the ranchers who lived nearby; Sandoval thought his name was Walker or Walters or something. "It's Jefe Sandoval all right, *cuate*. You know me."

"Yeah," the rancher said, "I know you, Jefe, but I'm going to give you a ride anyway. Just up to the turnoff to my gate, though."

Jefe Sandoval hobbled around and climbed into the truck and closed the door with a squeal of metal, and they started off.

"Where you headed, Jefe?" the rancher asked.

"Chasco," the old man said.

"Gonna have a ways to go after I let you off. 'Nother thirteen, fourteen miles."

"Yeah, I know. It's okay, I might get another ride, and anyhow, I got good feet. I ain't too old to walk. I'm only seventy-nine. When I get too old to walk, they can put me in a box."

The rancher chuckled, lighting a cigarette with one hand and guiding the pickup down the dusty road with the other, past infinite stretches of fence, and past cattleguards where little trails led off to nameless places in the desert. "Hell, Jefe, you'll probably outlive us all, if you quit poking big bloody holes in your liver with that crap you drink."

"Can't afford the good stuff, chief," Jefe said.

They rode on in silence for some time, perhaps another ten or twelve miles down toward Chasco, until the rancher pulled to the side, stopping on an unpaved approach to an open gate in the fence, an opening over the rough metal strips of a cattleguard. "Far as we go, Jefe. Wish I could take you all the way in to town, but I gotta get home and turn in. I don't lead no wild night life like you world travelers."

The old man got out of the truck and nodded to the driver. "You've been a help, *amigo*. No kidding. *'Chas gracias.*"

"Don't mention it," the rancher said, pulling the truck closer to the gate and waving. "Hope you get a ride the rest of the way. Say, tell me." He stopped the truck again, close enough to where Jefe stood so that they could still talk. "Why do you spend so much time over in Chasco? Damn near every time I see you, you're either headed to or from there. Place ain't got much of anything going for it, seems to me like. Kind of gives me the willies, to tell you the truth. Why do you go there?"

Standing beside the road, Jefe shrugged. "I know some folks there. *Buena gente.* Know some things about the place. You live in the streets, you hear stuff. You'd be surprised, *amigo.*"

The rancher shook his head and smiled. "Yeah, I guess I probably would. Well, you take care now, old man, you hear?"

Jefe nodded and started back along the road, turning from time to time to watch the rancher's pickup crawling like a disgruntled little insect along the side road to his ranch. By now it was nearly dark, and before long the truck was out of sight.

Trudging on along the road, Jefe hummed an old Spanish song to himself. The words said something about *cinco tequilas*, but he couldn't remember them all. When the sunset behind him faded from crimson to salmon-colored to a colorless uniformity of velvet darkness, the road was hard to walk at first, until a pale moon rose and cast a wan curtain of light out over the desert, bringing the road back into view in a kind of surreal reincarnation that scarcely looked like its daylight self. Nothing really looked the same at night.

Jefe walked for another hour or so, thinking about what the rancher had said about the town of Chasco. He wondered if the man knew that *chasco* in Spanish meant "disappointment," not a very complimentary name for a town. But there was a story behind that. Jefe wasn't sure he had all the details straight, but the way he'd heard it, it had to do with the time Coronado had come across the region and had stopped to build a bridge across the Pecos River, and one of his men had taken a sidetrip away from the main camp in search of some riches that were said to be in the area, about where the town of Chasco was now, but he hadn't found anything, and there had been some kind of trouble, and anyway, the whole thing had been a disappointment. Jefe figured the town was a disappointment to most people today too, but he kind of liked the place in a weird sort of way.

It was probably past midnight when, nibbling a piece of beef jerky as he walked, he reached the point where the main road turned south toward Roswell, and a smaller road led on toward Chasco, which was still probably six or seven miles further on.

Roswell. Now there was another whole can of worms. He knew things about what happened between here and Roswell back in 1947. Things he hadn't ever told anybody because it wasn't healthy, he gathered, to talk about them. To a lot of people he might be just a crazy old man to laugh at, but he knew what he knew. Right down the road here maybe fifteen, sixteen miles, there was a place you could walk out into the desert a few miles and find a ridge where something crashed to earth one summer night back then, more than half a century ago. Something strange.

He'd seen those army people the next day, surrounding the place, stationing soldiers with rifles along the fences, not letting anybody go cross-country off the highway. He'd been gloriously drunk the night before, and had been sleeping it off, lying out in the chaparral to the east of the road, maybe twenty miles north of Roswell, and had watched a big flatbed truck, carrying something covered with an olive-green tarp. The truck had lumbered on great dusty tires up to the roadway, and made its slow way down toward the air base at Roswell.

He knew what it was they were taking there, by God. It was a damn flying saucer, that's what it was.

And he knew other things. He knew about the little bodies that the army people had found scattered around the craft, and had taken away.

But he knew more about it than the army had ever known.

He trudged on across the road and headed toward Chasco, but by now his legs were rubbery with fatigue, and he was going to have to stop for the night. He could always go on into Chasco in the morning, and he could probably even get a ride then, from somebody headed into town. This hour of the night nobody was around. He hadn't seen another car or truck since the rancher had left him off, except for that little car parked off the road a couple of miles back. Walking past, he had thought maybe there was somebody in the front seat, but in the dark he couldn't be sure. *Lástima*, too bad, hell, maybe they could have given him a ride the rest of the way to town.

As it was, he was too tired to walk any further. He ambled over to the edge of the road, crawled over a low barbed wire fence, and found a patch of clear ground, as good a place to sleep as any. He lay down, curled his feet up under him, and made a pillow of one forearm, and closed his eyes.

But not before having one more look at the black dome of sky that hung over him, jewelled with a bewilderment of stars.

What lived out there?

It was too much for a weary old mind to ruminate about, just now, and he heaved a great sigh, and slept.

40

6

Driving from Midland, Texas into the desertlands of southeastern New Mexico was an unreal experience, especially with night coming on. Even to one who had grown up in West Texas and was used to the desert. There was desert, and there was desert; out here, the farther west one went, the more it was like being on Mars, with limitless plains of ruddy sand stretching away to the horizon all around, and miles and miles at a time without any sign of life. Then again from time to time a gaunt, angular windmill would poke its head up in the distance like some sardonic insect, or a pump jack would appear in the oil fields to one side of the road or the other, nodding and raising its great grasshopper head and nodding again to the earth in slow endless cycles of obeisance.

Lisa Jaramillo poked at the buttons on the car radio and migrated from one scratchy distant-sounding station to another, first country-and-western music whining its way out of the gathering night, then some border station dazzling the airwaves with Mexican music: saxophones, accordions, guitars, barroom ballads about gunfights and lost loves. After a while she realized that she valued the silence more than the sound, and shut the radio off.

It was almost night by the time she drove up through Hobbs and Lovington and turned due west, letting the town lights die away behind her, replaced by darkening seas of prairie where an occasional pump jack still reared its head in the gloom. She had thought of stopping in Hobbs, but somehow it didn't feel right. It wasn't quite far enough away.

Not far enough away from her problems. From her feelings.

"Correction," she said to herself as the car nosed its way through the gathering night and turned north onto a lonely stretch of road that would come out, according to what she remembered of her map, up near Caprock somewhere. "Correction, not far enough away from my ex-problems and my ex-feelings."

Were problems ever really ex-problems? Who could tell, maybe they would turn out to be, maybe she really was leaving it all behind. A divorce was a divorce whether you still lived where it happened or not, but it was done, and it was probably for the better. And ex-feelings? She wasn't sure she wanted to try to make sense out of that right now. It had all been over between her and Gary for a long time, the truth to tell, and if there were still some sneaky little feelings, subtle and furtive, feelings for him, hiding in the depths, who was she to try to make sense of the human heart? She was an idiot, she figured, to feel anything for him at all. It certainly didn't make sense to. Emotions might make sense in books and in movies, but they never made sense in real life. Anyway, Gary had cheated on her, and she couldn't handle that. Just couldn't handle it. She didn't want to still love him, not even a little; he didn't deserve it. If there was any mercy at all, those residual feelings would just smolder for a while, dying embers in a guttering fire, just smolder and wink out, leaving only the ash of memory.

Yet maybe in spite of everything, she did still care for him just a little bit.

"Just a squitch," she mumbled. It was her pet expression. ("Have some more coffee?" "Just a squitch.") Surprisingly now these words carried an unpleasant little wave of resentment through her mind, because she remembered Gary, good old pedantic Gary, giving her a hard time about the expression. "There's no such word as *squitch*," he had said, more than once. And when she had gently tried to explain that that was the charm of the thing, he had given her one of those poor-ignorant-creature looks of his, and had followed it with some remark to the effect that maybe anyhow she should be pronouncing it *esquicha*, in keeping with her ethnic heritage. It wasn't the only time he slipped. It wasn't the only time he made it clear, inadvertently, that he resented her being Hispanic. That part hadn't slowed him down a bit when they'd been nineteen years old and what he'd seen in her was a hot little *chiquita*, but there had come a time when even though she had pretty well kept her figure and her face, she wasn't hot little *chiquita* enough for him. A teen Hispanic was one thing, a maturing woman was something else, apparently. Men!

Well, by God, she wasn't Lisa Logan any more. She was Lisa Jaramillo again, and damned proud of it. Her ancestors had been here in the American Southwest since Coronado, and she wondered if he could say the same.

Divorce was nasty business, no denying it. It left scars in the mind, left aching wounds that rendered even what should be pleasant or at least neutral memories somehow unpleasant, left them emotionally colored in very disturbing ways.

The worst part of the whole experience, as it revisited her now, had been seeing the pain in Jerry's face, the incomprehension, the sadness. Jerry was pretty well grown up, but eighteen was only eighteen after all, for all the bravado that kids of his age liked to exhibit, and while he had had friends in school whose parents had split up, he must never have imagined that he would face the same miserable thing himself. He was a good kid, a bit sheltered if anything, a bit fragile when you got right down to it, and he clearly hadn't been ready for what had happened. Kids were never ready for it. How could they be?

This would be the first time, Lisa realized suddenly, that she had ever been apart from Jerry for more than a week or two. (*I'll come visit you, Mom.*) Dabbing at her eyes with the sleeve of her jacket, she sniffed and swallowed hard and snapped her eyes up proud and determined, intent upon the ribbon of road that wound ahead. Enough of this; she had cried all she was going to cry.

Whether that was really going to be true or not, it sounded good to her right now.

This stretch of road seemed to go on forever, meandering through a landscape that would have been featureless, she suspected, even by day, with only a rare windmill or pump jack to break the monotony. Her headlights might well have been the beams from some landroving robot exploring the alien plains and hills of a distant planet. She suddenly felt very, very alone.

But what was it Thoreau had said, at Walden Pond? That he had never found a companion so companionable as solitude? Something like that.

Lisa wondered if old Henry David Thoreau could have maintained that attitude out here in the desert at night, where it wasn't just a little stroll into town, and where if your car broke down it might be days before anyone found you.

At length she reached the turnoff onto the main road, west toward Roswell. Maybe she would stop there for the night. Or maybe not. Maybe she'd drive on up to Corona, or even on to Albuquerque. It was a warm feeling, just when she needed one, to realize that she could do what she damned well pleased.

A little after ten o'clock she passed through the sleepy streets of Roswell. Evidently her subconscious mind had decided, quite on its own, that she wasn't going to stop, not when she could press on. Maybe she would drive all night. She had never done that before, and it just might be fun. Maybe she would drive forever, like someone in a fantasy, to the ends of the earth, through swirling clouds of wonder that blended road with sky until one fell right off into the starry abyss. Out here, one could almost believe that that was possible.

The road north out of Roswell quickly became desolate, almost eerie, as the lights of town fell away behind her, and her enthusiasm began to flag a bit. She understood, after a moment's reflection, what it was. She was simply dog-tired. Her fatigue caught up with her surprisingly fast, making the lightless, undifferentiated land around her seem all the more spectral. Talk about bravado. All that brave inner monologue about driving all night, and going on to the end of the world, was fine and good, but she realized all at once that if she drove much longer, she was going to end up careening to the side of the road, crashing through a barbed wire fence, piling up in a pasture on some old boy's sheep ranch, and this was not her idea, actually, of finding a place to stop for the night. Suddenly Albuquerque seemed unimaginably distant. She wasn't sure she even wanted to go on to Vaughn or Corona. Wasn't there someplace closer?

Rummaging through her memory of the map (why hadn't she studied it more closely?) she thought she recalled a little town up this way, a little east of the turnoff to Corona. She couldn't remember what it was called, until she reached the point where the road forked, and a sign said Corona to the left and Chasco to the right. She turned toward Chasco and kept driving; the sign didn't say how much farther it was, but she had the impression it was only another few miles.

Then again, she thought after going another mile or so, maybe it was farther than she thought, maybe it was as far as going on to Corona would have been.

Damn. Why hadn't she got these things straight in her head when she'd looked at the map?

She pulled the car off the road, crunching the tires through a dry expanse of range grass and weeds, drew up beside a barbed wire fence, checked to see that she was safely off the pavement, shut the engine off, and clicked on the little light over her head. Where the hell was that map? She fumbled around in the mess of papers and other detritus in the front passenger seat, then turned toward the other, more elaborate mess in the back seat, where indeterminate gatherings of paper and other things showed mysterious corners and edges from beneath a jumble of suitcases and cardboard boxes. She knew the map was here somewhere. Everything, Gary used to say, has to be somewhere.

"Shows what you know," she said, startled at how hollow her voice sounded in the dead air of the car.

Well. She clicked the light off and sat for a moment. It couldn't be that much farther into Chasco, and she'd probably feel better about driving the rest of the way in if she rested her eyes for a minute or two. No use denying it, her eyes were tired.

Just a squitch.

She closed them, tilted her head back, and forced herself to relax.

And fell asleep, and dreamed.

Dreamed that something like a half-spider, half-woman was talking to her, drawing her along by the elbow, and trying to show her something hidden in the shadows, something in an obscure corner of a cellar, something that scuttered back out of the light because it didn't want to be seen.

7

So what did he care? It wasn't much of a job anyway.

By the time he was halfway from Artesia to Roswell, Bill Weston had said that to himself at least twenty times. Who could tell—maybe if he said it twenty times more, he'd start believing it. He was trying to be philosophical about it, but at thirty-two he just wasn't used to being treated this way.

Actually, maybe they had done him a favor, laying him off. Maybe he could do better, if something like this forced him to get off his behind and go find another job. He hadn't been dismissed for any lack of quality in his work, that was certain; it was what they called "downsizing" nowadays. (That usually meant: figure out whom you really need the most, and fire them.) In any case, he thought he was managing to keep his sense of humor about the whole thing. Otherwise why would he savor the irony in what he had seen on his pink slip?

Maybe only someone being let go from a small trade-newspaper proofreading job would have thought it was funny. The note had said, in part: *We regret that we are no longer in a position to avial ourselves of your services.* Unless people in high places (the Language Patrol perhaps?) had decided to reformulate the spelling of *avail*, Bill rather suspected that these folks still needed a proofreader.

"Your loss, you illiterate turkeys," he said, passing the turnoff to Dexter and heading on toward the outskirts of Roswell.

In town, he stopped for a bite to eat at a fast-food place on South Main, and it was well after dark by the time he was headed north out of town, past the Roswell Mall and out into sheep ranch country, bleak and endless even when you were driving by day and could see everything around you, let alone driving at night, surrounded by great fathomless seas of darkness. He wasn't even sure where he was going. Tucumcari maybe, possibly even Taos later on, who could say? For now he'd try to get as far as Fort Sumner or Santa Rosa and stop for the night. He had a little money saved, so he wasn't too worried. He'd let himself enjoy a little unscheduled vacation, a few days at least, then nail down a decent job somewhere.

His headlights cut twin cones of illumination into the night. Maybe this was just one of those times when things came to a sort of juncture, one of those points in life when it was time to rethink some things, start fresh. Certainly his romantic involvement with Cindi hadn't worked out the way he'd hoped. Breaking up with her and losing his job all within a couple of days of each other wasn't his idea of getting through the week in the best of shape, but then again maybe it was going to be for the best, on both counts.

Or that couldn't be a classic case of sour-grapes rationalization by any chance, could it? You didn't have Cindi any more, so you didn't really want her, you lost your job so it really never had been any good anyway.

Well, whatever the hell one could say about that, here he was, driving through the desert late at night, with no particular notion about tomorrow or the next day. If this sort of thing was really a necessary juncture in life, he could handle it.

And speaking of junctures, here was one, literally. He hadn't expected a fork in the road. "A spoon maybe," he said to himself, "or almost any kind of standard cutlery. But dear God, not a fork."

He slowed the car and peered at the sign: Corona and Vaughn one way, Chasco the other. If he remembered his map correctly, going through Chasco might be the shorter way to get to Fort Sumner or Santa Rosa, so he took the right side of the fork and kept driving.

A few miles further on, he just happened to be thinking about Cindi and some of the good times they had had together, when he passed a car pulled off on the roadside near a barbed wire fence. He couldn't see if anybody was in it or not.

"Teenagers making a night of it," he said, sighing. Suddenly he felt very lonesome, and Cindi's face refused to stop appearing before him in the magic-lantern dusty swirl of his headlights. The shadow of the roadside car fell away in blackness behind him, and he reflected: go ahead, screw your heads off, you balmy kids. He wasn't jealous.

Not much.

Why should he be jealous, just because he'd spent most of his teen years working his butt off in the oilfields with his uncle, and never had time to do much lovemaking? He'd made up for some lost time on that score, but then here he was, alone again. Well, life came in waves, sometimes up, sometimes down. Peaks and troughs. Better than being flat-line, he supposed.

Chasco, which he'd never seen before, probably wasn't really much of a town even by day, and at night the sidewalks were pretty much rolled up and nothing going on. The road on which he drove into town became Camino del Sol, apparently the main east-west street. Somehow the town kind of gave him the willies, on first glance. And on second glance. After only a few major cross-streets he found that he was already about to leave town again, but he turned right onto Chamisa street when he saw a sputtering neon sign a block south that said *Swan Hotel*. This burg didn't strike him as a thriving tourist metropolis exactly, and he hadn't seen any regular motels either in or outside of town, so the Swan Hotel just might have to do for now. He'd probably stayed in worse places. Drawing closer, he saw that the Swan was a venerable-looking edifice, an old-fashioned hotel several stories tall, with some really wretched-looking pseudo-art-deco work in front, a likeness, more or less, of a black swan, done in faded paint on stucco. *Rates daily or by the week,* another sign proclaimed, and: *Vacancy.*

That was the magic word. Bill Weston was one tired dude right now, and didn't relish any more driving. Fort Sumner and Santa Rosa and Tucumcari could wait. It was late, and he only hoped someone would be on duty at the desk in the lobby. It was going to feel good to rest his bones on just about any kind of bed.

He couldn't quite shake the feeling, though, getting out of his car and heading toward the entrance to the hotel, that there was something creepy about this town. A feeling like that usually meant that you had been reading too many horror stories.

Unless the feeling had a real source, but if it did, he couldn't put his finger on what it was.

8

The lights of Amarillo, Texas fell away behind him like a great constellation of fading stars, and he was in darkness again.

The evening was young. It wouldn't be terribly late even when he got to Clovis, New Mexico, so he could probably go on to Fort Sumner and maybe even all the way down to Chasco tonight, and get there before midnight with any luck. He still had the rental house in Chasco, the one Ross had used, and even though it wasn't anything too great, it would beat the hell out of staying at some dumpy motel.

So Truman Lloyd drove on into the night, looking forward to a gin and tonic and a halfway decent bed. What a life. Sometimes when he drove past lighted towns on such a night as this, doing his job, he caught himself wondering what it might have been like to lead a normal life, have a permanent house, a regular home, a wife meeting him at the door with that gin and tonic, the sound of kids playing in the yard (*Hey Dad, come play ball with us, Mom says it's going to be another hour before dinner*), the drowsy hum of a lawn mower next door, evenings spent talking to normal neighbors over a normal backyard fence on a normal afternoon about normal concerns. Maybe he would have liked that.

Na-a-ah. Who was he kidding?

That wouldn't have been for him. Oh, it might be interesting to live like that, experimentally, for a week or two, but he knew himself too well for that—he'd be busting at the seams to get back out on the road, on secret assignment, doing the kind of thing he had gotten into government service thirty years ago to do.

Yeah, thirty years ago, when (among other things) someone in a little windowless room had asked him, during one of the preliminary interviews: If your government asked you to ram an icepick up the nose of a newborn baby, would you do it? He had said yes, of course, and meant it. It was one of the reasons they hired him. The icepick scenario had been hypothetical, but he'd done almost equally reprehensible things at taxpayer expense over the years, and had no regrets.

Let people have their backyard cookouts and football-watching chips-and-dip parties and trips to Disneyland. And garage-cleanings and mortgages and family arguments and plumbing disasters and dentist bills. God, what pitifully circumscribed lives most people led when you got right down to it. Even most people with ordinary Top Secret clearances didn't have any idea what was really going on. There were senators, there had been presidents, who didn't know a lot of what Truman Lloyd knew.

Truman Lloyd, special senior operative—Group Epsilon. A government agency that officially didn't even exist. Not a cent had ever been appropriated for it in Congress in the usual sense, not a word about it had ever appeared in any document available to anyone without a security clearance a dozen notches above Top Secret. There *was* no Group Epsilon. It had an annual budget in the billions, but it didn't exist. Now *that*, by God, was the way to run things. Quietly and efficiently.

Lloyd passed through the town of Hereford and continued on toward the New Mexico state line. New Mexico—always a special place, always the locus of more

52

secret activity than anywhere else on the planet, Wright-Patterson and Area 51 notwithstanding.

He glanced down at himself in the wan glow of the instrument panel, and snickered at his dress jeans and Western shirt with the flap pockets and the fake pearl buttons, and his fake-turquoise bolo tie. This was the way to dress, out here, to be inconspicuous. It was a real laugh the way movies portrayed high-level secret government operatives as guys in sleek-looking off-the-rack dark suits and sunglasses, as if a mangy halfwit chimpanzee with his head in a bag couldn't spot somebody like that a block away in a sandstorm. Actually Lloyd was almost beginning to enjoy dressing like this; every time he came out here it seemed a little more natural. He'd always thought of himself as a Detroit boy born and bred, but you kind of had to give them some credit, these Southwestern types with their laid-back lifestyle. Of course there was still something kind of corny about the whole thing, this culture with its endlessly droning country-and-western music (if you wanted to call that music) and its cutesy little adobe houses and cactus gardens and cowboys and *Se habla español* signs on every damned used car lot and loan office in sight. It was all a little unreal somehow, when you were used to a cosmopolitan life back East. But maybe he could fit in for a while and at least look as if he more or less belonged in the desert.

He'd better, because he was apparently going to be spending some time out here, this trip.

It was after ten when he crossed the New Mexico state line and headed toward Clovis. Maybe he should have followed his alternative inclination, should have flown from Tulsa, but he'd had to deliver some paperwork in Oklahoma City and brief a couple of field operatives there on an upcoming project, so it was just as well he was driving. Anyway, this whole scenario had been put together without much advance notice; he'd been working on other matters and hadn't expected to be replacing Warren Ross right now.

Ross had spent a great deal of time in New Mexico and had been a good operative, but the dumb shit had let the big C catch up with him. There really wasn't any excuse for anyone at that level in secret government service to die of lung cancer, not when there had been a cure for cancer since 1948.

Lloyd drove on through the night, thinking about how things had developed since the Roswell UFO crash of July 1947.

God, the technological harvest they had reaped from that spacecraft. Truman Lloyd hadn't quite been the proverbial twinkle in his papa's eye yet, back in 1947 when a mysterious heel-shaped airfoil-type object, hit by lightning, crashed a few miles north of Roswell and the military came out and picked up the pieces. No, Lloyd wouldn't be born for another three years, but he probably knew as much about the whole thing as anyone now alive. He felt rather warm about the fact that his folks had named him Truman after the very president who authorized the security classification and coverup of the Roswell UFO crash. To be named Truman—it was fitting, now that he himself was one of the few people privy to all that information.

Yeah, the military had picked up the pieces, and God, what pieces they were. Some of the stuff hadn't made sense at first. Even though the analysis and back-engineering of the debris had subtly taken the world into the computer age and beyond, the irony was that it had been a sort of chicken-and-egg problem initially, in that humankind was being given a huge technological boost, but it wasn't really ready for it, and needed, a little at a time, to tune up its own understanding of a number of things before it could really get rolling, really benefit from all the new ideas. Those microchips that the Army had found in the Roswell craft had sat around for some time before anyone really began to comprehend what they were and how they could be replicated; at first when engineers had examined that technology, they might as well have been gorillas scrutinizing a Swiss watch and wondering what it was and how it worked.

Ah, but in time, think what kinds of advances the alien hardware harvest had yielded: microcircuitry, fiber optics, lasers—the list went on and on, and included, of course, that item that had gotten Lloyd to thinking this evening: the cure for cancer, a medical technique so incredibly and bizarrely advanced that it had to be kept Top Secret, because any public awareness of its nature would have made it obvious, to some people anyway, that it could not have been formulated by human agencies alone. Wildly divergent from all the strains of biochemical and genetic research being done on cancer on unclassified levels, it was a product of alien intelligence, and that fact would be all too clear if the technique were disclosed. So it had gone under wraps like everything else. The greatest medical advance in history, classified above Top Secret.

Too bad Warren Ross hadn't been able to benefit by it as he should have, Lloyd mused, nosing the car though the nearly deserted streets of Clovis, New Mexico. The cure was absolutely reliable unless the patient waited until the very late stages of the disease, in which case it simply didn't work. Lloyd had known Ross, knew how his mind worked, could just hear him thinking: no, these symptoms aren't anything serious, I won't believe that they are, I won't let myself think about it, I feel a little down but all I need is a good vacation, there's nothing really wrong with me. By the time the sappy jerk got himself diagnosed, he had only three weeks to live.

Lighting a cigar, and thinking how pleasant it was to be able to smoke with impunity, Lloyd passed beyond the farthest lights of Clovis and headed west, toward Fort Sumner. Yeah, too bad about Ross, especially when it was avoidable. You never needed to lose a man like that; there were too damned few people you could trust as it was, at this level of secrecy, and Ross had known a great deal about the problems that

Lloyd was coming out here now to work on. Ross could have taken care of all this. But Ross was in a box in the ground.

It all seemed so contradictory when you thought about it, and heaven knows, Lloyd had been thinking about it for a lot of years. At first the coverup of the Roswell crash had been a great success. It was orchestrated to the point of genius. The military had been tracking the object the night it crashed, and they were out in the desert retrieving the craft and the diminutive bodies of the alien crew before sunup the following morning, trucking the bodies to Roswell Army Air Field for preliminary autopsies, later hauling the craft itself out on a flatbed covered by a tarp and rolling the thing right the hell down Main Street in Roswell and through the gate to the air base, and later cleaning (even vacuuming) the ground at the impact site to a fine finish, so that nobody could tell anything had happened there. Later it had been almost a godsend when that rancher had brought in some small pieces of debris found on his sheep ranch some miles northwest of the crash site, because it just created more confusion in the mind of the public. Military authorities higher up directed the base commander to issue a "flying saucer" story, saying that such a thing had crashed on the rancher's land, so that they themselves could trash the story a few hours later, declaring the debris to be a fallen weather balloon, to end the whole affair once and for all. Military and civilian government officials of course gravely threatened everyone who had seen anything, making it quite clear to them that if they ever talked, they and their whole families would be killed. By the end of the week there was no story. Zip. Nothing.

But.

Things hadn't stayed as nailed-down, as quiet, as one would like.

It wasn't the popular furor over Roswell that came later on, it wasn't the books, the movies, the whole popular subculture that thrived on conspiracy theories. That wasn't any problem. It helped, if anything, because to a large sector

56

of the public all the talk about flying saucers and alien bodies just made anyone interested in the subject look all the more foolish. Indeed, Lloyd reflected with a smirk, the government itself had contributed a great deal to the ongoing hype about Roswell just to further discredit the whole thing. No, it wasn't the popularly revived interest in the Roswell incident that posed a problem now.

It was something else, something less tangible.

Loose ends, odd rumors, subtle suggestions, strange little bits of lore.

For some time now, Group Epsilon had been concerned about scattered and insubstantial but somehow disturbing little threads of innuendo that continued to surface now and then, or almost surface. Ross had been down here working on the problem, but hadn't made much headway. He had nosed around, tried to find out what he could, but the irony was, the coverup in many ways was still working, and all too well. What Ross had found was that when some people and their families had been told, even half a century ago and more, that they'd better never talk about things, then in many cases they didn't! You could try to get your seemingly offhand conversation with some old geezer on some park bench to drift around to the subject you had in mind, but if they knew anything they weren't talking. Sooner or later, of course, Ross would have found some source of information, would have fed it to Group Epsilon, but unfortunately Ross was busy now feeding the worms instead, and it was going to be up to Lloyd. Who no doubt was going to run into the same problem: that the threats made to people, to whole families, were still all too potent, because it kept them from talking even when you wanted them to.

It was after eleven by the time Lloyd passed through Fort Sumner and turned southwest and was soon out in the eternal desert again. Not much farther to go now, anyway.

As he drove, Lloyd thought about some of the rumors, some of the wisps of innuendo that he was going to have to try to track down and make sense of, however insubstantial, however subtle they were.

For years there had been rumors that the crash at Roswell had had some survivors, unaccounted for.

What sense that made, exactly, Lloyd couldn't have said, because the military and government retrieval team were on the impact site very promptly, cordoning off the area for miles and miles around, setting up diversionary (phony) crash sites nearby, doing everything necessary to confuse the public and recover the craft and bodies. And by and large that's what they found: bodies. One had lived for a while, but that couldn't account for the faint lingering rumor, repeated by some people, that the crash had had a number of survivors that the military had never known about.

Could that be true? If so, they had probably died, long since. But what other questions did this leave unanswered? Who had seen these crash survivors? Were there still people around who knew things they shouldn't know? Or people whose parents or grandparents had known things they shouldn't know? Were there alien bodies somewhere, bodies that Group Epsilon had never seen but other people, unauthorized people, *had* seen?

Lloyd was going to have to try to find out.

He had to, because this operation had been kept buttoned down for decades, had survived all kinds of challenges, and it wasn't going to be any different now. The public was never going to know the truth about Roswell. Not when disclosing that truth would mean that the government had been lying for more than half a century, had withheld information that every bleeding-heart liberal in the land was going to say humankind had a right to know. Not when the powers-that-really-be had assassinated a president to keep Roswell covered up. Not when scores of political careers and reputations, past and present, would be down the toilet overnight if the truth about Roswell were ever declassified.

No, Group Epsilon still made the decisions as to what people had the right to know. That's the way it had always been, the way it would always be.

But there were problems, and Truman Lloyd was going to have to try to sort them out.

It was a quarter to twelve when he drove into the dusky little town of Chasco, turned left off Mesa Street onto Camino del Sol, then right onto Chamisa Street, and drove past the Swan Hotel and on south another two blocks to the house, which sat on the southeast edge of town. Or such town as Chasco offered, which wasn't much.

He could almost taste that gin-and-tonic nightcap. Then tomorrow—well, in this business tomorrow was always an interesting prospect.

9

North of Roswell and east of Corona and south of Santa Rosa lies the town of Chasco, mostly a place of earth-colored adobe, low-profile round-cornered houses and buildings of earthen colors foregrounded against the desert that stretches endlessly all around. The town, which might strike a visitor unaccustomed to New Mexico as looking more like someplace in Mexico than the United States, lies dreaming in the yellow prairie like a natural excrescence, rather like a stand of mesquite or a cluster of cactus. Chasco somehow gives the impression of something that grew there, organically and naturally, but paradoxically also something that has been there always, and will always endure—unchanging, timeless.

A disembodied observer floating ghostlike through the drowsy streets of the town might find it a curious place. As this diaphanous observer, you would do well to visit Chasco at the onset of evening, when the heat of the day is subsiding and the shadows go creeping out over the land like great stretching fingers of darkness and the town subtly, quietly goes to sleep, like a tired old man on a park bench anywhere in the world, but not quite like that either, because when the town drifts off to its own well-deserved slumber, it does so with a sense of identity and propriety, a sense of belonging. Chasco in some ways, to some eyes, isn't much to look at, but there is no denying that it has its qualities.

Let us suppose that you, the ghostly visitor, have come into town from the west on Camino del Sol, the widest east-west street in Chasco. At first you see residential sidestreets—simple rows of unassuming houses, some of them adobe, some woodframe, some stucco, most with large rusty air conditioners on their roofs—and then you see the fire station on your right, across from a real estate office ensconced in what must once have been a nearly palatial adobe home with vigas in the walls and with windowsills painted turquoise. The north-south cross street here is Old Roswell Road, and crossing here and continuing eastward on Camino del Sol you see the Medical Arts Clinic and a beauty salon on your left, and Lucinda's Cafe on your right, flanked by the Town Hall; the cafe backs up onto a kind of plaza or town square adjacent to the Town Hall, with little paths lined with wooden benches beneath the domed heads of Navajo willow trees. The only other building on this block, down on the southeast corner facing Zia Street on the south and Mesa Street on the east, is Lonnie's Tobacco and News, which you don't see, coming along Camino del Sol, till you cross Mesa Street and glance back to your right. Mesa Street (which, to the north, leads to Fort Sumner) seems to be the major north-south street in the town, and the Town Hall, on the southwest side of the intersection of Mesa and Camino del Sol, frowns down on both streets with an exaggerated sense of superiority imparted by its being a two-story adobe building among more earth-grazing neighbors.

Continuing along eastward, you see a savings bank on your left, flanked by a large vacant field where twisted pipe and fragments of brick stick through dry weeds like the gnarled remains of some odd fossilized beast. On the right you see Melendez Park, with its quaint fountain in the center and its own array of paths and benches. After a few nondescript cross streets you come to the last sizable north-south thoroughfare (if any street in this town deserves so pretentious a description), Chamisa Street. After crossing this intersection, heading east and back out of town, you see on your right (but down a block, on the corner with Zia) the gaudy frontage of the Swan Hotel, taller than its neighbors but old and tired-looking, while on your left you see a strange little store called Paco's Emporium, with odd moon-signs and indecipherable designs painted in bizarre colors on the windows. If you were to hang around town long enough—and a day might be long enough—you might well discover that Paco's, presided over by one Paco Rojas, is a store with a rather dark reputation, though nobody seems to be able to say exactly why. In any event, this is near the east edge of town, and continuing this way just brings you out into the open prairie again, where you might find roads leading eventually to Clovis, New Mexico.

Back in Chasco, the east-west street below Chamisa del Sol, namely Zia Street, affords relatively few discoveries. At the intersection with Old Roswell Road there is a barber shop diagonally across from a gas station, and, on the corner with Mesa, a drugstore faces Lonnie's Tobacco and News across Zia Street. Continuing east along Zia you will find a meat market and another squalid-looking abandoned field, and nothing beyond that but residential streets with countless small houses redolent of quiet poverty. The only major east-west street below Zia is Old Corona Road, where you see a used book store on the southeast corner with Old Roswell Road and a grimy-looking bar on the northeast corner, and, some blocks further east, a tiny bus station with a rattletrap bus pulled up next to it like a tired old dog hunkered down for the night. Further east still, you see the last clear landmark in this direction: a farm machinery place on the corner with Chamisa Street. The rest is residential. '

Above Camino del Sol the next east-west route of any importance is Piñon Street, featuring only a laundry on the corner with Old Roswell Road and a large but dingy-looking hardware store on the corner with Mesa. The rest, where private residences don't take up the space, is all consumed by forlorn store fronts long closed and boarded up or whitewashed, except for a nondenominational church on the corner with Chamisa on the east side of town. Above Piñon there is only one major east-west street, Camposanto Road, so named because it runs past the town cemetery on the west side, featuring nothing the rest of its length but private homes of the poorest sort. It is the same if you go out of town to the north on Mesa Street, or on Chamisa—straggling rows of ill-visaged houses afloat in weedgrown yards where mangy dogs bark and where gaggles of children, puzzled, stare at you for a moment when you pass, then return to their nameless occupations. On nearly any road leading out of town, these impoverished neighborhoods linger for a few blocks before giving way to infinite vistas of open desert.

But going northward up Old Roswell Road, beyond Camposanto, one sees, instead of the usual wretched neighborhoods, only a funeral home (facing the eastern edge of the cemetery) and one large, somehow eerie-looking house on the northwest edge of town, with a lopsided *For Rent* sign in front; house and sign alike are lost in a sea of overgrown prairie grass. Evidently the house has been for rent for quite some time. Perhaps no one wants to rent it because of the proximity of Arroyo Encantado, a large dry wash running behind the house some few hundred yards. But if it's the threat of floods that anyone is worried about, any oldtimer in town could testify that there hasn't been any water in that arroyo in recent memory—and recent memory, for these oldtimers, is counted in decades.

Memory, when it concerns Arroyo Encantado, runs especially long and vivid, if you can get anybody to talk about it. But despite the sleepy-looking nature of the place, you won't find all that many people in Chasco who are inclined just to sit and talk. Sure, you might get a wild yarn or two out of old Jefe Sandoval or some of his ragamuffin cronies on the benches in Melendez Park or around the Town Hall, especially if you offer them a drink or a cigarette, but for the most part people here have their jobs, and they tend to stay quietly, unobtrusively busy doing whatever it is they do.

Altogether there might be eight hundred people living here in Chasco, maybe nine hundred, who could tell? The signs leading into town don't say, and one has the feeling that no one really cares. Hanging around here for a while, one would discover that there are few great passionate political concerns here. There isn't even a local school system; the children (there aren't too many of them) are taken by buses to Corona.

On most occasions, as a wandering ghostly visitor, observing but unobserved, you will find that by and large the people on the streets are simple little desert-town people, some Anglo, some Hispanic, all less than wealthy. But at times, depending on where you are, and when, you might notice that however ordinary most of the people in Chasco appear, some few of them seem to have an odd look about them, difficult to define, just a certain unusual something, as if some rather strange local family had left its genetic wake upon the sea of faces.

One person would stand out in a different way, should you happen to be passing through at the right time to see her: an old Indian woman whose walk, whose motions in general, would tend to give you the creeps for some reason, even making you lie awake a night or two, perhaps, wondering why the sight of her bothered you. And if you thought about it enough, you might come to the conclusion that it was because the old woman, at least the time you happened to see her, moved like a spider. In a way (at least this was probably your impression) she even *looked* like a spider when you saw her, with those gangly legs and those tatters that only a generous spirit would have called clothes. She isn't always in town, the locals will tell you, but if you come at the right time you may see this odd creature passing wisp-like through one quiet side

64

street or another, pausing from time to time for no discernible reason, muttering sometimes to herself in a language that isn't English and isn't Spanish.

If you're so inclined, you might even follow this old woman out to Arroyo Encantado some night. But you might end up wishing you hadn't.

In any case you will find that Chasco offers little enough with which to amuse oneself of an evening. The town goes to bed early, and scarcely even turns over in its sleep. If you walk the streets late at night you will see that the windows of Lucinda's Cafe, facing Camino del Sol, are lighted well into the evening, as are the windows of Lonnie's Tobacco and News, diagonally across the block at the corner of Mesa and Zia. Down on Old Corona Road the bar—a seedy establishment called Jim Ray's—is operating late, occasionally opening its mouth to vomit a polyglot gush of drunks onto the street. Otherwise, the storefronts of Chasco are mostly closed and locked and the windows are shrouded in a darkness broken only by the fevered sputtering of an occasional neon sign or the wan illumination, at wide intervals, of halfhearted streetlamps goosenecked out over the pavement like ridiculous birds standing at a loss in the night.

If you walk far across town, to Chamisa Street on the east side between Piñon and Camino del Sol, you may at first think that Paco's Emporium is open, because there is a suggestion of light and movement inside, but the store is in fact closed at this hour. If you cup your hand around your eyes and lean over and peer through one of the gaudily painted windows, you may see Paco Rojas himself, an Hispanic man of indeterminate age whose distinguished face might almost suit him to be a Conquistador. He will be sitting, on these occasions, at an old card table drawn up near the sales counter, and there may even be someone with him, though you will have little time to ponder this, as he will rise upon noticing you and let down the blinds. Somehow you will sense that this is not an unfriendly gesture, but merely Paco Rojas' way of saying that he needs his privacy.

If you hang around the streets of the town much longer, you will see the lights even at Lucinda's and at Lonnie's and at Jim Ray's go out as the last customers spill out onto the dusky streets and disperse. The curtain falls and the drama, such as it is, is over, at least until another day dawns, a day that may well be much like the one it has displaced.

But in the seemingly featureless progression of time in this little town lost in the desertlands of New Mexico, there is a certain nameless something, an undefined feeling that lingers in the corners of the mind.

A feeling that in some strange and secret way, Chasco, New Mexico is different from any other place on earth.

10

Lisa Jaramillo wasn't accustomed to sleeping in her car. She awoke suddenly, disoriented and uncomfortable. She had a terrible crick in her neck from having slept with her head back against the headrest, turned to one side. Evidently having had a more natural slumber, several birds twittered nearby, perched on barbed wire, and off in the distance she could just make out the grazing forms of sheep. She felt somehow very out of place as a human being, and wondered idly if that were a reasonable way to feel.

Upon her awakening, some strange dream had scrabbled down a hole in the back of her mind, like a spider—in fact hadn't the dream been something about a spider, in a dark place where something *else* moved uneasily in the shadows?—and in the afterglow of this dream it took her a few minutes to remember exactly where she was, and why. Hadn't she intended to go on into—into—damn, what was the name of that little town? Chasco. But after pulling off the road here, she had fallen asleep. It was probably just as well, because if she had been that tired, falling asleep while driving might have been a real possibility, and at the start of this, her new life, she had no intentions of wrapping herself around some fencepost at the side of some remote desert road.

So. Was this the way a new life started, then? Waking up achy and tired in the front seat of a car? With no clear idea where you were going or what you were going to do when you got there, if you got there?

Well, there were worse things.

"A sharp stick in the eye," she said to no one in particular, nodding in agreement with herself. "That'd be worse."

She looked at herself in the rearview mirror, ran a hand through her hair, and sighed. "Still being married to *him*," she added. "That'd be worse too."

She was hungry, and she needed to go to the bathroom. At least the latter was manageable, not exactly in any very dignified manner, mind you, but manageable nonetheless. She opened the car door, climbed out, and looked up and down the road. The end of the world could have come to pass overnight, for all the traffic that was whizzing by—not a car in sight in either direction. There was not a house on the horizon, no people, no sounds. Nothing. Just those sheep grazing in the distance, and she didn't think they'd mind if she answered the eternal call of nature. She squatted down behind the car, in the prairie grass, and tried not to think of her ex-husband with their (now his) newly tiled and freshly painted bathroom.

Back behind the steering wheel, she felt so much better that even the hunger seemed to have subsided; she could wait now, in any case, until she got into town and found someplace to stop for breakfast. She started the engine and pulled the car back up onto the road, heading toward Chasco.

And maybe a mile or two further along, she saw an old man hobbling along the side of the road. He was dressed in an assortment of rags that might almost have been comic if it hadn't been so pitiable, and he was so intent upon making his way along that he didn't even look up as she drove past.

Clearly the man wasn't hitchhiking, didn't expect her to stop, but he was obviously quite old and she really couldn't see just letting him walk the rest of the way to town, out here in the middle of nowhere. Heaven only knew where he had come from; as likely as not he had spent the night in a pasture. She pulled the car half off the road and stopped just a few yards past him, and waited for him to catch up.

When he came wheezing up to the car, she leaned across and popped the passenger-side door open and smiled to him. "You look like you could use a ride."

He climbed in and shut the door, and Lisa pulled the car back onto the road. The old man lifted his hand to tip an imaginary hat to her. "*Chas gracias, señora,*" he said. "I am Miguel Sandoval, *a sus órdenes.* They call me Jefe."

"Well, I'm happy to meet you, Jefe," Lisa said. "I'm Lisa Logan." She winced, catching herself too late. "Lisa Jaramillo."

The old man nodded, and they drove on in silence for a while. At length he turned and asked her, "If you don't mind telling me, *señora,* why in the world is a pleasant young woman coming to Chasco at this hour of the morning?"

She shrugged. "I'm not really sure, Jefe. Right now I'm just kind of—well, looking around. I'll probably just be passing through."

Jefe nodded. "Lots of people just pass through, on their way someplace. But *¿quién sabe?*—maybe you'll want to stay."

As unlikely as this seemed to her at the moment, she replied, "Sure, you never can tell."

They were coming into town now, past a fire station on the right; the signs told her that she was now on Camino del Sol. The town promised to be small but not tiny, as she could see cross streets stretching away into the distance, eastward. Just past the fire station, Jefe raised a gnarled old hand. "You can let me off here, *señora,*" he said.

"Are you sure?" she asked, slowing the car.

"*Sí, vale,*" he said, "and thank you very much for the ride." She stopped just past the fire station, and the old man climbed out of the car, tipped the imaginary hat to her again, and was off up the sidewalk.

Lisa started to drive on, but stopped just beyond the cross street (Old Roswell Road) and parked in front of a little place that proclaimed itself Lucinda's Cafe. A sign in the door said OPEN, and that looked good to her; she was hungrier now than ever. She wondered if the old man, Jefe, was going to be getting anything to eat this morning, and she was half tempted to go back and find him and slip him a few dollars, but when she looked back up the street, he was nowhere to be seen, so she went on into the cafe and got a seat at the counter. She looked around for one of those little newspaper-vending machines but didn't see one. Making a mental note to get a paper later, she turned her attention to the menu, looking down the counter to find someone to wait on her.

The place was fairly busy for a little town like this, so early in the morning, but a waitress took her order quickly, and soon she was ensconced over a plate of ham and eggs and hashbrown potatoes, not to mention a very welcome cup of coffee. All around her, the other diners were chatting in quiet undertones, some in English, some in Spanish, all in that subdued kind of way that for a lot of people is the natural tone in which to start the day. Now that she was assuaging her appetite, the crick in her neck had largely gone away; just a trace of it lingered to remind her of last night's odd sleeping arrangement, but only a little twinge. Just a squitch.

Back out on the street, she felt that something was bothering her, but she couldn't place what it was. Some impression. She turned and went back into the cafe and caught the eye of the waitress who had served her. "Excuse me, is there somewhere I can buy a newspaper?"

"Yes mam," the girl said, "go back out and go east on Camino del Sol till you reach Mesa Street, and turn right and go till you see Zia Street, there's a tobacco store on the corner there that sells papers, you can get one from Albuquerque or Roswell or Santa Rosa."

"Fine," Lisa said, smiling as she went back out the door to the street. "Thank you." She felt the smile fade a bit when she was back outside, because she had confirmed now what the unplaceable impression had been.

That waitress was damned odd-looking.

It wasn't that she was unattractive, exactly, just—strange, somehow. Her head seemed a little larger, or a little rounder, or both, than one would expect for the rest of her body, which was fairly short in stature, though not unusually so, and she had a funny way of sort of tilting or bobbing her head when she turned around. There was something, too, about the eyes; they were rather pronounced, not much larger than most people's, but somehow suggestive in the way they were shaped, rather like almonds. But suggestive of what? They weren't Oriental exactly. They weren't Hispanic or Indian either; the girl had a fairly light complexion, in fact. Overall it was a hard impression to analyze; the girl just struck Lisa as looking—different.

Anyway, there was no need to spend the morning woolgathering over such as that. Lisa got back into her car and headed east, the way she had been going, on Camino del Sol. Turning right onto Mesa Street, she spotted the place the waitress had mentioned, not far down, on the right on the corner with Zia Street. Lonnie's Tobacco and News was a long, low, brown stucco storefront, its windows bristling with a multicolor frenzy of magazines. She parked and went inside, noting the aroma of cigars and pipe tobacco before she even got all the way in the door. A number of customers and magazine-browsers were milling around inside, and she threaded her way among them and picked up a Santa Rosa newspaper and took it to the counter, where a busy but unperturbed-looking mid-fifty-ish man, evidently Lonnie, was ringing up purchases. For a moment she hesitated in front of the register, half thinking that she had forgotten something, but went ahead and paid for her paper.

"Thank you," Lonnie said, eyeing her curiously. "Haven't seen you in here before."

"No," Lisa said, "I'm just passing through. I might stay till tomorrow, actually. Is there a hotel or motel?"

"Only place in town is the Swan Hotel, on Chamisa. You go on down Zia out here and you'll see it when you get past Melendez Park."

"Okay, thanks."

Back outside on the sidewalk, she asked herself a question: Why in hell was she thinking about staying here today and tonight, instead of just going on?

And she didn't know. But suddenly she did know something else—she did know why it was that she had hesitated in there at the register, feeling as if she were forgetting something.

It hadn't been that she was forgetting anything. It was just that she had been struggling to place an impression, something nuzzling at the back of her mind. And when she realized what it was, she somehow found it a little disturbing.

Lonnie had a little bit of that odd look about him too.

Just a suggestion, enough to be noticeable when you thought about it. Something about his head, kind of rounder than most folks', with dark almond-like eyes that seemed somewhat too large. And did he move that way too, like the girl in the diner, sort of bobbing his head as if it were too heavy for the neck, or had she imagined it?

Was there some oddly pervasive family trait here, some kind of subtle trace of inbreeding?

Why did it matter?

Musing, she got in the car and drove east on Zia, spotting the hotel on her left a few blocks down, facing onto Chamisa Street. Still not knowing exactly why she was doing so, she parked in the hotel lot on the corner of Chamisa and Zia and went inside the hotel, thinking that the place looked

72

as if it had seen better days. It didn't seem *too* bad, actually, despite the gaudy pseudo-art-deco frontage; if it had looked really wretched she would probably have just gone on, but she had stayed at times in worse places than this. In the lobby the hotel actually had a kind of charm, with old dark wood trimmings and an air, overall, of fallen opulence.

Clutching her newspaper, she went up to the desk in the lobby. By now, though it made her feel foolish to reflect upon it, she half expected the clerk behind the front desk, an older Anglo woman with her hair pulled back in a huge bun, to have *that* look, like Lonnie and the waitress. The woman, however, looked normal, and Lisa was actually relieved. *You're losing it,* she thought. *Maybe Gary was right, saying you'd have a hard time getting along on your own.* She quickly followed this thought with another: *Gary right about anything? Bullshit.*

"—help you?" The woman's smile had grown a little strained, and Lisa realized that this wasn't the first time she had asked.

"Uh. Oh! Yes, I'm sorry, I was just—I'd like a room."

"Just for tonight?"

"Well, I'm not sure. I might want to stay longer."

The woman pushed an old-fashioned registry book across the counter to her. "We have plenty of room. If you decide you want to stay longer, that'll be okay. I can give you a room on the first floor, just down that hallway, if you'd like."

"That'd be—ah, great," Lisa said. She had hesitated because a man had stepped out of the elevator and walked up to the counter. My, my. Rather tall and trim, dark brown hair, pleasant-looking face with a lot of character written across it. Good-looking dude, more or less her own age. Just what she needed, to be windowshopping for men when she had scarcely gotten through shaking herself loose from one. She wasn't in the market, not at all. Still, he was attractive.

"I've decided to stay tonight," he told the woman behind the desk.

"That'll be fine, sir. Stay as long as you like." The man nodded to Lisa and headed across the lobby and out the door. "You see?" the woman said to Lisa, smiling mischievously. "Sometimes people find our little town irresistible."

Lisa laughed, signing the register. "I'm sure that's true." She wasn't sure of much of anything, really, but it sounded good.

When she deposited her suitcase on the bed and looked around her room, she found it unassuming but adequate, rather charmingly old-fashioned, in fact, like her impressions from the lobby. The bed was an old four-poster with bulbous pillows; an old bureau squatted in one corner on curly wooden legs. By the window (which looked out on the park) there was a little desk and chair. Some corner of her mind wondered: are all the rooms pretty much alike, do they all have the same furnishings, and are they all the same price (very reasonable for the times), and by the way, what floor was the man in the lobby coming down from?

"Go ahead," she told her reflection in the bathroom mirror, "think like a schoolgirl."

Outside again, she started to go for her car but thought better of it; walking around town might be refreshing. She realized that she hadn't even looked at her newspaper, which she still had folded under one arm. Maybe she'd stroll across the street to Melendez Park and find a nice quiet bench and read the paper. It was a pleasant day, and she realized with a flush of pleasure that actually she had all the time in the world. She'd have to find some kind of job fairly soon, but she thought her savings would carry her for as long as she would be likely to need. She walked across Chamisa Street and headed down a path into the park.

She found her bench soon enough, near the fountain in the middle of the park, and settled herself to read the newspaper, starting with the classified ads. Specifically, the employment ads. It wasn't much of a paper, but there were a couple of pages of ads to go through. You never could tell—

"HAY-fay, HAY-fay, crazy in the head! HAY-fay, HAY-fay, you look half dead!"

The voices came from over near the fountain, where several children, ten or twelve years old maybe, some of them Anglos and some Hispanic, were taunting a ragged old man. It took Lisa a moment to realize that it was indeed her new acquaintance Jefe. Angry, she rose from the bench, crumpling her newspaper, and started walking over there just as one of the younger boys tossed a soda can at the old man, barely missing his head. "You kids—" But her voice was lost in the tide of sound.

"HAY-fay, HAY-fay, crazy in the—"

"Listen, *niños.*" It was the old man himself, and, unlike Lisa, he had managed to make himself heard. For some reason, in fact, the kids had stopped yelling to listen to him, almost as if, in spite of everything, he commanded a certain aura of respect.

"You kids," he went on, "gonna be in a lot of trouble. You keep on acting like this, Arroyo's gonna get you. Now go on, *váyanse,* beat it." He swung his arm at the nearer antagonists, his rags flying like pennants. The children scattered, taunting him again as they went. Lisa came up to Jefe and took his arm, escorting him back to her bench.

"You okay?" she asked.

"Oh sure," he said, sitting down for a second but getting back up and starting off down the path, toward Chamisa Street. "Them kids gets smart sometimes, but I let 'em know they can't mess with me." He shuffled on down the path and was gone.

Lisa settled herself on the bench again and opened her paper back up to the employment ads, but found her attention wandering. For one thing, she had caught a glimpse of another ragged figure, more ragged perhaps even than Jefe, just an old Indian woman over beyond the fountain, but disturbing somehow. In the fleeting moments that Lisa had her in sight, the old woman seemed to move in a way that both compelled one to watch her and at the same time forbade understanding what one saw. From this distance Lisa couldn't see her too well, but it was as if the old woman, swivelling along on her bony legs, moved in more than one direction at a time, heading one way, lurching off-course as she went, yet still managing to get along. She reminded Lisa of something, but what was it? Something she had dreamed? In any case the woman was soon out of sight, and Lisa tried again to concentrate on the want ads, but in vain. Something nagged at her mind.

You keep on acting like this, Arroyo's gonna get you.
What in the world was that all about?

11

From out of a tangle of strange dreams—someplace dark and stuffy and unpleasant? vague shadowy things moving around? spiders?—Bill Weston struggled to a level of awareness at which he realized, with a sinking feeling, that he was going to be late, that he should be leaving for work by now. Sitting up in bed and opening his eyes, he looked around to find an utterly unfamiliar room. Then he remembered, and chuckled.

"Say, old son, you don't have to be in the newspaper office this morning. You don't have to be anywhere, actually. You're not a proofreader any more, remember? You're on the road. In the good tradition of Jack Kerouac. For whom a moment of reverential silence."

Still sitting in bed, he took a moment to analyze his feelings, now that he was awake and had remembered that he was unemployed. And to his delight, he noted that compared to that sinking feeling a few seconds ago, when he thought he was late for work, this wasn't all that bad a feeling, waking up as a gypsy.

"Keep in mind, though, lad," he said, swinging his legs onto the floor, "it's not forever. You're going to have to go to work before long." Wiping at his eyes, he made his way into the bathroom and regarded himself sleepily in the mirror. "Keep in mind also," he told his reflection, "that only crazy people are supposed to talk to themselves."

By the time he got washed up and dressed and took the elevator down to the lobby, it was nearly ten in the morning. On his way into town he had noticed a diner over on the west side, and he hoped they would be serving breakfast at this hour. He would grab some coffee and a plate of pancakes or something, maybe find a newspaper and start looking through the job-wanted classifieds. Very definitely in that order.

In the lobby, he walked over to the registration desk to find the woman there talking with an Hispanic lady seemingly his own age more or less, nice intelligent face with dark lively eyes, shiny black medium-length hair, most decidedly attractive. A corner of his mind remarked: splendid way to start the day, resting one's gaze upon a pleasant example of humankind. (A contrasting image flashed across his mind, a picture of his erstwhile boss Linda Jellison: beneath hair that looked like wilted straw, she had truculent closely-spaced eyes in a ruddy face, and a nose ring around which the tissue always looked diseased.) There was a lull in the exchange between the woman behind the counter and the Hispanic woman, so he paused in front of the counter and said, "I've decided to stay tonight."

Glancing at her room registration chart, the woman replied, "That'll be fine, sir. Stay as long as you like."

Bill nodded to both of them and headed toward the front door.

Driving back across town, past Melendez park with its bench-lined paths and loungers (an old man, a group of kids playing near the fountain), he found himself wondering what it was about this little town that tugged at his head, some unplaceable impression, a feeling that there were things beneath the surface, things that one ought to notice or remember, something that danced around a corner in the mind and vanished, taunting, elusive, gone. Ah well—he'd had that kind of feeling before. His own theory was that a sensitivity to language and literature gave one an enhanced and sometimes maybe misleading sensitivity to life itself. You sometimes tended to think that you were having a religious experience when in fact you were hungry, or horny, or maybe just needed to go to the bathroom. Still, he supposed it was better than attaching too *little* significance to things.

Lucinda's cafe on Camino del Sol was apparently doing a lively business even at this hour, between regular breakfast time and lunch, but he did manage to get a seat at the counter. The coffee wasn't bad (Linda Jellison's had always tasted vaguely like shoe polish) and in fact the pancakes were the best he had had for some time. He found himself watching his waitress as she darted back and forth setting plates and saucers in front of people and taking them away. There was something about her that was—different. Something in the way she moved. And when she turned her face toward him ("Some more coffee?") he worked in vain to analyze his impressions, to decide what it was about her that he found striking. Maybe it was just her rather birdlike way of nodding her head, maybe it was those large, dark eyes. In any case, he tried not to embarrass her by staring, and looked around for a newspaper, not seeing any. A large man in overalls and checked shirt, however, was getting up from the place next to Bill at the counter and was apparently going to leave his newspaper, which Bill saw was from Roswell.

"Oh, if you're through with your paper—"

"Welcome to it, young man. I done read the sports page, that's all I wanted to see anyway."

Back outside, Bill folded the newspaper under his arm and started to get in his car, but decided to walk around a bit first. There seemed to be no parking meters in this town, and he could leave the car parked in front of the diner indefinitely, so he strolled eastward, down to the corner, where the Town Hall stood looking across Mesa Street onto Melendez Park. He crossed the street and took a path into the park, admiring the large fountain that stood in the center. Just at the edge of his vision, far down on the other side of the fountain, he could just make out a solitary figure sitting on a bench, and he thought it was the Hispanic woman he had seen at the desk in the hotel lobby before, but she was getting up and leaving anyway, heading toward the other side of the park, so he couldn't be sure. He turned down a side path and walked around the edge of the fountain and surveyed the north side of the park, which lay along Camino del Sol. At the moment, there was nobody around.

He walked down toward Camino del Sol and stood for a moment, looking up and down the street, then turned back toward the path to the fountain, and nearly collided with someone.

Which was bizarre, because he'd been sure there was no one there.

She was old, withered, cadaverously thin, dressed in rags of appalling filth that gathered about her more like some sort of accretion than like clothes in any ordinary sense of the term. She appeared to be Native American. She took a step toward him—away from him?—to the side?—he wasn't sure. There was something unnerving about the way she moved, with a sort of jittering lilt that seemed to take her in more than one direction at a time. It half reminded him of something, but he couldn't have said what. Then the bottomless layers of creases in her wizened face melted one into another, fleeing, regathering, changing, as the parched lips formed themselves into speech.

"You sense it, don't you?"

He blinked at her. "Beg your pardon?" Her voice had had that broad-voweled quality that he admired in Native Americans, but what she had said had taken him a little aback.

She shook her head as if to dismiss his gesture of not having understood her. "You feel something. About this place."

"This town?" he asked. "Chasco?"

She eyed him craftily. "I said *place*. A place is more than a town."

For a moment he was speechless. She was just a ragged old woman, swaying there in front of him on bony legs protruding from tatters that might once have been clothing. Just a ragged old woman, but in some way, some unplaceable, irrational, preposterous way, she made you feel as if you were in the presence of royalty.

"I—well, yeah, the town. I mean, the place. It does give you a funny kind of—I mean, there's something about it."

She nodded, her rheumy eyes glowing like half-hidden little coals in their nest of wrinkles. "Yes. There is something about it. Not everyone can feel it. But you can. Araña knows."

He shrugged. "There's nothing special about me."

The old woman shifted closer to him, moving in that jittery, disorienting way that she had of seeming to go in more than one direction at a time. Involuntarily, he moved back a step, then felt embarrassed. Clearly she hadn't meant to pose a threat to him. How could she? Indeed she only seemed to have wanted to emphasize her next remark.

"There's something special about everyone. Not always the same way. Some people are special, different ways. You—feel things."

"We've never even met," he said.

"How do you know?" she replied. And he couldn't have said why, but something about this reply gave him a little chill that passed off in the morning sunshine like a mirage, but left its afterglow, a dim feeling like standing on the edge of some abyss in a dream. He sensed that her question was not intended to elicit an answer. She didn't wait, in any case, for him to give one.

"One day you will go to the arroyo," she said.

"The arroyo?" Out here, the desert was full of them.

"At the edge of town," she said, pointing across Camino del Sol toward the northwest. "What they call Arroyo Encantado."

"Why would I go there?" he asked.

"To feel what is there," she said. "Maybe to understand."

He studied her ancient face for a moment but found that it gave no further clue. One couldn't read her face; one simply had to comprehend her words, and he was discovering that that wasn't an easy thing to do, in spite of anything she said about his having some kind of insight that she thought she perceived in him. At length he turned in the direction in which she had pointed, gazing off across town, but there was nothing to see but a bank across the street, with other buildings huddled around and beyond it. The arroyo she was talking about must be a couple of miles away. He turned back around to say something further to her.

"But what—"

She wasn't there.

No one was there. Some twenty yards away, the fountain burbled in the sunlight, but except for Bill himself, the park was deserted.

No, off in the distance on the other side of the park flanking Zia Street, an old man hobbled along the sidewalk. But other than that, no one.

"Damn," Bill said to the morning air. Physically, the old woman certainly hadn't looked spry enough to make it out of sight in the few seconds he had been turned away from her. But she was gone.

He walked over to the fountain and leaned on the concrete rim, watching the water splash and sparkle in the sunlight. Somehow he felt that it didn't look the same to him now as it might have looked if he had just walked over and stood here fifteen minutes ago, or a day ago or a month ago, without talking to—what had she called herself?

Araña.

That was Spanish, but his Spanish wasn't all it should have been, and he scrambled in his mind for a meaning. Didn't it mean *frog?* No, that was—*rana* or something like that, he thought.

He walked around the rim of the fountain, feeling once again that even the innocent plashing and swirling of the water had taken on a darker quality, as if the sunlight itself were not so illuminating as it might be. At the edge of the walkway on the opposite side of the fountain from where he had talked to the old woman, he almost missed seeing a furry shape scutter down a small hole in the grass, rolling into a ball and pulling its legs in after it.

Suddenly, by association, he remembered what *araña* meant.

And he decided that if this was what a mini-vacation was going to do to his mind, it was time to sit down somewhere and read those employment ads.

12

When the little travel alarmclock went off, its soft burring was just obtrusive enough to draw Truman Lloyd gently back from dreams that fled when he tried to grasp them. Earlier he had dreamed of that girl in Chicago, the one with the skull-and-crossbones tattoo high up on her left thigh. What was her name? Monica? Veronica? God, that time when she——but the dream images that were withdrawing back into the darkness now weren't about Veronica or whatever her name was. He couldn't remember what they were, but he had the feeling he didn't like them.

Well, what the hell. Out of bed and into the shower. One of the wee creature comforts that his predecessor Warren Ross had added to this little house on the southeast edge of town was one of those water-stream massage attachments in the shower, nice for loosening up tight muscles in the back of the neck, and by the time he was washed and dried and dressed and had popped a couple of frozen breakfast burritos into the microwave in the kitchen, he felt very much like addressing a new day.

Heating a cup of water to make instant coffee, he walked back and forth between the kitchen and the living room, setting up the comm unit on the little side table by the sofa and plugging it into the electric outlet and the phone jack. He made another trip to the kitchen to retrieve his coffee while the comm unit was coming up, and when he got back, the left side of the double monitor-screen had warmed to a noncommittal gray. This unit was a new model and he liked it; the whole thing folded up into something that looked like a small briefcase, but when unfolded it was a microprocessor, double monitor, keyboard, video telephone, scrambler, microprinter, and pretty much everything a chap in Lloyd's esteemed profession might need. ("Gives you everything but a blow job," one of the tech support people in the Group had rather nonchalantly remarked.)

Lloyd picked the little telephone receiver up out of its cradle, held it between his ear and shoulder, pushed a couple of buttons, and dialed a number. When the characteristic electronic handshake response sounded in the receiver, he punched in the codes for circumnavigating the regular telephone networks, and dialed another number to enable the multiple scrambler sequencing, then dialed still another number. To the right of the gray screen, the other half-screen came alive with a nondescript design that looked something like a TV test pattern. This was quickly replaced by a light red question mark that nearly filled the screen. Lloyd typed in a long alphanumeric password. There was a pause. The large question mark contracted to a point, then returned to its former size, still red. Lloyd typed in the second password. The question mark flickered, turned pastel green, and vanished. The screen was blank for a moment, then filled with a Chinese face. This was Lloyd's colleague Charles Wu, head of the comm center in Ohio and one of the most powerful people in the world when you got right down to it.

Wu's pie-round face nodded on the screen, and gave just the suggestion of a grin. "Good morning, Tru. Glad to see you're starting your workday in time for lunch."

Lloyd snorted, feeling a grin begin to play across his own face. "I might point out that it's only eight o'clock in

New Mexico. You Chinky types never could get the time zones straight."

"I'll ignore the reference to the ethnicity of my forefathers," Wu said.

Wu's family went back several generations, to the days of the early railroads in the West, Lloyd well knew. No one could ever be cleared high enough for Group Epsilon unless their family were USA-born at least four generations back. "I think you have some briefing materials for me," he said.

"Yes I do," Wu replied, "and I'm going to upload those to you right now and leave you to ponder them, because I have a teleconference with the President and the Secretary of Defense and some other folks, coming up in four minutes."

"Well go ahead," Lloyd said, "see if I give a rat's ass."

"Have a glorious day," Wu said, "and as they say, don't do anything I wouldn't do."

"Pretty much leaves everything open to me, doesn't it?" Lloyd said.

"Up yours," Wu said, and the screen went blank.

There were soft telemetry sounds and the left screen filled itself with the first page of a document. Lloyd stared at it for a moment, then clicked a release button on the side of the monitor and a little chute came unfolding down. He pressed the *print* button, and several sheets of paper collected in the little tray. He retrieved them, shut the comm unit down and folded it up, and went to the kitchen to bring back his breakfast. Settling himself on the sofa with a burrito in one hand and the briefing papers in the other, he began to read. Aside from the date and the usual cryptic routing-data stamps, the document said:

TOP SECRET NOPAL
GROUP EPSILON/EYES ONLY
CONTROL 11J55377YB/K44296/8MX853
TRANSM. MULT. SCRAMBLE EPSILINK
PROJECT STARSIFT

Investigations by Warren Ross have delineated the following three major problems for Group Epsilon's ongoing consideration: (1) The long-standing rumor, among the populace in the Roswell/Corona/Chasco/Fort Sumner/Santa Rosa area of southeastern New Mexico, to the effect that in the matter of the Roswell UFO crash of 4 July 1947 there may have been crash survivors other than the one known by Group Epsilon to have existed; (2) The difficulty of separating folklore from fact in this matter, especially as threats made to the civilian populace by the Army/Air Force in 1947 have evidently rendered most people in the area still reluctant to talk to strangers about anything related to the question; and (3) The fact that, were rumors of unaccounted-for alien survivors to have any basis in truth, the implications for unauthorized knowledge among the general populace would be problematical in the extreme.

The folklore/rumors in question are well known to be centered, for whatever reasons, in the town of Chasco. The Group has identified three primary sources of possible information:

(1) Miguel "Jefe" Sandoval. Born 15 March 1920 in Corona, New Mexico. Hispanic male. Father Carlos Sandoval, mother b. Juanita Montoya, now both deceased. Height 5 ft. 10 in., weight approx. 140 lbs., hair gray-black, eyes brown. Existing clinic records Roswell, New Mexico indicate chronic alcoholism,

duodenal ulcer. No record military service. No record steady employment. No permanent address. Usual locations Corona, Chasco, Roswell. According to informants, known to tell stories apparently related to La Llorona legend with reference to Arroyo Encantado on outskirts of Chasco, embellished to form less well-known variants. Also vague accounts of witnessing crash retrieval in Roswell 4/5 July 1947, no consistent details.

(2) Araña, so called. Real name unknown. American Indian female, age unknown but suspected to be at least 80. Said to have been born at Nambé Pueblo, New Mexico but no details known. Height approximately 5 feet 8 inches, weight approx. 90 lbs., hair gray-white, eyes brown. Inhabitants of Nambé Pueblo reluctant to speak of her. Said to be nomadic because unwelcome in pueblo. Popularly said to be sorceress and "shapeshifter." Thought to be fluently acquainted with general folklore of area, hence Group Epsilon interest in her as possible link to strains of rumor worth pursuing. Often seen in streets of Chasco, occasionally in Corona, Roswell, Artesia, Fort Sumner, Santa Rosa, Lincoln, Capitan.

(3) Paco Rojas. Born 10 April 1939, Santa Rosa, New Mexico. Hispanic/American Indian male. Height 5 feet 5 inches, Weight approx. 150 lbs., eyes brown. Father Rolando Rojas, mother b. Mary Highcloud, both now

deceased. Proprietor of store Paco's Emporium, 117 Chamisa Street, Chasco, New Mexico since 1961. Residence apartment over store, that address. Local folklore, perhaps enhanced by strange inventory of store, suggests Rojas a kind of authority on legends of region. Not overly talkative, but at times evinces strong interest in regional folktales, Roswell crash, paranormal/preternatural phenomena, UFO lore.

Group Epsilon considers productive investigation of these leads to be Priority One. Probability of significant disclosures is high.

Sipping his coffee and munching the second of the breakfast burritos, Lloyd glanced back over the document and clucked to himself.

"Regional lore. Legends. Folktales. Damn, Sam. It sounds like I ought to have a degree in cultural anthropology instead of political science. And sounds like they need an egghead from Harvard out here, not me."

But he knew better. It might make you feel silly sometimes, checking these things out, but local legends and regional folklore could often be the springboard to discoveries of real importance. He knew of such cases. Listen to myth and legend long enough, and you could end up listening to hard cold facts. One thing, in the great and wondrous chain of being, would damn well lead to another, as sure as God made spies.

He cleaned up his breakfast debris, shredded and burned and reshredded the briefing document, packed the comm unit away in the camouflaged double-locked pantry his predecessor had devised, and got ready to go out, wearing the usual inconspicuous uniform: dress jeans, Western shirt, bolo tie, bluejean jacket, cowboy boots. His mother, back in the old neighborhood in Detroit, would have died if she'd ever seen him in this get-up. But then she had died anyway, *without* seeing him in it.

Driving north up Chamisa Street from the southeast edge of town, he passed the Swan Hotel, swung left onto Camino del Sol, and circled Melendez Park, coming around on its west side on Mesa Street. He parked there and got out and walked south along the edge of the park, turning east onto Zia Street, because he had spotted a ragged-looking old man over on the southeast side of the block when he had driven past, and he thought he just might know who it was. Small towns were nice; it wasn't like looking for somebody on the streets of L.A. or New York. Glancing to his left across the expanse of the park, he noticed a woman sitting far off on a park bench and a rowdy-looking group of children scattering away beyond the fountain, but his main interest was the old man, whom he soon caught up with, beside a bench near the corner with Chamisa Street.

"Warm day for October," Lloyd said, gesturing toward the bench.

The old man seemed to consider the gesture for a moment, then went and sat down. Lloyd sat beside him. The old man wiped a brow with his dirty sleeve and shook his head. "Right. Warm day, *amigo*. Sure can make a man thirsty." He seemed to wait for this to sink in. "Damn thirsty."

Lloyd, never one to be unprepared on such high occasions of state as these, felt in his jacket pocket and brought out a bottle, a fifth of whiskey, a brand that he himself probably wouldn't have used as a toilet cleaner. He handed it to the old man, who lost no time in uncapping it and taking a lusty pull from it, releasing it with a smack and handing it back to Lloyd, who sure as hell wasn't going to drink from it himself now, not if it was smoothest sherry.

"Feel better now?" he asked the old man.

"*Sí, con un buen trago van mejorando todas las cosas de la vida,*" the old man said, incomprehensibly. "Much better." He extended a withered but surprisingly firm hand. "My name is Sandoval. People they call me Jefe."

"Well, I'm glad to meet you, Jefe," Lloyd said, and it was the God's truth. "I'm Travis Lombardy." That wasn't the God's truth, but one out of two wasn't bad.

"Ain't seen you here," Jefe said.

"No, no, I'm just—visiting. Pleasant little town. I like it. It must have some interesting history."

"*Sí señor,*" Jefe said. "I been here most of my life, coming and going, you know, and I seen things around here you might not believe. *Cosas extrañas.*"

Lloyd nodded, careful not to seem too eager. "I'm sure you have."

For a moment he wished he had let himself be a little more eager, because the old man seemed to have lapsed into a silence from which he might or might not decide to emerge. Deciding to take a risk, Lloyd handed him the bottle again and watched him take another mighty swallow from it. For a while the old man still didn't say anything, but at length he turned to Lloyd and eyed him curiously.

"Place is haunted," he said.

Christ, Lloyd thought; what's this going to be? "Haunted?"

"Haunted," the old man repeated. "*Embrujado.*"

"I don't understand," Lloyd said. "You mean ghosts? Like in a haunted house?"

"*No se trata de las casas,*" the old man said rather vehemently. "Ain't got nothing to do with houses. It's the place. Always been haunted."

"What makes you think so?" Lloyd asked.

"You live on the streets, *amigo*, you see things. You know things. Even people living in them nice houses, they know things too, things they ain't talking about."

None of the houses Lloyd had seen in the town looked all that nice, but he supposed they probably looked that way to the old man. Lloyd handed him the bottle yet again and watched him take a swig, then took it back. Half of it was gone. At this rate—but it probably would take quite a bit of rotgut to make this old boy comatose, and in fact he was continuing to talk.

"You go out to that arroyo, northwest side of town, you might not come back," he said. "I seen *her* once, at night, out there."

"Who?" Lloyd asked.

Jefe looked at him as if the question were a pitiable species of ignorance. "La Llorona," he said.

Lloyd nodded. "Yeah, all right. I know that legend. A ghostly woman wanders arroyos and irrigation ditches and whatnot, at night, crying for her lost children." He was about to say that that story was told not only all over the American Southwest, but in Mexico as well. He stopped short of saying this, though, because he didn't want to discourage the old man's inclination to talk.

"You say what you want," Jefe said, "I seen her. And it ain't just *her* children she's crying about. It's got to do with what lives in the arroyo, too. She's afraid it's going to come and she's going to see it."

Oh boy, Lloyd thought, a fine crock of shit this is going to be. "What do you mean—"

"Some folks call it Arroyo, 'cause that's where it lives," Jefe said, letting his head sag on his chest. For a moment, Lloyd thought the old man had gone to sleep, and maybe he had. But Jefe popped his head up quickly enough and fixed Lloyd with a watery stare. "Some of them oldtimers, they say they seen it, years ago."

"How about you?" Lloyd asked. "Did you ever see it?"

"No, *gracias a Dios*," Jefe said, shuddering. "But I know it's there. I can feel it. I used to know some of them people that seen it, too. *Viejos.* Old folks. *Muertos.* Dead now."

Monsters living in dry washes, Lloyd mused. Why didn't this surprise him a whole lot? The Southwest always had some weird legend or other to offer. If it wasn't La Llorona it was Indian magic or something. Definitely kept life from getting boring. He returned the old man's stare. "You want to take me out there?"

Jefe cast an incredulous look at him, then turned away. "You wanna go out there, you go alone, *amigo.* I ain't going." His voice had dropped almost to inaudibility.

"Okay, okay," Lloyd said, "never mind. I wouldn't really ask you to go anyplace you were afraid to go. I was wondering about something, though. There are big arroyos all over the desert out here, so why should this one have some—thing—living in it?"

Jefe didn't answer for a long while, but finally turned to Lloyd and said: "*Debido a lo que pasó aquí.* 'Cause of what happened here."

"What do you mean, what happened here?" Lloyd asked.

Jefe was quiet again for a time, then said: "They killed him."

Lloyd blinked. "Killed who?"

"*El niño del cielo,*" the old man said, and got suddenly to his feet and started walking away.

"Wait a minute—" Lloyd protested, but the old man kept walking, not even looking back. Well, enough for now, there would be other chances to get him to talk. In a few moments, Jefe was across Zia Street and out of sight.

El niño del cielo, Lloyd thought. There were times he rather wished he had paid better attention in old Prof Mendoza's Spanish class back at the university, instead of trying to seduce that girl with the big *cha-chas* who sat nearby. *Cielo* meant *heaven,* didn't it? Ah, but he remembered, it was also the word for—

Well, Christ on a crutch in noonday traffic. He knew what *el niño del cielo* meant.

It meant *the sky-child.*

13

The job-wanted ads in the newspaper had turned up a surprising number of leads. Lisa pondered the possibilities, walking across the little park behind Town Hall. She had pretty well explored the main landmarks of the downtown blocks, and in between walking excursions she had settled on another park bench, after her encounter with Jefe, to read the paper in earnest. She was headed toward Lucinda's Cafe now, but it was too early for lunch, and she had other things to do first anyway.

Some of the jobs listed were in other towns—Santa Rosa, Roswell mainly—but a few were right here in Chasco, and in some odd way she felt drawn to this peculiar little town. It wasn't quaint exactly, or warm or endearing, or particularly inviting in any usual sense of the term; it was just—intriguing. She couldn't have said why. In any case, she might just stay here, for a while at least. With her varied experience (bookkeeper, receptionist, data input clerk, assistant loan officer, collector, customer service rep, you name it, at one time or another she'd done it) it shouldn't be hard to latch onto one of these jobs or another, right here in town. She was going to check on one or two of them this morning, in fact.

With this resolve, she doubled back through the park behind Town Hall and walked past Lonnie's Tobacco and News and back across Mesa Street to Melendez Park, where now a number of people were sitting or strolling, and some kids were playing frisbee on the grass. Past the park and across Chamisa Street, she headed back to the hotel, and in another half hour had freshened up, changed clothes, retrieved her resumé folder from her suitcase, and made ready to drive across town to the address on Piñon Street given in one ad, having given them a call first to see if it was all right for her to come by. She had the feeling that the job applicant pool wasn't exactly overflowing around here; this wasn't Albuquerque or Dallas or Phoenix, after all. Anyway, they had scheduled her right away for an interview. It was an insurance company, and the position was called "administrative assistant," which, in her experience, could be any number of things, all of them pretty manageable.

She found the place easily enough, a small stucco building on the northwest corner of Piñon and Old Roswell Road. Inside, the receptionist greeted her with a smile and ushed her in to see a Mr. Wieland, tall and lean and friendly in a halting kind of way, and the game was on. She'd been through this process many times before, and wasn't nervous in the least. It felt good to be footloose and have a lot of options open.

Back out in the parking lot, she felt very positive about the interview. The position itself would involve a combination of data entry and other office work, including some loan processing, and occasionally covering the switchboard. It was all *déjà vu* to her. The current admininstrative assistant was going to be leaving in three weeks, and while Mr. Wieland had only promised to let her know one way or the other within a few days, Lisa had the distinct impression that the job was hers if she wanted it, which she did. The pay wasn't too bad, and at the very least the job would no doubt be a comfortable niche for the immediate future, maybe even a nice resumé-enhancer when she applied for something else later on. You never could tell, she mused: today Chasco, tomorrow the world. She'd probably still check on that other job, the one at the Medical Arts Center, but not till tomorrow.

And with that thought, and a productive morning behind her, it was time for lunch.

She left her car in the lot next to the insurance company and walked down Old Roswell Road and across Camino del Sol toward the diner, but on the way she happened to glance westward and noticed the real estate office (Naranjo's) down on the far end of that block. She had seen it on her way into town, but hadn't given it a thought at the time. On an impulse, she crossed Old Roswell Road and walked down to Naranjo's and went in, feeling a little heady. Interview for a job, she told herself, and then go right out and look for a place to live; Lisa Jaramillo, the picture of unbridled optimism. But what the hell—why not? Didn't she have what it took to make it in the world on her own? (Without Gary, in other words?) These days, she firmly believed in that old bumper sticker slogan: *Just do it.*

Inside, the real estate office was pastel colors and smooth corners and curved arches and nichos in the wall, all beautifully Southwestern. The middleaged woman in the front office rose and introduced herself. "I'm Mrs. Betty Naranjo." She gestured toward a younger woman seated at another desk across the room. "This is Miss Cheryl Hobbs. How may we help you?"

"I'm Lisa Jaramillo. Very pleased to meet you. I'm at the Swan right now, but I think I'm going to be staying in town, and I was wondering about finding something to rent."

"We have listings on a few apartments," Mrs. Naranjo said.

Go for it, Lisa thought. "Do you have any houses for rent?"

The two realtors exchanged what Lisa thought was an odd sort of glance, then Miss Hobbs said, more to her colleague than to Lisa, "We do have that one house—"

Again it seemed to Lisa that a peculiar unspoken exchange passed between them, as if some reticence or some indecision had to be overcome. After a moment Mrs. Naranjo said, "Yes, I'd almost forgotten. There is one rental, an older house on the northwest edge of town, just up Old Roswell Road. It's not far from here. The owner lives in Albuquerque. We can quote you a very reasonable figure on the rent."

"Is it furnished? I'm—I don't have any furniture of my own."

"It's furnished," Miss Hobbs said. "Nothing too fancy."

"Could I see the house?" Lisa asked. Standing back in her mind's eye and regarding herself, she wasn't entirely sure she believed she was doing all this.

"Certainly," Mrs. Naranjo said, getting up from her desk. "It isn't far. Cheryl, if you'll hold the fort here for a little while I'll take Miss Jaramillo to see the—house."

They went in the realtor's car, and indeed it wasn't far, perhaps a mile and a half north on Old Roswell Road, past a few less than appetizing-looking residential streets that thinned out to occasional weed-overtaken houses by the time Mrs. Naranjo drove past the town cemetery. The house itself, bay-windowed and gaunt-looking, taller than it was wide, was only half a mile or so further on, and sat a considerable distance off the west side of the road, looking as if it were at a loss in its overgrowth of chamisa, sagebrush, and other rampant growth. It made Lisa think of that description, in Dickens's *Christmas Carol*, of the house that looked as if it had crept there while playing hide-and-seek as a young house, and forgotten how to find its way back.

"Sorry about the condition of the grounds," Mrs. Naranjo said, crunching the car up the gravel driveway through a parting sea of weeds. "If you do decide you want to rent it, we'll have the yard cleaned up for you." The yard was at least an acre in extent, roomy both in front of the house and behind, apparently, as Lisa could see, far in the rear of the house, a tottering fence that seemed to mark the boundary of the property. Beyond that fence, the land was cloven by an access to a large arroyo that wound its way out northwestward into the desert.

Lisa followed Mrs. Naranjo up the creaking but reasonably stable steps that led to the front porch, and soon they were inside, where in spite of the characteristically musty smell of a house long closed up, something about the place rather appealed to her. She had to weigh her feelings carefully. Did she really find the house livable, or would she have found any house, at this juncture in her new life, livable by default? Was she just taking whatever came, or was she thinking straight?

She judged that she was thinking straight.

"The upstairs is two bedrooms and a bathroom," Mrs. Naranjo said, leading her up the stairwell. Downstairs had been a living room, kitchen with small dining area adjacent, and a bathroom. Upstairs, like downstairs, was all clean but faded wallpaper and minimal but adequate-looking furniture. House and furniture alike appeared to be some decades old.

Back downstairs, they discussed the rent, which was indeed very reasonable. "I can pay the deposit and first month's rent with traveler's checks, I hope. I haven't opened a bank account here yet."

"Traveler's checks are fine," Mrs. Naranjo said. She seemed relieved to have rented the place, and a corner of Lisa's mind registered some concern about that, but she had checked the place out pretty thoroughly and really couldn't see anything seriously wrong with it. Anyway, she was renting it, not buying it.

Back at the real estate office on Camino del Sol, they took care of the paperwork, and Lisa took the keys and thanked Mrs. Naranjo and Miss Hobbs and walked toward Lucinda's Cafe with a new spring in her steps. One side of her mind said: you're doing too many things too fast. The other side of her mind said: horseshit. The side that said horseshit was dominant by the time she walked into Lucinda's and found a seat at the counter down on the left end, near where the counter took a dogleg turn back toward the wall, enclosing the grill area. She glanced around for the odd-looking waitress but didn't see her. Another girl waited on her, and Lisa ordered a hamburger and fries and large root beer.

It was 12:45, and the place was fairly busy. Around the corner of the counter, on the short section that ran back nearly to the wall, a late-forties-ish guy in a good-looking Western shirt was working on his own plate of all-American food, and glancing at Lisa from time to time. Again her mind was divided. One side said: you're a divorcee, kid, and you've got a few miles on you, and it's kind of nice to know that men still look at you. The other side of her mind said: horseshit, you don't need men, lady, you're doing just fine all by yourself, thank you very much. The horseshit side of her mind seemed to be coming out in the lead pretty consistently today.

So much had happened this morning, though, that it felt good to just sit at the counter and eat her lunch and take a little time to reflect on things. She was about halfway through her burger, and a lesser fraction of the way through her reflections, when a familiar-looking chap sat down on the stool to her right. Where did she know him from?

"I'll have a ham and cheese on rye," he said to the waitress, "and coffee."

Ah, she remembered, as much from his voice as from his face. He was the guy she had seen in the hotel lobby this morning. And she had taken just a little too long in figuring this out, because he had noticed that she was looking at him.

He returned the look, evidently trying to sort out in his own head where he knew her from.

"Excuse me, didn't I see you at the hotel?" he asked.

She nodded, putting down her hamburger and dabbing at her lips with a napkin. "Yes," she said. "I didn't mean to stare, but when you sat down, I thought I'd seen you somewhere." Out of a corner of her eye, she noticed that the other man, around the corner of the counter to her left, was looking up from his food from time to time, as if idly half-following this conversation. What did it matter?

"I imagine you're just passing through town, like me," her acquaintance from the hotel said.

"Yeah," she said, then caught up with herself. "Ah—no, actually. I'm going to stay here for a while. I had an interview this morning, think I might have got the job. My name is Lisa, by the way. Lisa Jaramillo."

The man smiled apologetically. "Pardon my manners. They need the dust shaken off them once in a while. I'm Bill Weston. And good luck on getting that job. I'm going to be doing some jobhunting myself, I'm afraid."

"Oh?"

"Sad but true," he said as the waitress was bringing his food. "I used to be a proofreader on a little farm-and-ranch trade newspaper down in Artesia. A few days ago they decided they'd rather misspell every other word and decorate their front page with dangling participles than keep handing me a paycheck, so here I am."

"I'm sorry," Lisa said.

"Well, they may have done me a favor, who knows? I just might find something better, now that they've forced me to get out and look."

"So you came to Chasco?" she asked.

"Well, you know, I'm passing through. Chasco is a place everybody just passes through." He glanced sidelong at her and smiled at his mistake. "Nearly everybody."

Lisa was finding that she enjoyed talking to this fellow. He was articulate and polite, two things she liked, two things she didn't always find. "Bill—can I call you Bill?"

He looked at her with mock incredulity. "I've been called infinitely worse," he said. "I don't believe in formality. It's like wearing a tie, it leads to brain damage."

"I was just wondering," she said, "do you find this town kind of—"

"Kind of strange?" he supplied.

"Well—yes. I can't put my finger on it, but kind of strange."

"Funny you should mention it," he said.

14

Group Epsilon operative Lloyd, sitting three or four yards across the corner of the counter from the people who had identified themselves as Lisa Jaramillo and Bill Weston, was managing to listen to their conversation over the general hum of talk that pervaded the room. And when the subject turned to the strangeness of the town, he began to find the conversation more interesting. When you had an agenda of your own, however vague or oblique, sometimes relatively innocuous remarks could turn intriguing.

Of course he had been intrigued by Lisa from the outset, for other reasons, seeing her walk in wearing that short skirt and that very becoming blouse. Great legs, nice contours all around, matter of fact. Pretty face, too; classic Hispanic, with probably an admixture of American Indian back there somewhere. Without overburdening the ever-busy synapses of his brain in the least, he could imagine crawling into the sack with this rather fetching lady. And who knew, maybe it might come to that, in this ongoing saga of normal life in a small American town. In the meantime this guy Bill Weston had come in, and they seemed to be chatting it up right and left. Boy meets girl, Truman thought; how very touching.

"Kind of strange?" Weston was asking.

"Well—yes. I can't put my finger on it, but kind of strange," Lisa replied.

"Funny you should mention it," Weston said. "I've had that feeling ever since I got here. It's not anything unpleasant, exactly, but it makes me feel as if I'm missing something."

"Missing something?"

"Yeah," he said, "some—I don't know, some elusive impression that I ought to be picking up on, but I'm not."

"I think I know what you mean," she said.

Lloyd continued to listen. This might not end up being very productive, coming from a couple of out-of-towners, but one never knew. Anyway, it kept his mind off this wretched hamburger.

Weston was eyeing the woman curiously. "Did you say your last name is Jaramillo?" he asked.

"Yes. It was Logan, until recently. Now it's Jaramillo again. I've just been through a divorce."

"I'm sorry," he said.

"I'm not," she said.

"Ah. Well. So that's why you're here, kind of—"

"Starting over," she said. "A person can do worse. But why did you ask me if my name—"

"Oh, I was just remembering something," he said. "When my dad was in the service back in the forties, he was stationed down at Roswell Army Air Field, and he knew a man named Ruben Jaramillo. They were close friends, I guess. Dad always talked a lot about him."

The woman was looking at him with surprise. "You're kidding. I had an uncle named Ruben Jaramillo. My dad's older brother. I don't remember much about him, because I only saw him a few times, and he died when I was in the fourth grade, but from what Dad said I know Uncle Ruben was in the army, and he was stationed at Roswell."

"Be damned," Weston said. "You don't know if your father ever mentioned his brother having a friend named Herb Weston? My dad."

Lisa appeared to be trying to remember. "No, not as far as I recall. But that doesn't mean anything. I bet you're right, the man your father knew was my Uncle Ruben. Wow. It sounds corny, but you know what they say about a small world."

"My dad used to tell me some interesting stories about Ruben Jaramillo," Weston said.

"Really?" She was obviously very excited about the prospect of hearing more about her uncle. I know where *this* will probably end up, Lloyd thought—vomitously endless family reminiscences—but he kept listening. He knew that the prospect *could* conceivably be a fruitful one for him too, for different reasons. "What kinds of stories?" Lisa was asking.

"Well," Weston said, "it had to do with that business that happened in Roswell in 1947. You know, the UFO that was supposed to have crashed in the desert north of town, right down the road here. My dad was in the army in Roswell at the time, and he didn't have anything to do with all that flying saucer business, but Ruben Jaramillo did, apparently. He was part of the retrieval team that went out and picked up the pieces. And the bodies."

Lisa was all eyes. "So that's what—you know, I remember my dad always acted kind of funny when he talked about those days, kind of like there was a lot that Uncle Ruben knew but couldn't say anything about. I never really knew that it was about that UFO thing. You said bodies? I've heard people *say* there were alien bodies—"

"Well, your Uncle Ruben told my dad there were," Weston said. "Four of them. And that's not all. He said there were some live ones."

"Oh well, I've heard that too," Lisa said, smiling skeptically, "but I never really took it seriously. I mean, people have said all kinds of weird things."

"Dad said Ruben Jaramillo told him the army picked up one live alien at the crash site, but he didn't know where they took it or how long it lived," Weston said. "But he did know something else."

Truman Lloyd chewed less vigorously, and listened.

"He told my dad," Weston went on to say, "that the army retrieval people thought there might have been some other crash survivors, some that got away or were hidden, or something. I guess when the army was at the crash site they thought it looked like there should have been more creatures than they'd been able to find. He said there were vague rumors among the locals, too, but nobody would ever say anything much about it, and no other survivors were ever found, even though they went over the desert out there for miles around."

"*Dios mío*," Lisa said. "I never heard a word about that from anybody in my family."

"Well, the military threatened everybody, told them not to talk about it," Weston said. "I guess your Uncle Ruben did talk about it early on, to my dad, the way people will do, but by the time it was all over, he was probably afraid to talk about it to anybody else. They transferred all those people out, you know, and my dad was sent to New Hampshire and never heard from Ruben again, never found out where he'd gone."

Lisa seemed to be trying to remember something. "I think Dad said Uncle Ruben was sent to Oregon or someplace after he was at Roswell. It's all—kind of scary."

Weston nodded, finishing his lunch. "Matter of fact. Well. I've got some things I ought to go and do. I've enjoyed talking to you. Are you going to be staying long at the hotel?"

"No," she said, "actually this is crazy, because I don't even know if I'm going to get the job I applied for, but would you believe I've rented a house? I plan to stay here in town for a little while at least. I always was a risk-taker."

Weston nodded. "Good for you. I'm one too, but my risks don't always work out. I guess they wouldn't be risks if they did. Anyhow, I really think you ought to let an unemployed proofreader take you to dinner tonight. Unless you're going to be too busy moving in. I could even help you with that."

"Oh, there's not much moving in to do. Everything I own is in my car. When I start over, I really start over. But you know something? I'll take you up on that dinner. Could we make it tomorrow night, though? The house I rented has been sitting empty for a long time, and I think I'm going to have to spend tonight cleaning."

Weston was clearly pleased, Lloyd observed. "Tomorrow, then. I saw a little restaurant that doesn't look half bad, out east on Zia Street on the edge of town, kind of behind the hotel."

"I think I saw it too," she said. "Mexican food place. Casa Linda or something? I could meet you there."

"No," he said, "let me pick you up around six. Where do you live?"

"Up Old Roswell Road on the northwest side, last house on the way out of town, left side of the road. It's a little two-story house, kind of Victorian looking. But you almost can't see it from the road, for the weeds."

Lloyd thought he saw a few people nearby give Lisa odd sidelong glances at the mention of the house, but he might have imagined it. God, that would have been like something out of one of those half-assed horror movies, where the out-of-towner says the wrong thing (like "I'm going to the castle to meet Count Dracula") and the villagers cross themselves and gather their children in and close the shutters. Maybe the desert sun was starting to bake away his brains, but he did think people looked at her funny. In any case, both Lisa and her lunch companion were leaving, and as the conversational murmur in the rest of the room swelled up to fill the vacuum, he found nothing half as interesting as the things he had already heard.

Uncle Ruben, eh? Dead for quite some time, he remembered the woman saying. Good old Dead Uncle Ruben. Well, well. At least Dead Uncle Ruben wouldn't be running off at the mouth any more, but—there were loose ends here and there, nonetheless. Who could say what kind of bundle one would get in the process of tying them up?

He plunked down a fistful of taxpayer dollars and left the cafe.

15

The day grew toward evening, and Araña knew where she would go. Where she must go. She felt drawn there.

Crossing Camino del Sol, she walked up Mesa Street, making her way across town north of Melendez Park and angling toward the northwest. People sometimes stared at her, sometimes not; she was, after all, a fairly common sight hereabouts, jittering along the sidewalk with her oddly multidirectional gait. Naturally she could have chosen some other way to get to where she was going, besides walking. Such choices were the privilege of a shapeshifter. Right now she could conceivably be soaring on crisp ebon wings over the streets of the town, unnoticed, but Crow had never been her preferred Shape-Ally, though she probably could become him if she wished. No, it was good sometimes just to walk, even in the rather awkward impediment of the human form, in which she was rather old and infirm. She could move in a much more agile fashion as Spider Grandmother. But there was no hurry. Only the impoverished of spirit, only those out of touch with the magic of the land, were in a hurry.

She crossed Piñon Street and walked west along its length, passing a hardware store, a weedy vacant lot, and any number of little storefronts boarded up and forlorn-looking at the corner of Piñon and one cross-street or another. At length she reached Old Roswell Road and turned north, hobbling past the graveyard and continuing on. About half a mile farther along, where the town was giving up its pretence and becoming desert again, she spotted her usual landmark, the solitary old two-story house far up off the road on the left, and just short of this piece of land she angled off the road, crossing a stubbly waste of range grass and yucca and prickly-pear cactus. Perhaps a hundred yards in this direction lay the opening of the great dry wash that she sought.

Arroyo Encantado.

At first its walls were shallow, barely rising above the sandy old riverbed, but as one progressed along the dry rivercourse a little farther, the sides of the arroyo rose canyonlike to become walls of gnarled cedar-root high enough to block off the view of the land around. It was like walking in a maze, because the course of the riverbed divided here and there into side-channels that dead-ended in blank walls with yucca and chamisa nestled at their bases, and one would have to back out and try another route if one made the mistake of venturing into such a blind alley. Araña knew her way, and kept to the main course. From time to time she saw a rattlesnake hole burrowed into the base of a mesquite bush in the arroyo floor. The rattlesnake was an ally, of course, though a feisty one, whom Spider Grandmother had to keep in line on occasion. It was all part of the Way.

Some distance into the deeper-walled arroyo, the old woman stopped at a place where the sandy walls curved out a little wider than elsewhere, and she stood for a while and watched the sun-spirit make his fiery way to the distant western horizon, sending ghostly shadows of the left-hand arroyo wall creeping out over the sand. Araña lifted her bony arms in tribute to the setting sun, and her own regal shadow, thrown upon the opposite wall of the arroyo, might have been a folk-legend cast into the quiet faces of listeners. She was the Storyteller too, but her stories were not always composed of words that the common ear could discern.

At length the sun descended beneath her line of sight and she dropped her arms and sat upon a low rock in the riverbed, and contemplated what her most recent dreams had told her of this special place.

She stirred the sand with one sinewy foot and crooned a song that had been old before the siege of Troy. This is where it was, where it had happened.

Where the Sky-Child had fallen to the brutality of one who served spurious gods, one who could not possibly have understood.

She knew, she saw what had happened. Her dreams last night had told her, and dreams belonged to the magic of eternity; they were the song of the soul.

Here in the drifted sand of the rivercourse, here somewhere, she knew, the fragile little bones lay buried. The people, her people of a time centuries ago, must have covered them over and their medicine-man must have pronounced sacred words over them; her dreams spoke only vaguely of this, but it must have been so, as this would have been the Way. It was a holy place, a place for prayer and singing, but also an accursed place, a place where great wrong had been done. Whether the wrong could ever be set right, even she could not say.

The western sky, aflame with a salmon-colored memory of the sun, gradually grew muffled in darkness, and the night came along the arroyo like the advance of a river, filling its length with shadows that slowly revealed, once again, more faintly, the contours of the land they had concealed, as a bewilderment of cold stars came out to encrust the sky and cast their pallid radiance abroad. Araña sat in the riverbed and watched the night come on, and her feelings were mixed.

This was a place of memory, of chanting, of song, of uncertain possibilities of atonement, but also a place of dread. She was not so much afraid for herself, just afraid in an objectless kind of way, afraid to see what one day soon was going to come from the farther dark reaches of the

111

rivercourse. It was not that she would be harmed, and what if she were? Her spirit would seep back into the land and live eternally. If her concern had been for herself, she would not even be here; she did not have to be here, after all, in this spectral place. No, she was not afraid of harm that might come to her; her mind recoiled only at the hideousness of what might come upon the land, the terror of what had lain here, waiting, biding its limitless time, since that night so long ago when the Sky-Child had been slain, since the curse had been pronounced.

Something disturbed her reverie, brought her back to the present. Without warning, a low, keening sound had come upon the night like a stirring of wind. Indeed a wind had arisen, soft and subtle, to whirl the dust at Araña's feet. She merely listened, then rose in odd angles to stand upon her ancient legs and face the direction from which the sound was coming. She knew what it was. Who it was.

She had only to wait a few moments, and the expected form appeared, some distance off, from deeper in the arroyo, gliding in its unearthly way along the sandy rivercourse, illumined like a pale ghost in starlight.

What undulated in the arroyo was an eerie play of gossamer fabric, the folds and contours of a white dress floating upon the sighing wind, weightless and pallid like moonbeams.

And above the phantasmal white dress that flowed and curled on the wind, a woman's face floated into view, from out of the shadows, and the tragic mouth opened, and the sound of crying filled the rivercourse, ululating, finding its way into obscure corners, riding upon the wind like a nightmare. The face fixed Araña with a gaze that would have frozen the blood of an ordinary person.

Araña just stood and watched and listened, rapt, as the woman, transparent in starlight but as real as the sand underfoot, came gliding along the riverbed, crying frightfully for her lost children.

16

Lloyd roamed about town for a while during the early afternoon but encountered little else of interest at the moment. The overheard conversation at the diner was (no pun intended) food enough for thought, and would require checking on. And of course that little chat with the old drunk, Jefe Sandoval, had provided some few things to ponder as well. Children of the sky, indeed. By all appearances, this was going to be a more intriguing assignment than he had anticipated. Life was full of surprises.

Around three o'clock, back at the house, he set up the comm unit again in the living room and started to connect to Charles Wu by video, but thought better of it; Charles would probably be off the floor by now and he'd have to talk to that asshole Wendell Sims, whom Lloyd suspected of having gotten his credentials out of a box of breakfast cereal, as a prize only slightly more impressive than the usual plastic whistle or baseball card. Sims was a nerd. As much as Lloyd liked to give Charles Wu a bad time about being of Chinese extraction and so on, he very much admired the man's solid grasp of the job. No, he'd get what he needed from the system without a video link.

After typing in the appropriate codes, he sat back and waited, mixing himself a gin and tonic. Before long, the comm unit was chattering with life again, and paper was issuing from the little printer. He sipped his drink and watched as the report appeared, capped by the usual TOP SECRET NOPAL heading and myriad routing data.

Group Epsilon databases contain the following information on William J. Weston:

Born 20 August 1966 in Lovington, New Mexico. Caucasian male. Father Herbert Weston, mother b. Lorraine Daly. Height 5 ft. 11 in., weight approx. 165 pounds, hair brown, eyes brown. CIA files (see routing data above) include photo from crowd surveillance, El Paso, Texas, during antiwar demonstration, Persian Gulf War, 19 January 1991. Minimal routine surveillance since that time shows no further suspicious activity. Employment since July 1993: proofreader for Artesia (New Mexico) *Daily Guardian*. Unmarried.

Group Epsilon databases contain the following information on Lisa Jaramillo:

Born 10 November 1961 in Seminole, Texas. Hispanic female. Father Carlos Jaramillo, mother b. Guadalupe Carrillo. Height 5 ft. 5 in., weight approx. 120 lbs., hair black, eyes brown. Project Starsift file exists due to minimal routine family surveillance, as subject's father's brother Ruben Jaramillo (see cross-references above) was present at crash retrieval, Roswell, New Mexico, 5 July

> 1947. Lisa Jaramillo married Gary Logan
> 16 June 1978, Midland, Texas, one son
> Gerald Logan b. 3 August 1980. Lisa
> Jaramillo Logan divorced (Midland, Texas)
> 8 October 1998. No suspicious activity to
> date.

Lloyd was a little annoyed to see that the files were slightly out of date or incomplete on a couple of points, according to the conversation he had been privy to in the diner. First, Weston was no longer employed at the newspaper in Artesia. Second, the computers should have picked up on the fact that Weston, a known antiwar demonstrator and subversive, had a family member (his father) who knew someone present at the Roswell UFO crash retrieval: Ruben Jaramillo, the girl's uncle. Sloppy, the system not noticing such a connection, however slight or indirect a connection it was. He'd have to talk to Charles Wu about this. Meanwhile, he busied himself typing a report into the files, on the overheard conversation. Very fortunate, that stop in the diner; the information garnered thereby almost made it worth having struggled through a decidedly vomitous hamburger. He'd go back there, though, because evidently the place was a kind of social crossroads for the town, a good spot to listen to loose talk.

Shutting the comm unit down and packing it away, he finished his drink and made ready to go back out. So far it had been a productive day; besides the intercepted talk at the diner, he'd had that little chat with Jefe Sandoval, and though he hadn't run into Araña yet, the old Indian woman, he was sure he'd see her about town soon enough. Meanwhile, there was the one other major lead, and he could follow up on that directly: the store Paco's Emporium, and its reportedly rather unusual proprietor Paco Rojas.

He drove north on Chamisa Street. Paco's Emporium, a sprawling two-story stucco building on the southwest corner of Chamisa and Camino del Sol, took only five minutes to reach, and the oddly painted windows were taking on stranger hues now that the sun would be setting soon and the daylight was growing more diffuse. What in hell were these designs supposed to mean, anyway? Some of them looked vaguely runic, some were moon-signs, some looked like Indian petroglyphs, all done up in bizarre shades of purple and orange and green and less identifiable colors. Whatever the window decor might mean, Lloyd figured he'd better not lose too much time pondering them, as the time was already 4:43, and the sign on the door said that the Emporium would close at five. He pulled the door open with a clang of the little bell attached, and stepped inside.

The light in here wasn't any too intense, and it took his eyes a few seconds to adjust. To the left of the door, a battered-looking little counter reached across that corner of the room, and a man sat behind the counter on a tall wooden stool. From what Lloyd could see in this light, the man's complexion was dark, his hair black going over to gray, his face an almost classic mix of Hispanic and Indian heritage. So this was the Paco Rojas of government-surveillance legend and song. Nothing suspicious, in particular, was recorded of him; he was simply supposed to be one of those walking repositories of local legendry, and he did reportedly have more than a passing interest in UFO lore.

Lloyd nodded to him. "Afternoon."

Paco Rojas nodded back. "How may I help you?"

"Oh, nothing in particular," Lloyd said. "I was just driving by and thought I'd stop in."

"Please feel free to look around," Rojas said.

Lloyd turned to survey the interior of the room, which was lined with display racks and shelves, stretching back some considerable distance into the gloom. The things displayed were of a rather incredible variety. Some shelves held bric-a-brac that might have been imported from Mexico: wooden icons decorated in silver, clay carvings of Mayan or Aztec gods,

116

wooden flutes. Nearby, a whole section of the wall was festooned with little plastic bags containing powders of various colors; the labels were in Spanish. *Pulvo del diablo,* one of them said. These bags were interspersed with various odd and obscure religious statues and charms and pungent bundles of incense and tall multicolored candles. There were paperback books, both English and Spanish; *Avatars of Zeta Reticulae and Channels to Wisdom,* one of them was titled, whatever the hell that meant. Wandering a little distance toward the back of the store, Lloyd wondered what the market was, around here, for all this peculiar merchandise, as he was the only browser in the place at the moment. The store might have gone over big in Harvard Square, but here?

He had scarcely formed this thought when the bell clanged in front and the door opened and closed. Glancing back toward the counter, Lloyd saw that the newcomer was none other than old Jefe Sandoval. Not much chance of good old Paco ringing up a big sale there, Lloyd mused. But the proprietor didn't sound at all annoyed to see the old man.

"Jefe, my friend. *Bienvenido.* How are you?" Rojas' voice barely carried far enough back in the store to reach Lloyd; the place seemed to muffle the sound.

"Pretty well," Jefe was replying. "And how about you, *cuate?*"

"Can't complain," Rojas said.

Continuing to listen to their conversation, Lloyd edged farther into the back regions of the store. In the very rear a rather massive wooden door lolled a little open, and a musty odor, admixed with some other smell, drifted up to suggest that this door led to a stairwell into the cellar. Unusual; most buildings in this part of the country didn't have cellars. What was that *other* odor? Not exactly unpleasant, but certainly not pleasant either; he'd never smelled anything quite like it.

"It's getting to be time," Jefe was saying, back up at the front of the store. The voice called Lloyd back from his reverie.

117

"Time to close?" Paco Rojas replied.

"Naw, you know what I mean," Jefe said. "Time. Time for Arroyo. He's getting *inquieto*. Restless. The stars are coming right for him to move."

Lloyd had been moving back toward the counter, and though he was still halfway down the aisle he was in, when Jefe made this remark, he could see the two men, one behind the counter, one leaning across it from the other side, and he distinctly saw Paco Rojas jerk his head toward the back of the store, as if to gesture to Jefe that he should watch what he was saying, someone was listening. Maybe, Lloyd thought, that's a doubtful interpretation; but he didn't think so. In any case Jefe had turned around to peer into the room and had seen Lloyd, who was stepping back up toward the counter now.

"*Señor* Lombardy," Jefe said, nodding stiffly.

"You're good remembering names," Lloyd said. Even phony ones, he could have added. He noted that Paco Rojas was watching him with a glint of what just might have been suspicion, or perhaps it was just a small-town reluctance to warm up to outsiders, hard to tell.

"I got a good memory," the old man said. "Ain't that true, Paco?"

The man behind the counter nodded. "True, *amigo*." He glanced at his wristwatch, and the gesture gave Lloyd the feeling that the fact that it was nearly closing time simply made a ready excuse to shut this whole conversation off.

"I know you gotta close up," Jefe said, addressing Paco, and he shuffled over to the door and went out, mumbling a goodbye over his shoulder. The proprietor, left alone with Lloyd, nodded to him again and said, "I hope you'll stop back in, Mr.—Lombardy?"

"Oh, I will," Lloyd said, taking his leave with a jangle of the bell on the door. Count on it, he added silently; I'll be back. Soon.

At the house he popped a frozen dinner into the microwave and fixed a pot of coffee. He had a feeling that it might be a rather long evening, as he had some things he wanted to keep an eye on.

Not the least of which was Paco's Emporium.

He couldn't have said exactly why, but something about the place stirred vague responses in the back of his mind.

When it was good and dark he took the necessary equipment, drove back up Chamisa Street, parked the car in an unobtrusive spot around the corner, and settled himself in the weedy vacant lot across Chamisa Street from Paco's store, training a pair of binoculars on the windows. It was a good setup for surveillance. He had clumps of mesquite on his left and right to block himself off from view, and nothing but the blind side of a bank building behind him. He was hunkered down low enough on the ground so that the weeds in front of him, though low enough to allow him a clear view of Paco's window, would also hide him from anyone who might happen to stroll past.

First he scanned the window across the way with his binoculars, noting that while the blinds were partly closed, a low light filtered through from behind them, enough to allow him to see that Paco was indeed there, moving about; he seemed to be puttering around, near the sales counter. He was probably going over the cash receipts for the day, though Lloyd could scarcely imagine what anyone, especially these cowboy types around here, would want with any of Paco's recondite merchandise. At any rate, there Paco was, working late.

And now there was somebody else, too.

Paco's head had come up as if in response to someone's coming near, from the interior of the shop. And indeed there was another figure moving about now, though Lloyd couldn't see clearly enough through the blinds to make out who it might be. Time to unlimber some other equipment, as this promised to be a conversation now. He reached into the canvas bag beside him on the ground and drew out the rifle mike, a new model that he had been itching to try out anyway.

Positioning it out in front of him on its little tripod legs, he aimed it toward Paco's window and slipped the earphones on. An observer might have thought he was setting up a sniper routine, but no bullets would be fired here. The rifle mike, about a foot shorter than the older models, very compact and now extra sensitive, would pick up a whisper, would pick up the sound of someone swallowing, the sound of their stomach grumbling. Worm farts, distinct and clear, at a hundred yards, the training session leader had said, and he had no doubt spoken truly. Lloyd lay very still and listened through the earphones. This conversation might turn out to be about as interesting as a church luncheon, but then you never could tell.

"You came up early tonight," Paco was saying.

"Mmh," another voice said. Lloyd, still training the binoculars on the shop window, could see only a vague, shadowy suggestion of someone else moving around near Paco. Someone rather short? A child, or a midget? That was the impression.

"Jefe Sandoval came in today," Paco was saying. "He thinks something is going to happen, very soon."

"Mmh," the other voice said again, a nearly toneless kind of hum that had an odd quality about it, something not readily pinned down to familiar associations. The shadowy figure moved a little closer to the windowblinds, but Lloyd, squinting through the binoculars, still couldn't quite make out who it was. After a few seconds Paco spoke up again.

"I don't know, I don't know," he was saying. "Who can tell? Maybe nothing can stop it." This was odd, Lloyd mused; Paco made it sound as if the other party to the conversation had said something, but Lloyd hadn't heard a word. "Whatever powers can be brought to bear—" Paco said, but he apparently scooted a chair or something across the floor, and the sound drowned out the rest of the sentence.

120

After a few moments silence, Paco continued: "Yes. Frightfully potent." Again, it was as if the man were responding to some unheard remark. Lloyd wondered momentarily if there was something wrong with the rifle mike, but he knew better than that. A tentative hypothesis was beginning to form itself in the back of his mind, but it would take time to pursue it. Meanwhile, Paco was saying: "Yes, good night. Is there anything you need?" But Lloyd heard no response. Straining, he seemed to catch a glimpse of the other figure, much shorter than Paco's shadowy outline against the blinds, and saw this vague form move away from the window and become lost to view in the interior of the store. After a few minutes Paco himself moved away from the window too, and the lights went off. Lloyd listened for a while longer, but there was nothing to hear.

Sighing, he packed the rifle mike back into the canvas bag, got up, dusted himself off, and walked to his car. What he was beginning to think would scarcely have been even a remotely acceptable hypothesis to most people, but when you knew the sorts of things Lloyd knew——

It was going to take some time to be sure. Meanwhile, he had other things to check on. He drove west on Camino del Sol and turned onto Old Roswell Road and headed north.

He remembered, of course, from the conversation at the diner, where she lived. Lisa Jaramillo, whom he was going to get to know better, one way or the other.

17

Lisa didn't really have all that much stuff in her car, but it was nearly dark by the time she had carried it all up the porch steps and through the door to the living room, where she piled things on the sofa and chairs with a weary resolve to sort them out later. She did feel weary suddenly. Maybe she was finally feeling the psychic drain that a divorce and a move to another place and a lifestyle change were supposed to impose on a person. Or maybe it had just been a long day. What with her going by the hotel to let them know she was checking out, stopping off to make arrangements for telephone service, and then swinging by the market at the corner of Zia and Mesa to pick up a few basic groceries, the afternoon had been busy, and she thought the it's-just-been-a-long-day theory had a lot going for it.

In any case she flopped in a chair for a minute and caught her breath. Probably, she reflected, she was expecting too much of herself, as usual. When you thought about it, how could a person feel energized up to the eyebrows at this time of day, given all that had been happening? Here she was, about to settle into a new house, when not very long ago—mere days—she was still under the same roof with Gary, out in Midland. (And with Jerry, she thought, and felt a dry lump in her throat, and resolved not to think about her son right now. It hurt. As soon as she got her phone put in, she'd call.) Good old rat-bastard Gary, doing his best to be unobtrusive while she packed and made ready to leave, watching her all the while with that well-whose-fault-is-it-anyway look in his eye. Yes, only days ago she still lived in Midland, close to friends and acquaintances, still had her old job, still had never really been out on her own. Now here she was, away in a strange place, a new town, a different house, soon a different job perhaps, and certainly a different set of faces and names—everything different. The very walls here, dressed out in faded wallpaper, frowned at her and said it again: different, different, different.

Casting her glance around the silent room, she wondered idly which was more trying: to have only slight changes in one's life, or to really go for it and have changes all around? Which scenario would have been easier to take: experiencing just a single change (a divorce only, say, but stay in the same house while he moves out, keep your same old job, follow mostly your same old routine) or experiencing, on the other hand, a multitude of changes all at once?

Mulling it over, she decided, at least for the moment, that it was more comfortable, in a way, to revise everything at the same time: dump your cheating husband, move out, drive to another state, look for another job, make new friends. She might change her mind later, but right now she thought it would most likely turn out to be better, this sweeping alteration of her life, as opposed to just getting rid of Gary and then trying to conduct the rest of her affairs unaltered, as if nothing had happened. She allowed herself to feel just a twinge of optimism—just a squitch—to the effect that she would soon come to like this house, would ease into a new job and find herself liking that too, would rather effortlessly make new friends.

Still, she was rather glad she had persuaded that Weston fellow to wait until tomorrow night to go out to dinner; she would have been too tired to enjoy it tonight, and anyway she still wasn't sure how she felt about getting involved with anybody right now.

"*On the rebound* is what I think they call this stage of existence," she said to the four walls of the room. They didn't answer, which was just as well. Don't tell me, she thought, that I'm already going to start feeling spooked, right away the first night, being alone in a house out on the edge of town—not a healthy way to think. She would definitely get this place fixed up and make it feel like home. But it was going to take some time. Home wasn't just a place, it was a state of mind, and a state of mind needed nurturing. She got up with a sigh and made her way to the kitchen.

The entree at dinner tonight was going to be meat loaf *à la* frozen dinner. Easier than cooking. She wasn't really too well set up right now to do that. Most frozen dinners, in her experience, tasted pretty much like camel shit, but for now the easy way out would have to do.

Eating her rather cheerless dinner at the little table in the kitchen at the back of the house, she stopped chewing for a moment and listened.

What was that?

Some odd sound from back behind the house? She sat still and listened. Nothing.

No, there it was again.

A high, thin, keening sort of wail, like a child crying, or a woman perhaps. Down in the middle of town she wouldn't have thought it too odd, probably would have assumed it was just someone passing on the street, but here on the fringe of town, the sound was unaccountable; there really shouldn't be anybody out there.

Especially behind the house.

"*Carajos,*" she muttered, getting up from the table and fishing a flashlight out of a paper bag of odds and ends on the counter. She half realized that she was striking a pose of annoyance to keep her response from seeming like something

124

else altogether. Meanwhile, the barely audible but undeniable wailing went on and on. Someone was definitely out there.

She pulled a jacket on, opened the door, and stepped out onto the back porch, switching the light on out there as she came out. She stood and listened.

There, off in the night somewhere, the crying.

Something about it, some elusive quality, made her skin crawl. For a moment she didn't think she was going to be able to muster enough courage to move from where she stood, transfixed and listening, as the ineffably sad wail went on, on, in long ululations, somehow dreadful to hear.

Well. Like it or not, she had to find out. Someone could be in trouble out there. A lost child, maybe, or someone hurt. She snapped the flashlight on and descended the porch steps.

Out behind the house, the ground was bare, featureless, but became gradually covered with low range grass and occasional clumps of cactus as one went farther back. She trained the wan beam of light on the ground ahead of her and picked her steps carefully. Far off in the dark, or maybe not so far off as it seemed to be, the crying sound continued, a sound like a lost soul.

She came to the wire fence at the back of the property, and found it sagging so low at one spot that she simply stepped over it and kept going.

The farther she went, the denser the undergrowth became: mesquite, prickly-pear, here and there a yucca with spikes that the flashlight caused to cast long, eerie shadows out across the sandy ground. After what seemed like a long time but probably was not, she stopped and listened. She had thought for a moment that the wailing sound had stopped, but no, her own footfalls had somewhat covered it up. It was still there, floating ghostlike on the night air. By now Lisa was perhaps a hundred yards out from the house, and when she turned and looked back, the house was huddled angular and gaunt against the darker backdrop of night sky, and the light from the back porch and the kitchen window, though they should have looked warm and cosy, only made her feel all the more foolhardy for being out here at night by herself, with only a feeble flashlight for comfort.

Ahead, farther on, she could just make out the faint outlines of the entrance to the arroyo, its sides gnarled with shadowy ghosts of cedar and piñon. The sides were at first only a shallow rim for the sandy floor of the wash, then they would gradually deepen to become canyonlike walls too tall to see over, so that one was walking in a sort of maze.

These things had always rather fascinated her, these great dry washes that carved their way across miles of desert, and though she had never walked in one of any size, she knew enough about them to know that they were scary places to venture into at night, when each branching of the main course of the wash would become a dark mystery, its farther reaches so little illuminable by the beam of a flashlight that the nocturnal wanderer would have to regard them as forbidding. A fall over twisted roots or clusters of cactus could mean a nasty mishap, and of course there would be rattlesnake holes here and there, little harbingers of menace. Lisa hoped that there would be no reason for her to enter the arroyo.

But now the high keening wafted to her once again on the night air, its tones heavy with an undefinable strangeness, a kind of melancholy, and she froze in her tracks and listened, placing the sound somewhere ahead of her, within the shadowy confines of the arroyo. To see what the situation was, she would have to go in.

Swallowing hard and training the flashlight ahead of her, she resolved to do what she needed to do before she lost any more of her nerve. Taking a deep breath, she walked toward the entrance to the arroyo, trying to go softly.

A corner of her mind nagged: are you trying to walk softly so that you can hear, or so that you can avoid being heard?

Pushing this unwelcome thought away, she stepped into the wash and scanned the scene before her as well as she could in the feeble light. Off on the horizon the moon had risen, but a scudding froth of black clouds had largely hidden its chalky face, and the desert was dark except for her light. She could just make out the further walls of the wash where they turned, up ahead, and the dry watercourse twisted out of sight. Beyond that point, somewhere in the unimaginable dark, the low crying continued. Lisa shuddered to hear it, closer to it now; there was something about it that was positively unsettling.

She walked slowly into the arroyo to the point where the sandy floor took a swerve to the left, around the ragged corner of the arroyo wall, and soon she was far enough around to see something of that next portion of the wash, which was now an unbending stretch for perhaps some hundred yards ahead, and perhaps some thirty or forty feet from wall to wall. A low, moaning wind had sprung up, and the odd crying off there in the night somewhere blended eerily with the tones of the wind. Lisa trudged on, following odd-angled turns in the dry rivercourse, sometimes fetching up against dead ends when she entered a side channel that had no egress, and backing out and finding the main course of the wash once again, following it through further twists and turns until, after what seemed like a good half mile inside the arroyo, she came out into a relatively wide place in the sandy riverbed, where the root-gnarled walls might now have been some sixty or seventy feet apart. The moon was coming out a little from behind its veil of clouds now, and she could see a little more.

She wasn't sure she understood what she saw.

Near where she stood, and near the lefthand wall of the wash, there was an odd kind of confusion, as if she could almost see something, but not quite. She had the fleeting impression of someone standing there swathed in rags, but that must have been a trick of the light, because now that she

127

blinked and looked again, no one was standing there. Instead, lowering the beam of her flashlight, she saw a rather large tarantula scutter down a hole in the sand. She shuddered again, involuntarily; she hated those wretched things, in spite of herself—she knew they were harmless, but they were so *damned* ugly. She cast her light quickly around to see that there weren't any others.

But what dominated her attention now was the *other* impression, the impression from farther down the arroyo, where the beam of the flashlight played out to a hopeless diffuseness of inadequate illumination.

She thought someone was standing there.

Someone in a kind of gossamer robe or dress? It was confusing to the eye, this impression, because the dim contours of this vision seemed to blend problematically with the pale moonlight, making it impossible really to know what one was looking at, if anything.

But whoever or whatever was there, eerily outlined in wan lineaments of moonlight, was moving.

Lisa had the impression that the robes, or whatever they were, fluttered and waved in the sighing wind, and that the figure who wore these robes was receding into the shadows behind her. Yes, Lisa had thought just this thought: behind *her*, for the ghostly figure was almost certainly that of a woman, tall and lithe and spectral. Her robes and the woman herself in this uncertain light looked almost translucent, as if one could see right through to the sandy wall behind her, a wall nearly hidden in a dense shadowy blackness that looked alive and restless. The weirdly plaintive crying went on, though intermittently, as if it became lost from one moment to the next in the dismal sighing of the wind.

If the woman was in trouble, Lisa had to try to help her, though her pounding heart urged her to stand her ground, pleaded with her not to get any closer to this apparition, whatever it was.

Against her better judgment, she walked toward the figure in the moonlight.

And she was perhaps fifty feet away from the vision before her, when that pallid figure seemed simply to fade back into the shadows altogether. But not without turning its head and casting a final look, square into Lisa's face.

And in that instant, what Lisa saw in the leprous moonlight was a bone-white face aglow with horror, its eyes fastened black and penetrating upon her. Then, with one last dreadful cry, the figure was gone.

But Lisa's terror was not, for in that moment the whole thing came crashing down upon her mind—the hideous figure that had floated before her, the soul-chilling cry that had come to her on the wind, the sudden realization that no one should be out here, under any imaginable circumstances, at this time of night, and the even more sudden and mind-numbing realization that Lisa herself was indeed here, unaccountably, in this lonely and unseen place, and if anything happened to her, no one would even know she was here.

The whole realization came upon her with such force that she wheeled about and ran, clutching the flashlight spasmodically, dodging around rocks and clumps of mesquite and cactus. It was like one of those nightmares where one tries to run through the deadly fog of dream but cannot—the cold, thick sand seemed to clutch at her feet, the very night air seemed to thicken against her. Ahead, in the jittering beam of the flashlight, the lines of the arroyo wall were incomprehensible; she couldn't tell which way to run. Rounding a corner, she bolted into a narrow stretch of riverbed that ran straight for what felt like an intolerable distance before it veered to the left, and when she ran that way, she found herself in a cul-de-sac, a blind offshoot of the rivercourse, where uncompromising walls of sand raised their sightless faces before her and offered no way through.

Spinning back around, she headed back out of the side-channel, and for a heart-stopping moment she thought that this way too, the way she had come in, was an impasse, and she only now realized in some panicked corner of her mind that she was crying. But when her vision cleared she saw that there was a clear way out after all, and she ran all the faster, showering sand to both sides as she went. Could she find her way out? This arroyo was like a natural mirror-maze where one might conceivably wander lost forever. Farther on, the contours of the dry rivercourse grew unclear again, and once again she darted into a blind, where only tangles of cedar root greeted her. A dry burring filled the air, and turning around and directing the flashlight beam ahead of her, she found her way out of the side-channel blocked by a five-foot rattlesnake, coiled and ready to strike, its triangular head gleaming terribly in the quavering light.

Someone was moaning, and she only dimly realized that it was she herself. Her chest ached from running and from this new access of fear. She thought there might just be enough room to slip through between the snake and the wall of the side-channel, maybe a space of four or five feet, enough room for her to get back out into the main rivercourse. Pressing as close to the root-choked wall as she could, she edged through, watching the snake as it undulated and drew back to strike. In one ghastly motion it did strike, but by now Lisa was past it, backing her way out into the main channel, and the snake connected only with empty air. A strangely lucid part of her mind prattled about something she had read somewhere about a rattlesnake's only being able to strike a distance equal to half its length. Abandoning these thoughts, she ran for all she was worth, caught her left foot in a tangle of mesquite, and sprawled to the ground, burying her face in the sand and driving the flashlight into an outcropping of rock with a sickening crack. The light was off, gone, and now only a pale wash of yellow moonlight illumined the ground about her. Was that the rattling of the snake, or another

130

snake, that she heard now, or just some trick of the blood singing in her ears? Spitting out a gritty mouthful of sand, she rolled to one side, pressed her hand into a prickly-pear cactus, and cried out with the pain, but sprang the rest of the way to her feet and kept running.

The rest was a nightmare kaleidoscope of impressions, running, dodging this way and that, running again, running faster, trying desperately to make out where she was going in the near-dark, for another armada of cloud had sailed across the moon and she could see barely anything at all. Her skin, her clothes were torn, her lungs ached for air, her legs felt sluggish and unable to carry her further, but she ran on, snuffling, a hot river of tears coursing down her cheeks. She would never find her way out of the arroyo, she was miserably, hopelessly lost. But after an eternity of running, she came into open desert, chaparral country that stretched limitlessly around her under the re-emerging face of the moon. Even now, though, her heart wouldn't stop pounding, her feet wouldn't rest, and she bolted toward the distant house.

And ran square into someone standing in the way before her.

18

Moonlight spread a pallid and somehow sickly radiance down the meandering length of the arroyo, whose walls sprouted ragged gnarls of cedar and piñon root that cast eerie shadows out onto the sandy floor of the wash. It wasn't clear what was happening. At one point, a female figure in rags seemed to stand wavering on shaky, spindly legs, looking down at herself, then raising her gaze to the stretch of dry wash before her, where the darkness down there writhed as if it were conscious and fitful. Out of that churning blackness came a diaphanous suggestion of another female figure, lithe and ghostly, trailing white raiments about it like whispers of dream in the wan light of the moon, whose face hid itself from time to time behind sinister black clouds but reappeared to spread a patina of spectral moonglow over the figure that was struggling to emerge from the blackness down the arroyo, where a frightful face now showed through the gloom, its mouth agape and moaning now with a chilling tone of horror and sadness, its eyes glowing darkly like fat, avid beetles. The point of view seemed to collapse to the sandy ground, and seemed to grow multiple and fragmented, as if the figure down the way were seen through shards of glass.

Suddenly someone else was on the scene, another woman, someone vaguely familiar. She held a flashlight, training its feeble beam shakily down the arroyo, where it fell upon the dreadful face that was swimming out of the darkness. The sight engendered an effect of such raw hideousness that she wheeled about and ran, and fell, and got up and sprinted away again, and ran into someone, and screamed.

And *Bill* screamed, bolting upright in bed.

Damn. What a dream. He ran a hand over his face and through his hair, finding himself drenched in sweat. He couldn't remember ever having had such a nightmare as this, and hoped he never had one again. But he couldn't place exactly what it was about the dream that so disturbed him, and indeed could remember the dream only in fragments. Swinging his legs off the bed, he stumbled to the bathroom, used the toilet, washed his hands, and ran a wet washcloth over his face and the back of his neck. This action, which should have relieved him, suddenly made him feel ineffably disconnected and lonely. He realized, then, that depending on what is going on in one's life, there are moments when a hotel room can be damnably impersonal and cold.

Getting back into bed, he chided himself silently for feeling this way. Hell, it was only a dream, and in the real world things weren't going so terribly bad when you got right down to it. He'd met a nice lady just today, and was taking her to dinner tomorrow night. He didn't have a new place to live yet, but he could scarcely expect to, this soon. The fact that he was unemployed wasn't really an issue right now; he could find another job fairly easily, he suspected. So he shouldn't let himself be disturbed by a dream.

Except that it came to him, unbidden, that the other woman in the dream vision, the one who came to the arroyo and saw what she saw and ran away, was Lisa.

He lay in the dark, eyes wide, and pondered this. Well, so what? So he had met her just today, had been impressed by her in a variety of ways, had been unconsciously thinking

133

about her when he retired for the night, had peopled his dreams with the fresh memory of her. Nothing so strange about that.

Now that he thought about it, he was pretty sure that the other, earlier impression of the woman in rags was a reflection of the strange crone he had met in the park. She was a little scary in real life, actually, but there wasn't anything so outrageous about this either. No subtle dream symbolism here for the psychoanalysts to have fun with, for sure, just nocturnal memories of very real daylight experiences.

But he was avoiding the other parts of the dream.

He was avoiding the part about the face emerging down there in the shadows of the arroyo wall, the face that glowed like something impure, something dead—"a dismal light about it, like a bad lobster in a dark cellar." The words from Charles Dickens came back to him with a shudder. And he was avoiding the part about the person whom Lisa ran into in the dream, to him only a fleeting impression of someone rather tall and unsmiling. Bill sat back up on the side of the bed and tried to massage the back of his neck.

What else? What else, in the dream? Something else. He struggled to remember, though he wasn't sure he really wanted to.

He knew what it was. It was the darkness itself, behind the dreadful apparition in the arroyo. The darkness itself had seemed to stir, writhe, quiver, as if something in it were alive. Almost as if *it* were alive, the very darkness itself.

That couldn't be anything so remarkable, dreams were often like that.

Weren't they?

Or was this a nightmare vision so singular, so unique, that it meant that his subconscious mind was trying to tell him something? Or that other forces were trying to tell him something, forces so incomprehensible that he was scarcely in any position to imagine them?

Christ, he was going to have to get hold of himself, this was crazy, he needed his sleep, and he was behaving like a child, letting a nightmare rattle him this much.

But maybe behaving like a child wasn't so unreasonable sometimes. Maybe when children recoil from nightmare, he mused, they recoil from a Great Unknown that the rest of us have learned not to let ourselves think about. Children start out close to a great many truths in their untrammeled awareness, then let themselves have this insight bred out of them, perhaps for peace of mind, perhaps for social reasons less defensible. Maybe behaving like a child, at times, meant having an honest, square look at what was going on.

In any event, if it was childish to let this dream disturb him so much, then so be it—he felt convinced, now, that the dream meant something more than the random reverberations of nightmare in a tired mind.

And he felt frightened. Not for himself, but for Lisa.

He wished he could talk to her just now, but he figured she had no phone yet. Maybe he ought to get up, get dressed, and drive over there, to her house, and see that she was okay.

But that would mean clomping up onto her porch, knocking on the door, waking her up and probably scaring the hell out of her at this hour of the night. He'd better wait. Surely she was okay.

But he was worried, and guilty about his own irresolution, and when the sun came up, he had had only a little fitful sleep. Exhaustion overcame him at the point when he might have gotten up, and in spite of himself he fell back asleep and didn't rouse himself till nearly noon.

19

Jerry Logan turned over once in bed, tried to get comfortable again, turned over once more, and gave it up. He hadn't slept worth a damn, but there wasn't anything he could do about that now. If he didn't get a move on, he was going to be late for work.

Swinging his legs off the bed, he shot a glance across the room, where his reflection in the mirror over the bureau did the same for him. God, he really did look like he felt. Pushing clothes and various other clutter aside with his feet, he trudged to the bathroom, resolving to clean his room sometime. What would Mom think if she saw this mess? Dad had only glowered at him, shaking his head, as much as to say: why bother talking about it?

When you got right down to it, he and his father didn't bother to talk about a whole hell of a lot these days.

Which was just as well. Their last conversation, if you could call it that, was largely one-sided. *You should be in college, not working at a damn car wash. You give me one reason in the world why you couldn't have signed up for some courses at the community college this fall? You could still have worked parttime, for Christ's sake. What's gotten into you?*

He had tried to reply something like: I don't know, I guess I just needed some time to get——. Whereupon Dad had said: *I know, get your head together. Typical damn kid response.* And if that wasn't a typical damn Dad response, he'd never heard one.

"What I wanted to say," Jerry mumbled to his reflection in the bathroom mirror, "was what do you expect? With you and Mom breaking up, I'm supposed to go jump into a bunch of classes and shine my ass off?"

That was what had "gotten into him," all right. He tried to tell himself that it didn't really bother him all that much—hell, just about everybody he knew had folks who'd done the old split—but that was crap. It did bother him. Mom ought to be here. Instead, she was God knows where, out in New Mexico someplace. Maybe she was okay.

Maybe she wasn't.

Well, wherever she was, it probably wasn't all that far from Midland, not as if she'd gone to the moon or something. Maybe she'd call soon.

And maybe not.

That was what he loved about life: all of its wonderful certainties.

By the time he showered and picked his room up a little and made it to the kitchen, Dad was almost finished with breakfast. "Nice of you to put in an appearance, Jerry. Aren't you going to be late?"

Jerry shrugged, pouring himself out a glass of orange juice and popping some bread into the toaster. "I'll make it."

His father shook his head, smiling ruefully. "Another day setting the world on fire at the car wash, eh Jerr? You've got a great career ahead of you."

Jerry retrieved a piece of toast and started buttering it, standing at the counter. Sitting down with Dad didn't seem like the right gesture just now. "Do we have to get into this again? I don't plan to work at that place forever. And I don't plan to stay in Midland forever either."

"Oh, no," his father intoned, crimping up his mouth as if to suggest that staying in Midland would have been the blackest of atrocities. "I guess you'll want to go charging off one of these days and become a damn nomad, like your mother."

"Might be better than hanging around here," Jerry mumbled, chewing his toast. "Anyway, if Mom picked up and left, whose fault was that?"

"You watch that mouth of yours," his father said, getting up from the table and going for his briefcase. "I don't know who you think you're talking to. Whatever you think, I'm still your father, and you might do well to remember that."

"Dad," Jerry said, sighing, "this is beginning to sound like a soap opera. Why don't we just drop it? I—look, I'm sorry if I said anything out of line. But this whole thing with you and Mom hasn't been easy for me, you know."

His father headed out the door. "Yeah, yeah, yeah, children of broken homes get their psyches bruised and all that bleeding-heart bullshit. I've heard it all before."

Jerry wiped his mouth with a napkin. "But were you listening?"

His father shot him one last irritated look as he left. "Like I said, you want to watch your mouth."

"I will," Jerry said to the empty room. "Who knows, my mouth might say something true one of these days, and we couldn't have that, could we, Dad? The truth don't go down sometimes in good old corporate America, does it?"

Mom hadn't been too happy either about his not starting college this fall, but she had understood. Say what you wanted about being a mama's boy or whatever, he missed her, and he wasn't ashamed of it. He didn't know why, exactly, but he was worried about her, too. It was just a feeling, stupid probably, but that didn't help. She'd better call pretty soon, or he was going to go looking for her.

20

Lisa had emerged from the arroyo and started to sprint toward the house, when she ran full-tilt into someone standing in the dark. Whoever it was, she hit them so hard that it nearly knocked the wind out of her. She screamed, but it came out as a sickly-sounding wheeze. She spun on one foot, wheeling her arms to regain her balance, and managed to end up standing rather than sprawling. She blinked through the gloom, where an emerging moon was just beginning to give shape to a tall, slender figure standing beside a clump of mesquite, maybe five or six feet from her.

She struggled to get her breath. "Who the hell are *you?*"

The light from the moon grew a little more pervasive, and in a moment she could see a man's face, late forties or early fifties maybe, a face whose contours were marked in shadow in such a way that whatever the man really looked like, in this light he appeared positively ghoulish. But he was smiling now, and extending a hand.

"Are you all right? I didn't mean to frighten you."

She declined to take his hand. Again, as before, back there in the arroyo, the implications came crashing down frightfully: here she was, out in the chaparral, probably beyond

139

earshot of any human soul except this stranger, and nobody else knew she was out here, so if anything happened to her—

"I—no, it's all right. I mean, you didn't frighten me," she ventured, feeling uncomfortably as if she sounded like an unstrung high school girl to this macho-looking newcomer.

"Well," the man replied, "you could have fooled me. I thought you looked pretty scared."

She hesitated for a moment, but finally said what she said because she couldn't think of anything else. "I said *you* didn't frighten me."

The stranger seemed to consider this. "Ah. Then what did? What were you running from?"

The moon had fully emerged now from its veil of cloud, and she could see that he was a rather distinguished-looking fellow who somehow seemed familiar to her, she couldn't have said why. "I don't know what I was running from," she said, again feeling that she probably sounded rather foolish.

"I guess it isn't any of my business," the man said, "but what are you doing out here anyway, at night? Person could get hurt stumbling around out here."

"Especially a woman," she said, trying to make it both a question and a statement.

He shook his head. "I didn't mean to make it sound like that. All I meant was, it isn't safe, wandering around out here in the dark. Anything happens to you out here, nobody would even be around to help you."

It gave Lisa a bit of a shudder to hear her own thoughts of a few minutes ago, echoed in the words of this unaccountable newcomer. Was what he had just said, about there being nobody to help if something happened out here, just a flat commonsensical statement, or had there been the covert tinge of a threat in it? In any case she heard herself saying: "It's my turn to ask. What are *you* doing here?"

The man shrugged. "I was taking a walk, back out there on the road, and I thought I heard somebody cry out.

Thought maybe I'd better go look, somebody might need help."

This made her feel a little foolish. "Well, thank you, but *estoy bien*—I'm okay. I don't know if it was me you heard, anyway."

"Oh? Who else?"

She shook her head. "I don't know, that's why I came out here. I live in that house over there. I thought I heard someone crying or something, sounded like a woman maybe, or a child. I took my flashlight and walked into the arroyo—" In having been engaged in this unexpected conversation, she had almost forgotten about what she had seen in there, and the memory came back to her now. She shuddered, and hoped that the stranger hadn't noticed, but she thought he had.

"Well? What happened in there?"

She mulled this over. What indeed *had* happened in there? "I'm not sure. Look, can't we walk back toward the house? This place gives me the—"

"Willies?" the man supplied, half smiling.

"Yes. Can't we go?"

"Fine with me," the stranger said. "Oh, I'm sorry, I ought to mind my manners. Name is Travis Lombardy. I'm a salesman, just in town for a few days probably." He offered her a hand again, and this time she took it dutifully.

"I'm Lisa Lo—" There I go again, she thought, old habits die hard. "Lisa Jaramillo."

"Pleased to meet you," the man said, as they started to walk toward the house, picking their steps by moonlight to avoid clumps of cactus and yucca. "But you never did tell me what scared you back there. Did you just get spooked, being in the arroyo in the dark?"

She wondered if she were overreacting a bit to consider this question a little condescending. "No, no. I don't spook that easily. Like I said, I went in there because I heard somebody crying, and I saw her."

141

"Saw who?"

"Her, the woman, the one who was crying."

"What would anybody be doing out here—" the man started to ask.

"I don't know, but I saw her. And the funny thing was, it was like you could look right through her in the moonlight. Like you could see the wall of the arroyo behind her. I know it sounds crazy."

The man walking beside her shrugged again. "Trick of the light."

"I guess so," Lisa said, though she knew, with a queasy feeling in her stomach, that it hadn't just been a trick of the light at all.

"And," the man added as they were coming up to the house, "it sounds to me as if maybe the folktales they tell around here are getting to you."

They stopped a few yards out from the back porch steps. The light spilling out from the kitchen looked fetching to Lisa, and she wished she were back inside, alone. "What folktales?" she asked.

"Oh, I don't know," the man said, "they tell some kind of a story about a woman who wanders the arroyos searching for her lost children."

She thought this over for a moment. "Yes, I think I've heard that. But it wasn't my imagination. Somebody was out there."

The man nodded toward the house. "Live here long?"

"No, not long," she said. She didn't feel comfortable giving out information to him, however harmless it seemed.

"Ever hear anything like that before, from the arroyo?"

"No," she said, rather relishing the irony inherent in the fact that this might only be because it was in fact her first night in the house.

"Well," the man said, "if you're jittery about being here alone—"

"No, no," she hastened to reply, nervous about where this might be leading. "I'll be okay." Suddenly it dawned on her that, wittingly or otherwise, he had managed to get her to divulge that she was alone in the house. Nice going, Lisa, she chided herself. Nice going.

"Well," he said, "if you're sure."

"I'm sure," she said. "Thank you anyway for your concern." She started up the porch steps, more than half afraid that he was going to follow her up. What in God's name was she going to do if he did?

But he didn't. Turning to walk back down the drive toward the road, he waved to her. "Okay. If you hear anything else weird, I'd call the police."

"I don't have—" she said, wincing at yet another blunder. "I'm not worried, but yes, I'll call them if anything happens. *Muchas gracias*, Mr. Lombardy. Good night."

She stepped across the porch and through the door, which she closed and locked behind her. A dingy little kitchen had never looked so good, but she worried if the man out there had really gone. Why did she think that? Of course he would go. Wouldn't he? And why did she still have an odd feeling that she'd seen him before someplace? Did it matter?

With these questions rattling about in her head, she drew the blinds, made some coffee, and sat at the kitchen table sipping it.

At one point she thought she heard, somewhere in the night, a brief keening sort of cry, but it stopped almost as soon as it started, if she hadn't imagined it. Anyway, it could have been a coyote.

Or it could have been that gossamer wisp of a figure floating out there in the arroyo. And it came back to her now, how *alive* the very darkness behind her, behind the floating woman, had looked.

Lisa poured herself another cup of coffee; she wasn't likely to sleep well tonight anyway, so why not? Was she really ready for all this? It made her blush to think it. She suddenly had a mental image of Gary, smiling and clucking, asking her: *So tell me, what made you think you could make it on your own?*

Well, screw him. She could make it on her own perfectly well.

Couldn't she?

After a while she went up to bed, finding the unfamiliar bedroom creepy and imposing in spite of her using her own sheets and blankets and pillowcases. It wasn't home yet, and now she wondered if it ever would be.

And if it wasn't, was that a reflection on her? Her dependence on familiar settings, comfortable routines? Time would tell, she supposed.

She did sleep, in spite of the coffee, and in her dreams she saw, again, the wispy floating woman in the arroyo, a chalky face teetering atop a flowing confusion of gown, undulating in the wind, a spectral face with mouth open in a plaintive cry that even in her dreams made Lisa's forearms turn to gooseflesh. And behind this apparition, the blackness of the night seemed to churn and moil and push the ghostly woman along as it came up the arroyo, seeking the dreamer.

21

It was a new day, and in this business it might always prove to be an interesting one. Truman Lloyd settled himself in for a good morning's work.

Normally he preferred to do this kind of surveillance at night, but the time was right, daytime or not. There wasn't any easier time to set up this kind of wiretap than during a new telephone installation.

Lying on the ground in the weedy field across the road from Lisa Jaramillo's house, he felt even more comfortable with the setup than he had last night, across from Paco's Emporium. Over there, there had been the danger that someone might walk by, might even see him, and that would make things awkward. Out here on the edge of town, even in daylight, there wasn't much chance of anybody walking past, and anybody driving past would be unlikely to spot him here, as he was a good fifty or sixty feet off the road and had mesquite and chamisa on both sides of him. He aimed the device at the appropriate spot on Lisa's house.

He loved these things. Gone were the days of the horse-and-buggy wiretap, where you actually had to do physical things to the telephone hardware. With this thing, somewhat resembling a rifle mike but smaller, you just zeroed in and did it all from a distance. Watching the screen now, he could see that the telephone company was indeed flipping the right switches, going through the process of activating her phone installation—a window opening now on the tiny computer screen actually said: *circuit activation in progress*—and when it was done, all Lloyd had to do was monitor her calls from here. Once this was set up, he could even monitor them from his house, or route them to another operative. For now, he wanted to hear for himself what she was up to.

It was bizarre, this whole business. La Llorona indeed. The eerie thing was that the woman seemed to have experienced something of the sort without being too familiar with the legend. *Yeah, I think I've heard that,* was all she had said. One thing was certain: you had to keep an open mind out here in the desert. This might not have anything to do with the matters he really needed to be watching, but one could never tell. What was it old Jefe Sandoval had said—something monstrous was living in the arroyo because of what happened there. *They killed him,* the old man had declared: the sky-child. This might just be a load of crap. And it might not. In any case Lloyd was going to go have a look at that arroyo himself pretty soon. Like today.

Circuit activiation complete, the message on the little screen said. A dialog box appeared, asking: *Continuous monitor?* He clicked the *yes* button, eased the headset on, and settled down to listen.

He didn't have to wait long. A message appeared on the screen—*dialing*—but he was hearing that for himself. The number she was dialing appeared on the screen too, along with an address in Midland, Texas. There was a soft click in the earphones, and someone said, *"Hello?"*

"Jerry! It's so good to hear your voice," Lisa's own tinny voice said in Lloyd's ear.

"Mom? God, I was worried about you. Where are you?"

"I'm in a little town in New Mexico called Chasco."

The earphones filled with the disembodied but lilting sound of laughter. *"Yeah, it's not a place anybody would know about. It's between Roswell and Fort Sumner."*

"I don't know New Mexico. But I'll look on a map. Are you okay?"

"Well, I miss you, querido, but other than that I'm okay."

"When are you coming home?"

"Jerry, please, darling, we've been all over that before. You know your Dad and I can't ever—"

"I know, I know. It's just, you know, I just wish—"

"Say, it just occurred to me. I didn't even think, when I called. It's Wednesday. What are you doing home?"

There was a silence on the other end. Then: *"Jake canned me this morning."*

"What? Fired you? But why?"

"Aw, I was late for work again."

"Oh, Jerry."

"It was only the second time, Mom. Jake didn't even give me another chance. He said he had a bunch of job applications on his desk, and he didn't need me around if I wasn't going to show up on time."

"This makes me mad, Jerry. Doesn't your father even try to keep you—"

"It's not his fault. Nobody's fault but my own, I know that, Mom. Anyway, what's a job in a dumb car wash?"

"Well, it was a job. This makes me feel bad, like if I had been there I might have—what are you going to do now?"

"I'll find another job, don't worry about me. The question is what are you going to do?"

"Don't worry about me either, hon, I'm doing okay. Got a place to live, and I think I've got a new job, should know in a few days."

"You're going to stay there?"

She laughed. *"Well, for now anyway. It's not much of a town, but—"*

"Can I come out and see you sometime?"

"Oh, querido, *you don't know how much I wish you would. Let me give you my phone number here, and my address."* She repeated the number and the address a couple of times. *"I'd better go now, but you take care. I need to know that you're okay. And I do want to see you."*

"Me too, Mom. I'll call you in a couple of days."

"Do that, please. I love you."

"Love you too. Bye." And the line was clear.

Well now, wasn't that sweet, Lloyd thought, lighting up a cigarette; he didn't think anyone would see the smoke. Hell of a lot of vital information came out of *that* conversation. Now Group Epsilon knew that Jerry Logan had lost his job at the car wash. Oh well. You couldn't expect pay dirt every time. The Wandering Mom hadn't said a word about her weird experience in the arroyo, he noticed. Probably thought there was no use worrying the kid.

Lloyd set the portable cover up over the unit (which was waterproof, but no use taking chances) and checked the unit itself to see that it was firmly planted in the ground and still pointed at the house across the way. He checked to be sure that it was set to record whenever a connection was made. Lisa Jaramillo might indulge in nothing but puerile family chitchat, but whatever she said in the near future, there was going to be a file on it.

Lloyd was just beginning to wonder if he could walk back to where he had parked his car, farther up the road to the north, without attracting attention, when he saw that he was in luck. From across the road came the sound of a door closing. Looking over there, Lloyd saw that she was getting into her car. Perfect. He could walk back to the arroyo without there being any chance of her seeing him. He waited till her car came down the drive and pulled out onto the road and disappeared to the south, then he stood up, dusted himself off, and walked up the road to his car, where he took off his jacket, slipped his shoulder holster on, and replaced the jacket over it. Why he felt better going to the arroyo in the company of his .44 magnum than without it, he wasn't sure, but what the hell.

Skirting the house—he was virtually sure no one else was there, but again, no use taking chances—he walked back to the arroyo and started making his way up its sandy course. How many jobs, he found himself wondering, paid this much for walking up a dry riverbed? Soon the root-entwisted walls rose on his left and right like the sides of a little canyon, and he could see nothing but the twists and turns of the arroyo ahead of him.

Something about the place bothered him. Maybe it was just that there was something a little too primordial, a little too primitive, about it, a dry wash in the desert, when you were a city boy. Sometimes he wished he was back in Detroit, where all you had to be mystified about was the possibility of getting mugged.

He made a turn and found himself in a cul-de-sac, a deadend side-channel terminating in a confusion of mesquite and cactus. Were those rattlesnake holes, there in the sand? Not the sort of critters he'd prefer to meet in a blind alley like this. Backing out, he found the main course again, and walked until he came to a wider place in the rivercourse. Further on, he could see that the arroyo walls narrowed again, but here they seemed to curve out from each other to form a kind of opening.

And for some reason it was here that the feeling of strangeness was the most potent.

Letting things get on your nerves unnecessarily, Tru old lad. Bad sign. Ease up a bit, take a deep breath, relax.

Something moved in the corner of his eye.

He spun around in time to see a large tarantula fiddling its ugly legs up over the edge of a little hole in the sand, lifting itself out and meandering away. Disgusting things, spiders. Lloyd turned back in the direction he had been looking, and walked a little into the center of the opening. What was this?

At his feet, something seemed lumpy under the sand. He kicked at it with one foot and uncovered a little projection of brittle-looking bone. Scuffing with his foot in the surrounding sand he saw that there were apparently other bones here as well. Some kind of small animal, apparently. Coyote probably. He looked ahead, up the arroyo, again, but there was nothing to see but more rivercourse stretching on into the desert, an endless fissure in the earth, a path to nowhere. He turned to start back out.

And almost ran into her.

"Jesus jumping Christ, where the hell did you come from?"

It was an old Indian woman, her bony form swathed in a tangle of dirty-looking rags. Something connected in his head, and he realized all of a sudden that he had just met someone of whom he'd heard. This, no doubt, was Araña.

"I was here all along," she said, and some quality in the high, cracked voice sent a shiver up his spine. He really *was* letting this assignment, this place, get to him.

"Well, I didn't see you," he said, and hearing his own tone of petulance made him feel a little foolish. "What are you doing here?"

"I could ask you the same," the old woman crooned. That might have been an ironic little smile, but he couldn't tell; her face was one inscrutable nest of wrinkles.

"I asked you first," he told her.

The old woman shifted a little on her feet, and the sight of it made him giddy. She seemed to move in more than one direction at a time. Again the creases of her face fled apart to form a speaking mouth. "I live here," she said.

"Here? In an arroyo?"

"Does that seem strange to you?" she asked, inclining her head.

He snorted. "Well. Huh. I mean, a place with a roof would have seemed more like home to me, but then what do *I* know?"

"The sky is my roof," she said. "You do not answer my question. But I already know."

"Know what?"

"Why you are here," she said.

"And why is that?"

"Because," she said, "you have heard that this is a special place."

He shook his head. "I haven't heard anything of the sort."

Undaunted, the old woman continued. "You have heard that something happened here. Something bad."

"Go on." This was getting interesting.

"A long time ago, someone was killed here," she said.

"Who?"

"I cannot tell you," she said, and something in her voice made it seem almost as if she were taunting him.

"Can't tell me, or won't?" he asked. There would be ways of making her talk, if it came to that.

"Sacred things happened here, long ago," she said, "but then there was the killing, and a spirit-brother put a curse on the land."

"No kidding," he said. "A long time ago. How long is that? Couldn't be about fifty years ago, by any chance?" Was something knitting together for him? Possible scenario: an unaccounted-for alien survivor of the Roswell crash finds his way up here somehow, hides or is hidden, maybe for a few years, then someone comes upon him, is understandably scared out of their wits, and they kill the creature—

"Fifty years?" the old woman echoed, and actually laughed this time, a dry, husky sort of sound that was dreadful to hear. "Is that what a long time ago means to you?"

He could scarcely analyze his reaction at being mocked in this way. He was angry, but the anger was tinged with something else. Was it fear? Of a spindly old Indian hag? Not a chance. Still, he struggled with his feelings for a moment before replying: "Well, what *did* you mean, then, by a long time ago?"

The old woman cackled again, raising her arms and beginning to sing tunelessly. He couldn't believe his eyes, or his ears. It was some kind of ritual chant, and she had no sooner started it than a brisk little gust of wind came up, casting a whirl of sand into the air, stinging his face, his eyes.

"Damn!" He wiped at his eyes, but when his vision cleared, the old woman was gone. He looked up the arroyo and down, looked carefully around the edges of the riverbed, anywhere that a shadow or a clump of brush might conceal her. Over toward one wall of the arroyo he thought he glimpsed something move, down close to the sand, but he couldn't be sure. Anyway, the old woman was really gone.

And so was he going to be too. "I don't need this shit," he muttered, heading back toward the entrance to the arroyo. Wait till he met up with the old bitch again. She'd talk to him and make sense, by God, next time.

22

Lisa drove into town with a strange medley of feelings and thoughts playing about in her head. Damn, but it was good to have talked to Jerry! One would have thought that it had been years instead of days, the way she had felt, hearing his voice. But in a way it *had* been years, emotionally—this was all such a radical change for her that it was as if her normal life, her life before the divorce, lay on the other side of some impenetrable mental mountain range, hidden away and too distant to be readily imagined. In any case Jerry's voice had been refreshing, revitalizing, especially after her experience in the arroyo.

Of course, she reflected, turning onto Camino del Sol and parking in front of Lucinda's Cafe, she would have felt better if Jerry hadn't told her he'd just been let go. It might have been an inconsequential job, but it was a job, and this wasn't a good pattern for him to be building up at his age. What was his father going to say? It wasn't pleasant to ponder.

Inside at the counter she studied the menu, and looked up to see that same odd-looking waitress that she had noticed before. *Yolanda,* the nametag said. The girl smiled at her with those large, dark eyes. "May I take your order?"

"Oh," Lisa said, "I'll just have a grilled cheese sandwich and a cup of coffee."

She waited for her lunch, absently fingering the menu and only dimly aware of the drowse of conversation in the air about her. Her hand suddenly gave a twinge where she had hurt it, falling on that cactus, and her thoughts took a turn that she scarcely welcomed but couldn't avoid. What had she really seen last night in the arroyo? That eerie, translucent, wailing figure in the night, that unthinkable woman with the floating gown, and with the very darkness shifting and restless behind her—

"Never saw a menu that was *that* interesting." Feeling an elbow nudge her elbow, she looked up to see Bill Weston sitting next to her.

She laughed and shook her head, replacing the menu in its holder. "No, I wasn't really reading it. Guess I was just thinking about a lot of things. I always seem to see you here."

"Yeah," he said, "as they say, we're going to have to stop meeting like this."

"Oh, I don't know," she said, "I think it's kind of fun, if you don't pay too much attention to the food."

She noticed that his smile had faded, and that he was watching her with evident concern. "Are you all right?" he asked.

She shrugged. "I—" But the girl was back with her sandwich and coffee.

"May I get you anything else?" Again, that peculiar nod of the head, those oddly dark eyes, that overall unplaceable impression.

"No, thank you," Lisa said. She noticed that Bill seemed to be studying the girl's face with some curiosity too.

"And you, sir?" Yolanda asked.

"Ah, that looks good," Bill said, nodding toward Lisa's plate. "I'll have the same." When the girl went away, he turned to Lisa. "There's something about her."

"Yeah, I know," Lisa said. "I feel that way every time I see her. But why did you ask me, before, if I was all right?"

"I just thought you looked kind of—worried or something," Bill said. "Besides, I had a peculiar dream about you last night."

"¿De veras? You dreamed about me?" she laughed, and it felt good to laugh, though she was rather forcing herself not to think about some things. She tried to turn the conversation away from those things. "What kind of dream?"

"Oh, no you don't," he said, "I asked first. What's worrying you?"

"Well," she said, taking a bite of her sandwich and waiting till she could decently continue, "last night I heard somebody crying outside, I thought, and I took a flashlight and walked back to the arroyo behind my house to have a look. I went into the arroyo a good distance, and I saw some things. First, only a big tarantula. I'm not too crazy about spiders, but that's not what bothered me. I looked farther down the arroyo, and I saw—somebody. It was like—"

"A woman," Bill said. "Kind of floating like, and wispy and transparent in the moonlight. And there was something wrong with the darkness behind her. Like it was moving around by itself."

Lisa stopped chewing.

"Am I right?" Bill asked.

"You have a way with words," she said. "How in the world did you—"

"I told you," he said, "I had a dream." The waitress was setting his lunch down in front of him, and they waited until the girl was out of earshot again.

"Come on, Bill," Lisa said, "are you sitting there and telling me that you saw what really happened to me, in your dream?"

"You know what's strange?" he replied. "What's strange is that I'm not too surprised that I'm right. Somehow, I don't know, it's not really surprising."

155

"Huh," she said, "speak for yourself. It surprises the hell out of me."

"You know what you saw, don't you?" he asked. "You know the folktale."

"You mean the story they tell, you know, about—what's her name?"

He nodded, washing down a bite of sandwich with coffee. "The weeping woman. La Llorona. That story is told all over the Southwest. Everybody's heard it at one time or another."

"Well there you are," she said, "that probably explains everything. I mean, I thought I saw her because I'd heard the legend, and you dreamed about me seeing her because you'd heard it too. It was just a funny coincidence, the legend working on both our minds at about the same time."

He eyed her narrowly. "A coincidence. Do you really believe that?"

"What do you mean, do I really believe that?" she asked, a little petulantly, then shrugged and looked into her coffeecup. "Of course I don't."

"Well then," he said, "don't you think we ought to start looking into what makes this place so weird?"

"Looking into it?" she asked, finishing her sandwich. "What can we do?"

He put half of his own sandwich back on the plate untouched, and wiped his mouth with a napkin. "For starters, we can go back out there. To the arroyo."

He followed her back out to the northwest edge of town, driving with a sense that he was getting into something far stranger than he yet knew, and maybe getting Lisa into something strange too. Her experience of the previous night had seemingly been pretty disturbing for her, so maybe he should have just let it go, maybe he should have avoided involving her further.

No, that wasn't honest thinking. Whatever was going on, there was nothing for either of them to do but to face it with an open mind.

He pulled his car beside hers, next to the house, and got out. She was out already, standing beside her car and looking a little indecisive. She nodded toward the porch. "Want to see the house?"

"Later," he said. "What I really want to do is go right out to the arroyo."

She shifted from one foot to the other. "I knew you were going to say that."

By the time they were walking into the dry rivercourse far enough for the sides to loom too tall to see over, he seemed to have reconsidered a bit. He reached and took her hand, and they stopped walking.

"Look," he said, "I was thinking. Who am I to tell you—I mean, if it really bothers you—"

"No," she said pointedly, giving his hand a little squeeze and wincing, as the cactus-bite from the night before still hurt. "I think what I do need to do is go back and see. Maybe looking at the place by daylight will make it seem different."

"You're sure it doesn't bother you?" he asked.

She shrugged. "Well, just a squitch."

"Just a what?"

She laughed. "Just a squitch. That's something I say. My ex-husband Gary hated it."

Bill smiled ruefully. "That's too bad. I think it's neat."

She resumed walking, pulling him a step along before letting go of his hand. "*Vámonos.*"

They followed the dry rivercourse farther along, threading its mazelike twists and turns, occasionally blundering into a cul-de-sac and backing out again. On both flanks, the sides of the arroyo rose like little canyon walls, their sandy surfaces knotted with cedar and mesquite roots. On the way, they came upon the shattered remains of a flashlight, and a little farther along they saw the arroyo widen ahead of them, until they were standing in a sort of quasi-circular opening, beyond which the rivercourse narrowed again.

Lisa looked all around her, then met Bill's gaze. "This is where it was," she said.

"I know," he said. "Remember, in a way I was here too."

"*Mira*," she said, scuffing at something in the sand with her shoe. "Here's something I didn't see last night." Dislodging a silting of sand, she uncovered what appeared to be a bone, about an inch in diameter and perhaps nine or ten inches long.

Bill knelt over the object and whisked more sand away with his hands. There appeared to be several bones, disarticulated but lying close enough together to suggest a single source. "Some little animal," he said. "A fox, maybe, or a coyote, or even a small dog."

She sat in the sand beside the bones and uncovered them a little more. "I don't know," she said, "doesn't look like a dog or a coyote. The bones are kind of—"

"Intact," he supplied. "Yeah, that's what I thought too. Like they haven't deteriorated much." The visible bones were numerous now, jumbled and incomprehensible but somehow almost new-looking. Bill dug a little deeper in the sand. "Damn, look at this." His fingers had reached another osseous surface. Scooping sand out from around it, he lifted it carefully out into the air. It was a skull.

But Lisa knew, at one glance, and thought that Bill knew as well, that it wasn't any familiar kind of skull. "*Extraño*," she whispered. "Weird."

"Yeah." For some reason, he was whispering too. It was as if they were in the presence of something that made whispering the proper thing to do at the moment.

"Did you ever see anything like it?" she asked out loud, and her voice felt harsh and intrusive on the desert air.

"I don't know, I don't think so," he replied, holding the skull in one hand and running the fingers of his other hand over the chalky surface. The skull was roughly the shape of a football, perhaps fourteen or fifteen inches long. Two overly large eye sockets perforated the face, oblong in parallel with the contours of the skull itself. The rest of the face showed only a narrow slit for a mouth and two tiny holes where a nose should have been.

"What kind of a head is that?" Lisa asked. "It seems too big for the rest of the bones. Maybe it's more than one animal, all mixed together." She was brushing sand off the smaller bones and prying them up out of the ground.

"No," Bill said, shaking his head gravely, still fingering the skull. "No, I think it's one set of bones. One organism. But what?"

She took the skull from him and examined it, then handed it back to him. "Does it remind you of anything?"

He pursed his lips, evidently rummaging through his memory for some impression. "I'm not sure. Does it remind *you* of anything?"

She pushed herself up onto her feet and stood brushing sand off her slacks. "Never mind, it doesn't mean anything. You'd think I was crazy if I mentioned it."

"Try me," he said. "With some of the things I've started thinking lately, I can't afford to call anybody crazy."

"Remember the girl at the diner?" she asked. "The waitress?"

He looked at her in amazement. "The one with the odd—"

She laughed, but it came out rather hollow and humorless. "I told you you'd think I was crazy."

"You're not," he said. "Well, maybe just a squitch."

This time her laugh was more heartfelt, but strange feelings welled up around the feeling, dispelled it, replaced it. "It does make me think of her. The long, oval head, the big eyes," she said. "There's a guy over at that newsstand on Zia

Street too, that looks like that. Some kind of local family trait?"

"Could be, I guess," he said, "but what about *this* thing?" He held the skull up to let sunlight reflect off it. "This isn't even human. I don't know what the hell this is. The way it's situated here it doesn't make any sense, looks like it's been scattered around over time. Maybe if we could gather up all the bones and try to put them together—"

Without another word they started digging, exhuming a bewilderment of small bones and piling them up. Bill took off his jacket and made a kind of sling in which they carried the bones back to the house. Inside, they spread them upon the kitchen table and sorted through them, trying this way and that to articulate them. But nothing seemed to make sense, and after a while they gave it up for the time being.

"I know someone who could probably put this puzzle together," Lisa said, thinking of Jerry's countless childhood projects, plastic skeletal models of dinosaurs, bears, horses, and other animals. "I wish he was here."

"Yeah, well, we could use some help I guess," Bill said. "I never was much good at puzzles. Funny, right now I feel about as insightful as a turnip, but this crazy-looking old Indian woman I ran into in town yesterday told me that I see things, know things."

"Like your dream?" Lisa asked.

He seemed to be thinking this over. "Now that you mention it, yeah, maybe like the dream. Hey, you never did show me where you saw the vision of the woman, out there in the arroyo."

"Oh, it was right there in the clearing," she said, "just ahead of where we found the bones. Funny, I forgot all about that too, looking at this thing." She moved a few bones around on the table in another attempt to make sense of them, then let them be. Bill watched her with no evident desire to try again himself.

"Listen," he said, "if I'm going to take you to dinner tonight, I'm going to need to go back to the hotel and get cleaned up and changed."

She nodded. "Don't change too much. I think I'm going to kind of like you the way you are."

He headed for the door. "That's only because you haven't seen me yet at the full moon."

"I'll take my chances," she said, showing him out onto the porch.

"I get the feeling we both took our chances," he said on his way down the steps, "coming to this town."

23

Truman Lloyd was still pissed off about the old Indian woman when he finally got around to having lunch. Sitting down at the counter in the diner, he half hoped he would see the old crone, and that she would give him another one of those I-know-more-than-you looks out of that nightmare mess of wrinkles that she called a face; it would give him a good excuse to get up and throttle her right here, with an audience.

Tru, old man, you're losing your composure.

He took a deep breath and scanned the menu. Nothing on it looked too spectacular. He wondered if there was a world record for how long anyone could live on food like this, on the road. When was the last time he'd had a home-cooked meal? While he was trying to remember, a waitress appeared. "Yes sir, what would you like?"

Lloyd stared at her, then realized that he was staring at her and consciously tried to soften his gaze, though not without noting that her nametag said *Yolanda*. "I, ah, I'll have a hot dog and fries and a cup of coffee."

"It'll be right out," the girl said, departing.

Damn, but that was one peculiar-looking young lady, he thought, replacing the menu in its holder and watching the girl from across the room through a haze of cigarette smoke.

She wasn't unattractive, certainly; in fact, in an odd sort of way he found her rather appealing. But those big dark eyes, that vaguely birdlike way of moving, that oval head that somehow seemed to nod in a manner suggesting that it was almost too large for the frail neck that supported it—it all added up to a striking impression, or set of impressions.

Especially from a certain point of view.

He studied her again, subtly, when she brought his food. "Will there be anything else?" she asked.

"No, thank you," he said, and watched her write out his check. The handwriting looked normal. He watched her walk away to clear up a pile of dishes and cups down at the other end of the counter.

Something about her.

When he was through eating, and had gone to pay his check, an older woman was at the register; the Lucinda, no doubt, that the diner's name implied. Her nametag confirmed it, and reminded him of that other nametag. "Was everything okay?" the woman asked.

"Everything was fine," he said, smiling. "You have a very helpful crew here. The young lady who waited on me, ah, what was her name—" He nodded toward the girl, who was waiting on someone a few seats away.

"Oh, Yolanda Anaya?" the woman supplied.

"Yes, that was it, Yolanda. She's very courteous. I wanted to commend her."

The woman returned the smile. "Well, thank you, we're always glad to hear good things about our people. I'll be sure to tell her."

Back outside, Lloyd felt lucky that the woman had mentioned the girl's last name; if she hadn't done so, Lloyd would have had to fish for it a little harder.

When he got back to the house he mixed himself a gin and tonic to wash away the taste of that ghastly hot dog, and set up the comm unit, going through the usual security procedures. Before long, a Chinese face appeared on the

163

little screen. Good; he always preferred working with Charles Wu.

"Truman," Wu said, grinning. "You still haven't been eaten up by tarantulas?"

"Oh, I'm sure it'll come to that, sooner or later," Lloyd said. "I've always known I'd end up as tarantula shit. I don't mind. It's as good a way as any to end up. But they'll find me to be a pretty unsavory meal, I'm afraid. I take too much digesting. All that muscle, you know."

Wu rolled his eyes, shook his head, reached over and picked up a clipboard. "So how's it going?"

"I think I'm going to have some very interesting things to report, before very long. I'm taking my time, sniffing around. This is a sleepy little town, a person could expire of inactivity here and nobody would even notice, so things are relatively stable. There are undercurrents, but things are stable. When I decide to make the move, we're not going to have any trouble."

"You said undercurrents. What sort of undercurrents?"

"That's where I need your help," Lloyd said. "I've started checking up on the sources you listed before. When I learn a little more I'll have some specifics to get back to you with. Right now, I need you to run a background check on a young woman named Yolanda Anaya."

"Spell that," Wu said. Lloyd spelled it, and Wu, on the little screen, looked to one side and nodded. "Just take a minute."

Lloyd waited, and even he was a little surprised how fast the information came back.

"Yolanda Maria Anaya," Wu said, reading from a sheet he had attached to his clipboard. "Born 27 April 1976 in Chasco, New Mexico. Graduated high school Corona, 1994. Employed Lucinda's Diner, Chasco, New Mexico from 1994 to present. Father unknown. Mother Elisa Anaya, born 22 July 1949 in Corona, New Mexico, still living, residence Seminole, Texas. Unmarried. No other pertinent records."

Lloyd took a sip of his drink and scribbled on a notepad. "You did say father unknown?"

"That's right," Wu said. "You want hardcopy on this?"

"No," Lloyd said. "I've got what I need for now. What operatives are on line near Seminole, Texas?"

"Just a minute and I'll check," Wu said, pointing to someone offscreen. After a moment he said, "We can get you Jespersen if you need him, he's just finishing an assignment in Lubbock."

"Okay," Lloyd said, "I'll contact him myself."

Wu eyed him narrowly through the comm unit. "You going to keep me in suspense, Tru?"

"Not for long," Lloyd said. "Just till I'm sure about a couple of things."

"I'm going to need something more substantial pretty quick," Wu said. "Some of the folks upstairs are getting a little nervous."

"Tell 'em don't get nervous," Lloyd said. "It's bad for the digestion."

"*You* tell 'em," Wu said.

Lloyd snorted. "No thanks. Catch you later." He disconnected.

Damn, he hated it when they started putting pressure on. There wasn't any hurry. Whatever was going on here, whatever those undercurrents were going to come to, things hadn't changed in this dipshit little town for years, and weren't going to change in the next day or next week. He was on top of it. Didn't they know him that well by now?

He finished his drink, ran the comm unit back up, and made a call to Texas. Then he mixed another drink, drank it, and made ready to catch a little sleep, even though it was only mid-afternoon.

Unless he was mistaken, it was going to be a long night.

24

Jerry Logan wondered, among other things, how far this old heap of a Ford would make it into New Mexico before falling into pieces on the road. He would just have to hope for the best.

Looking in the rear view mirror as he swung onto the Andrews Highway, the quickest way out of Midland in this direction, he regarded the bruise on his cheek with a sense of humiliation and sadness mingled with impotent rage. Good old Dad, yessir, always good for a laugh when you needed one.

It wasn't as if he *wanted* to lose his precious job at the car wash, for Christ's sake. Dad had come home for lunch, already in something of a foul mood because of some problem at work; he had found Jerry unaccountably home early, and the shouting had started. If only it had stopped with shouting.

This was going to be a beauty of a shiner, or Jerry was much mistaken. Well, no more. He might be back or he might not.

Out on the open road, in the oil fields, he began to feel a little better, pushing the car toward New Mexico as if that were some sort of Promised Land. Maybe it was, in effect. After a while the pump jacks became more frequent, their great narrow heads bobbing into and out of and into and out of the earth like hungry, probing insects. Mom had always liked them. Good old Mom. All the poetry in the family was up to her, no question about it.

Damn, it was an ugly scene to remember, the falling out with Dad, and he tried not to think about it, but the thought kept sneaking back, nagging at his head.

Things had been getting worse between him and his father for quite some time, even before the divorce, which only made *everything* worse. It hadn't been so bad, when Jerry had been younger. Dad had seemed more or less to approve of him then, when he was a cute acquiescent little kid and not an angular and complex teenager who had the audacity to have his own mind. Growing into his middle teens, Jerry had found his father to be less and less approving, no matter what he did. *Study hard in school, make something of yourself,* Dad had urged him, but when Jerry's instinctive interest in biology had led him to start spending long days and nights in his room putting together all those plastic models of animal skeletons, instead of spending the hours out on the baseball field that his father would have preferred, the animosity started to grow. (*Sure, sit in your room like a lard-ass, and never mind that I'm the only man in my office who doesn't have kids playing ball. How do you think that makes me look?*) Had Jerry indeed started classes this fall at the community college, his father would have wanted him to major in business, of course, which might be fine for some people, but it would never occur to his father to wonder whether it was really right for Jerry or not.

He'd go to college, somewhere or other, when he felt good and ready. And the major would be biology.

He headed farther and farther into desert country, noticing that after a while the pump jacks at the sides of the road were punctuated by yucca and cholla. It was only mid-afternoon, and with any luck he might be able to reach Chasco by nightfall. Wherever that was, exactly; he still wasn't sure, but he had some maps if he needed them. He had a couple of cans of soda, too, and some candy bars. The great American meal.

The scene with his father insisted on replaying itself, painfully, in his head.

Sure, go ahead, run to your mother. That's all you ever know how to do.

Not true, and not fair.

Stupid bitch'll probably congratulate you on losing your job.

That really sucked, that remark. Really sucked bigtime. How could people say things like that about people they had once married and professed to love?

Anyway, when you come back here, you just might find your bags packed and set out on the steps.

That might not be a bad deal, all things considered, Jerry thought, taking a turn westward in the town of Seminole and heading toward Hobbs, New Mexico. From there he would find his way however he could manage. Mom had given him some idea where Chasco was, up north of Roswell someplace.

Later, he threaded his way through the streets of Hobbs and back out into open prairie, and by the time he was seeing signs for Roswell, he was driving into a beautiful desert sunset.

25

An uninformed observer would have noticed, in Jespersen's drive from Lubbock, Texas to the little town of Seminole, nothing of particular interest. Jespersen was driving a recent-model Plymouth hatchback, all very ordinary, and looked very ordinary himself. He kept within the speed limit, obeyed the traffic regulations when passing through towns, and drew no attention to himself.

Jespersen wasn't his real name, of course, and indeed in his work he went by so many different names that he almost had trouble, at times, recalling his real one, especially since (if one were to put it charitably) he wasn't terribly bright.

But he was loyal, devoted, dedicated, and that was something that Group Epsilon valued immensely in work such as Jespersen's, especially in combination with a generous endowment of stupidity. Dumb and dedicated, and informed just enough to know the essentials bearing upon his duties, that's the sort of person it took to get this job done.

He was very good at what he did for a living, and they paid him well. *They* being shadowy, nameless figures whom he had never seen, and about which he was scarcely even curious, as long as the checks kept coming.

Arriving in the little town of Seminole, Texas, he drove around, looked around to orient himself a bit. He had been here before, but it had been several years ago. Stopping at a traffic light and idly watching a kid in a beat-up old Ford turn in front of him and head out of town toward Hobbs, he spotted a gas station across the way, and pulled in there and bought some gas and a map of the town. It didn't take long to find the name of the street he was looking for.

He drove through town and turned down a side street, quickly finding himself among narrow residential lanes lined with simple frame houses whose yards were speckled with broken plastic toys and barbecue cookers and flowerpots. These scenes always annoyed him, because he hated people who lived their pitiful little lives in pitiful little houses when a real man, like Jespersen, lived his life on the road. He hated them for their simple pleasures. He hated them just for the hell of it, when you got right down to it.

Ah, here was the street he needed. He turned onto it, noting that it was still early enough in the afternoon for most working people not to be home from work yet. Good. Then Elisa Anaya probably wouldn't have a lot of nosy neighbors around poking their noses into things. There. That house.

He pulled the car into the driveway, shut off the engine, got out, and walked across the scrubby grass toward the door. The wooden porch rails were lined with dusty-looking flowerpots and other bric-a-brac, and some of the window screens facing out onto the porch were torn and curling. What a dump. Well, it did look as if nobody was out and about in the immediate neighborhood; the houses on each side had their shades drawn, and everything was very quiet. Perfect. He stepped up and rang the doorbell. A fifty-ish Hispanic woman, thin and tired-looking, pulled the door open a few inches. "Yes?"

"Sorry to bother you, mam, but I got car trouble, and I wonder if I could use your phone?"

The woman looked doubtful. "Well—" But Jespersen pushed his way through the door, crowding into the room and shoving the woman back. She gave a startled little cry but was apparently too surprised to say anything, or even to scream.

"Elisa Anaya," Jespersen said. It was a statement, not a question.

The woman caught her breath and spluttered, "Y-yes. What do you want? Please don't—"

Jespersen, nudging the door closed behind him, edged farther into the room. The woman tried to back away from him, but his strong arm shot out and clapped a hand around the back of her head and drew her closer.

"All I got is one question. It's about your daughter Yolanda. Who's her father?"

The woman's eyes grew large and frightened. "I don't know what you're—"

The muscles in Jespersen's arm rippled, the grip on the back of the woman's head tightened. "I *said*, who's her father?"

The fear in the woman's eyes partly shaded over into anger. "¡*Qué bárbaro!*"

Jespersen jerked her head forward so suddenly and so hard that she uttered a dry little cry of pain, and started to whimper. "I didn't ask you about no Barbara, lady. Here it is, one more time. Yolanda. Who's her father?"

Now the woman's eyes, though brimming with tears, flashed with anger. "*Chingado cabrón, atende a lo tuyo.* It's none of your business."

Jespersen took this in stride, having more or less expected it. "None of my business. Okay." He dragged the woman into the adjoining kitchen and pushed her down onto a chair at the table and sat down beside her. She started to bolt and run, but he pushed her back down, and when she tried to jump up again and run, he slapped her so hard that a trickle of blood oozed out of one nostril. "Let's see," he said, "if I can *make* it my business, what do you say?"

Holding her down with one brawny arm, he reached with his free hand into a jacket pocket and brought out a pair of pliers.

The woman's eyes filled with terror. "What are you doing?"

"Oh, just trying to make conversation, lady. Sometimes people don't like to talk to me, so I kind of have to loosen 'em up a little. Like you, now. I think you really do want to talk to me, you just don't know it."

"I told you," she whimpered, "I don't know what you're——"

But Jespersen took one of her hands in his, made a deft move with the pliers and fastened upon a fingernail, swiftly and smoothly ripping it out. He had to raise his voice now over the woman's wailing.

"Who's her father?"

But she only blubbered incoherently, shaking her head.

"I see," Jespersen said, shaking his own head ruefully. "Well, we got plenty of time." He went in with the pliers again and found another fingernail and tore it out. Now the woman screamed all the louder, and he hoped he was right about the neighbors being gone, as this kind of thing could get awkward otherwise.

"Please——" the woman sobbed.

"Who's her father?" Jespersen asked, quietly, as if he were talking to someone at a hospital or in a confessional.

"I——God, please help me, I don't know."

"Well now, that's too bad." He swooped once more with the pliers and ripped out another fingernail, and slapped her to quiet her screaming. "You know, lady, you only got ten of 'em. When we run out of 'em, I'm going to have to start on your teeth."

"*Madre de Dios, ayúdame,*" she cried. "I don't know, I can't tell you."

"Oh, you know, okay," Jespersen said, tearing out another fingernail.

172

"All right, all right, all right," the woman said, nearly choking with pain and nausea. "I'll tell you. Only please don't hurt my daughter."

"Lady, I wouldn't hurt your daughter for the world," Jespersen said. "Do I look like that kinda guy? Now talk."

It took the mother a moment to regain enough breath and composure to speak. Clutching her wounded hand and wiping at the blood, she looked up at him with a face tragic with pain and despair. "Her father——"

"Go on," Jespersen said, absently fingering the pliers.

"Her father was—I mean, he wasn't——"

"Go *on*, lady," Jespersen said, snapping the pliers together. "I ain't got all day."

The mother put her hands over her face, then drew them away, leaving her cheeks streaked with blood. "Her father wasn't human."

"Tell me about it."

She wiped at her eyes and shook her head. "I don't know, I don't know where he came from. I think some Indians brought him to town, late at night, hid him away or something. He chose me. *No sé por qué*, I don't know why, but he chose me to have his child. Then I never saw him again, I swear before God."

Jespersen rose to his feet, towering over her. "Well now, see, was that so hard? I didn't want to have to hurt you." He put a gruff hand on the side of her face. "Why'd you have to go and make me hurt you? Nice lady like you." He caressed her face, and then let his hand slip down around her throat and tighten. Her eyes bulged with horror, but now the only sound she could utter was a kind of squeal that subsided into a dry, expiring breath.

"You women. You always make me hurt you."

In a moment it was done, and Jespersen let her fall forward onto the tabletop, where he left her looking as if she had simply put her head down for a nap.

He made his way back to his car, noting that there was still nobody around. Good. No curious stares, no trouble.

There were calls to make now, but first he drove across town, watching for a nice place to stop for a bite to eat. His work always made him hungry.

26

The burring of the phone on the comm unit brought Lloyd out of an uneasy sleep. The dream had had something to do with the arroyo where he had met the old Indian woman, and something to do with the farther reaches of the arroyo itself. Something had looked wrong with the *air* down there, as if it were too dark, too restless. He was glad to wake up and answer the call; he had been expecting it, and had left the comm unit within reach.

"Yes."

"Hey, chief." Jespersen's loutish face swam into focus on the little screen.

"What do you have for me, Jespersen?" Lloyd asked.

"Pay dirt, chief."

"Don't call me chief."

"Right. Anyhow, I, uh, interviewed Elisa Anaya. At her house. Like you said, I asked her who the father was. Had a hard time getting her to tell me." The face on the screen grinned, and a hand appeared, brandishing a pair of pliers.

"Spare me the unnecessary details," Lloyd said. "What did she say?"

"She said the father wasn't human. Said she thought some Indians brought him to town at night and hid him

175

someplace, and he picked her out to have his kid for some reason. Said she never seen him again." Jespersen looked pleased with himself.

"And?"

"And so I snuffed her," Jespersen said. "Nothing more to tell."

Lloyd sighed. Not that he was surprised at the man's lack of imagination. "Jespersen, you dumb fuck. Haven't I told you again and again that dead people can't keep telling us things? Didn't it occur to you that there might have been some more things you could have asked her?"

"Like what, chief?"

Jesus, Lloyd thought, what has happened to the gene pool? "Like whether there were any *other* mothers like her, any other children like Yolanda."

Jespersen looked a little sheepish. "Didn't think of it, chief."

"Evidently not," Lloyd said. "And if you call me that one more time I'm going to have you transferred to toilet detail in Papua New Guinea."

"Sorry, ch—" But Lloyd hung up and switched the screen off.

Lloyd picked up his glass from the bedside stand. It contained only a trace of melted ice and a ghost of gin, but he drank it, and sat trying to think. At least the report from Seminole, Texas was a start. The girl Yolanda would have to be taken into custody, of course. In good time. No particular hurry; she'd been around here for over twenty years and wasn't likely to go anywhere, and in any case they'd find her even if she did. The real problem was exactly the issue he had brought up to that cretin Jespersen. To wit: were there others like Yolanda and her mother?

If an alien survivor of the Roswell crash had been hidden away, had sired a child hereabouts—as a biological experiment? as something less comprehensibly motivated? you never could assume you knew anything about alien psychology—if an alien sired a child here, how many other mothers were there, how many other children?

It might mean, at the very least, taking a close look at every face in town, as discouraging a prospect as that was. In the end, when he decided to draw the noose and go for broke, he might well have to direct the military to take not just a few people into custody, but the whole town. (At least he hoped it was only this town.) Yeah. Could be done. Could be done. Especially out here in the prairie. Do it silently, quickly, nobody would be the wiser. Everything under wraps. Move the whole population to a secret underground camp someplace (there were several possibilities, like Station 7 at Holloman), examine them at leisure, and do it properly: DNA tests, that sort of thing. Check to see what loose threads there were, like relatives in other towns. Keep the part-aliens for further study, dispose of the others.

But one thing at a time. Maybe it wouldn't come to that, at least not right away, if he could find out the right information through a more limited operation. Tonight he had work to do, and he needed to catch a couple more hours' nap before he started.

He drifted off to sleep thinking of cover stories to explain, if things ran to the full scenario, what happened to the town of Chasco.

27

The Mexican cuisine at the restaurant behind the hotel proved to be simple but quite good. Lisa and Bill lingered for a while in their corner booth, enjoying the opportunity to just sit. There was a little lantern on the table with a candle in it, and the effect was cosy, warm, pleasant. Mexican music was playing somewhere, a rendition of *La Paloma*.

"Best damned enchiladas I've had in years," Bill said, dabbing at his mouth with a napkin.

"Mm, and those tamales," Lisa said. "Just about as good as the ones my mom used to make. And that's saying a lot."

They fell silent for a moment, listening to the music. Finally Lisa noticed him looking at her with that concerned expression on his face again. He confirmed it by saying, "You seem a little—I don't know, preoccupied. Not that I could blame you, after the last couple of days."

She nodded. "You know something? And don't laugh at me. It made me nervous, being in the house alone with those bones." It should have sounded funny, but nobody was laughing. "They're still there on the table, you know, in the kitchen."

He shook his head. "Thoughtless of me. I could have cleared them away for you, at least put them in a sack or something."

"Not your fault," she said. "I didn't know they were going to give me the creeps when I was alone with them."

"Well, I really think I ought to dispose of them when I take you home. Of course you realize that's just my sneaky way of trying to be sure you invite me in for a nightcap."

She laughed. "A pile of weird bones does make a ready excuse, I guess. I can't offer you much of a nightcap, though. I do have a bottle of wine, nearly empty I think. May have enough left for a taste."

"Just a squitch?" he asked.

"Now you're making fun of me," she said.

"Oh no I'm not," he said. "I wouldn't dream of making fun of you." He took her hand.

"You'd dream *about* me, though, seeing scary things in an arroyo." He squeezed her hand, and she winced. "Ow. Careful. That hand's still a little sore. Cactus bite."

"Sorry, I forgot. Yeah, I still can't believe I really saw all that in my dream. I don't know which is more bizarre—that you saw La Llorona, or that *I* did, when I wasn't even there. It's all crazy. I mean, first, I've never believed in telepathic or precognitive dreams or whatever the hell this was. Second, I always assumed La Llorona was just a legend. A folktale. But now I don't know. I'm beginning to think anything is possible, around here."

Lisa gave his hand another cautious squeeze. "Take me home?"

They were halfway across town in his car, heading west on Zia Street and turning north onto Old Roswell Road, when she turned to him and asked, "Didn't you say you saw something else in your dream? Like the darkness behind the floating woman was—kind of alive?"

"Right, it did seem that way," he said.

"I saw it too. In a way it was scarier than the woman herself," she said, as they were nearing the house and then pulling into the drive. When the headlights washed across the house, she drew in a sharp breath at what she saw.

Someone was sitting on the porch steps.

There was another car, too, parked on the other side of her own, but Bill's headlights didn't illumine it, and all she could see was a shadowy outline.

Bill's car was scarcely stopped when she got out and hurried over to the house. Behind her, Bill had left his headlights on, so that they wouldn't be in complete darkness. The person sitting on the porch steps grinned, laughed, and got up and came down the steps to hug her.

"Jerry, *querido*," she said, pressed almost windless in his embrace. He was four inches taller than she was now, and very strong. "God, I'm glad to see you."

"Me too, Mom."

She leaned back to look in his face, and saw an angry-looking bruise on one cheek. "What happened to you?"

He looked down, as if he rather wanted to avoid talking about it. "Aw, you know. It was about losing my job."

She bit her lip to keep from saying: *That bastard.* In spite of everything, she didn't believe in trashing the boy's father in front of him. Anyway, before she could say anything further on the subject, she noticed now that Jerry was looking over her shoulder. She had forgotten, for the moment, about Bill. Jerry was looking at him with just a trace of an expression on his face that might have said: way to go, Mom, a new boyfriend this early?

"Oh, Jerry, this is my friend Bill Weston," she said, watching her son's face, a little apprehensive about what he might be thinking. But whatever was really passing through his mind, he only extended his hand to Bill and said, "Glad to meet you."

"Let's all go inside," Lisa said. "Bill, turn your headlights off."

They soon found themselves gathered around the pile of bones that covered the kitchen table.

"These bones look almost new," Jerry said, thoughfully fingering a few of them. "They kind of don't seem like bones. I mean, it's like they're made of different stuff." His dark, intelligent eyes were studying the bones with growing avidity. Clearly, he was hooked. "So, what is this?"

"That's what I hope you can help us find out," Lisa said. A corner of her mind registered that by saying *us*, she was knitting a little more of a connection, in Jerry's mind, between her and Bill.

"Yeah," Bill said to Jerry, "we went out to the arroyo behind the house here to check on—well, it's a long story." He turned to Lisa. "Why don't you tell him the whole thing?"

They sat down at the table. Any other time, Lisa would have found it hilarious, this scene, three people seated solemnly around a table bearing a pile of bones, like the aftermath of some unthinkable dinner. But recalling her experience in the arroyo, and telling Jerry the story, vanquished all thoughts of levity from her mind. Somehow, the account of La Llorona got more spectral, felt more creepy, every time she retold it. At length, Jerry regarded her solemnly for some time, turned his gaze on Bill, then back to his mother.

"No shit," he said.

Lisa cast him what she hoped was a no-nonsense mother-to-son look. "Young man, a week ago I would have given you a real bad time for talking like that."

"A week ago we weren't sitting here staring at a bunch of bones that look like they belong in a science-fiction movie," Jerry said.

"You don't think this is any ordinary animal, then," Bill said.

The boy whistled. "Not with a head like that."

"Well," Lisa said, putting a hand on Jerry's arm, "who was it that was always good at putting together stuff like this?"

"Is that a hint?" the boy asked, grinning.

"What do you think?" his mother replied. "Go to it."

She and Bill watched the boy work. She could tell that Bill was impressed with Jerry's methodical nature, the care with which he picked through the bones, trying them in various combinations, looking for a way to rearticulate them. Why did she give so much thought to what Bill and Jerry thought of each other?

An hour passed, and Jerry still worked on the bones. Parts of the puzzle were beginning to knit together. Lisa at some point got up and made coffee, and they all had some while the job continued. It was after eleven when Jerry slid one last frail-looking cluster of bones into place, and they all stood and looked down at what lay on the table. Involuntarily, they all edged a little away.

Nobody spoke for quite some time. It was Bill who finally did.

"What in holy jaywalking Jesus's name is that?"

It was a diminutive figure, this nearly complete skeleton, perhaps three and a half feet in length—or height, had it been standing up—and essentially humanoid in its contours: two spindly-looking legs, a compact little torso, two arms in which the forearms were a little longer than the upper part; each arm terminated in a spidery-looking four-fingered hand. The neck was long and thin, and the skull atop it argued an oversized, heavy, oval head out of which two large eyes must once have stared with an expression that somehow, one felt, could only have been placid.

"*Sea lo que sea*," Lisa said, "whatever it is, it isn't human."

"But it's not an animal either," Bill said, "at least no kind of animal I've ever heard of. The thing is, it's *like* human. Like a little grown-up child."

Lisa got up and started making another pot of coffee. She turned to Bill. "You must be thinking what I'm thinking."

Jerry looked a little annoyed at being left out. "What? What are you guys thinking?"

Bill nodded, clapping Jerry lightly on the back. "Your mom doesn't mean to be mysterious. It's just that—well, right down the road here a ways, to the south, is the place where something's supposed to have happened back in 1947. You must know the story: the Roswell UFO crash."

"I know about that," Jerry said, "I mean, I know about it, doesn't mean I know how I feel about it. I guess it could've happened." He looked at the thing on the tabletop, then met Bill's gaze again. "So what're you saying?"

"What he's saying is," Lisa replied, "there have been aliens here, on earth." She came over and put an arm around her son. It should have looked like a melodramatic gesture, but it didn't. "This thing on the table. *Es de otro mundo.* It's something from another world."

The desert wind rose a little around the eaves, and as if in eerie response to Lisa's words, a thin, ululant cry came on the wind, plaintive and shocking, a cry in the night, mournful and somehow hideous to hear.

A cry from the arroyo.

And everyone froze around the childlike bone-figure on the table, and Lisa thought: there she is again, moaning for her lost children—but who were they, the lost children of the legend, who were they really?

28

It was good and dark now. Getting up from his nap, taking a quick shower, doing a remote-check on the phone tap at Lisa Jaramillo's house (no phone traffic recorded), and packing himself a sandwich and a can of soda from the fridge, Truman Lloyd drove north up Chamisa Street, parked his car around the far corner on Piñon, and set up rifle mike surveillance again in the weedy field across from Paco's Emporium.

Tonight he planned to do more than listen.

For now, though, he simply settled down in the shadowy little hollow where he had set up before, fairly well sheltered from view by clumps of mesquite on both sides, and trained the rifle mike on the store window across the street, peering through night-vision binoculars at the traces of light filtering through the slats in the drawn blinds. As before, he could see the outline of Paco Rojas moving around near the front of the store, busy at vague tasks.

And, as before, after a while he could see, barely, that Paco Rojas was joined by a diminutive form moving about near him, rather like an inquisitive child.

But unless Truman Lloyd's esteemed mother had produced offspring with no discernment at all, this was no child.

Lloyd settled the earphones more firmly on his head and tweaked the controls on the rifle mike to be sure he was getting maximum receptivity. He listened to Rojas' tinny voice in the headset.

"...feel it more than ever now," Rojas was saying. "Something is going to happen. Very soon."

Another voice: "Mhhhh."

Silence. Then Rojas speaking again, as if in response to an unheard remark: "I know, I only wish I could share your calmness of mind. But I'm afraid. What if nothing can be done?"

A moment's silence. Then a voice that made Lloyd's flesh crawl, even though he had heard such a voice at length, on tape, once before, years ago: *"W'mhrra l'yedhh yi-hsul, yi-p-k'twohh, m'lueh."*

"Be damned," Lloyd whispered. "Suspicions confirmed."

Yes, he had heard tapes years ago with such a voice, speaking such a language. The language was one spoken by only one or two human beings in the world, so far as he knew; it was the language spoken by an early survivor of the Roswell crash, and Group Epsilon called it L-1. Interestingly enough, good old Paco Rojas seemed to understand it well enough.

"Yes, but I'm only human, I can't help being afraid," Rojas was saying. "Remember, I cling to life with a different kind of tenacity than you. I don't like to think of dying."

Long moments of silence, in which Rojas seemed to grunt a kind of agreement under his breath, then that other voice again: *"W'hsimh-la rh'kweh t'sillh."*

And Rojas: "I know, I know." Evidently Rojas' companion often communicated without using sound at all, and sometimes lapsed into speech for purposes of emphasis, or who knew what other purposes. "It's late," Rojas was saying. Lloyd strained to hear anything further, but all was silence. The vague figures beyond the windowblinds moved out of sight, and after a while the lights in the store went out.

Beddy-bye time, Lloyd thought. For human and alien alike, it would seem.

He waited in the sandy field for nearly an hour, giving it plenty of time. Let everyone drift off to dreamland. He had things to do. Things he had to see.

At length he packed up his surveillance equipment, walked across the field to his car, packed the equipment away, and walked down Piñon to the corner with Chamisa and crossed the street. He stood for a moment on the steps of Paco's Emporium and gathered his thoughts. His clip-loader was safely nestled in his shoulder holster, and all was well with the world.

Well, that remained to be seen, but in any case it was going to be a very interesting night. The situation was pretty clear: Paco Rojas had been harboring an alien UFO crash survivor for heaven only knew how many years. Some Indians, he gathered, had gotten to the crash site before the military and had taken away one or more survivors, leaving one for dead that actually revived later in government hands. Probably the unaccounted-for survivor or survivors had been moved around over the years, hidden here and there, to keep their existence unknown to the government. In any event the one in the Emporium was evidently old friends with Paco Rojas. Were there others? Was this one the father of the girl Yolanda, by Elisa Anaya? Were there other hybrid children? Too many questions.

This much was certain: Truman Lloyd was going to have an alien in custody before sunrise. Then the rest of the operation would come into play. The whole town would be interned if need be. It was going to get a little messy, but what the hell. Big problems had always called for big solutions, ambitious solutions.

He began to work on the lock on the Emporium door.

29

Lisa and Jerry and Bill stood around the skeleton-draped table like the witnesses to some weird, long-overdue autopsy. There was something pitiable about the osseous figure on the table, as if its limbs, its enigmatic face, its birdlike ribcage wanted to radiate the warmth of life but had been stilled all too soon, tragically, a fallen traveler far, far from home, lost and alone.

Lisa found herself wondering which was more frightful, this unthinkable creature whose remains were sprawled upon her tabletop, or the wailing cry that had wafted to them on the desert wind, keening for a few moments, then subsiding.

It was finally Jerry who broke the silence. "I just noticed something."

Bill and Lisa looked at him quizzically. "Here," he said.

He ran his forefinger along one side of the chalky skull, and for the first time Lisa noticed a kind of groove or indentation there. She had missed it before, in her reaction to the overall strangeness of the skull's contours.

"Yeah," Bill said, feeling the skull himself with a gesture that looked almost reverent. "It's as if somebody dealt the thing a blow to the head. Probably how it died."

Lisa nodded, taking her own turn at fingering the crease in the skull. *"Pues, ¿qué pasó aquí?* What happened here?"

They were all silent again for a while. At length Bill said, "I don't know what happened here, but I know one thing. If these are really the remains of an alien life form—"

"What else could they be?" Jerry asked.

"Well, if they are," Bill said, "and if the wrong people find out, we may all be in a lot of trouble."

Lisa didn't like the direction this talk was turning. "What do you mean, trouble?"

Bill pointed to the thing on the table. "I mean, if you think about it, this is a real find. This is proof. They've denied it, all these years. The government. The military. They've all said there are no aliens, no flying saucers, no crashes, no close encounters, nothing. They've denied everything, and they've made fun of people who believe in such things. You know that. Well, this is proof."

"And we have it," Lisa said, and heard her voice tremble a little as the realization of what he meant began to creep over her awareness. It was a chilling thought. "We have the proof."

"That's right," Bill said, "and if they find out—"

Jerry snorted, shaking his head. "How could they find out?"

"You might be surprised the things they can find out," Bill said. He addressed himself both to Jerry and to Lisa. "Don't you remember all those stories about the things that happened after the Roswell UFO crash, back in 1947? The military swarming all over the place, threatening people, telling them if they talked about anything they'd seen, the government would kill their whole families? Haven't you heard those stories about people who've taken good pictures of UFO sightings and had somebody come to the door—"

"The Men in Black," Jerry supplied.

"Yeah," Bill said. "They take your photos, tell you you'd better keep your mouth shut and don't pry into things you ought to leave alone. Sometimes they threaten you outright."

"I always thought those were just a lot of wild stories," Lisa said. She looked long and hard at the thing on the table. "Until I saw this thing."

"So what're you saying?" Jerry asked, fixing Bill with a stare that had something in it, Lisa thought, of fear. "Are you saying we ought to—"

"I don't know, I don't know, Jerry," Bill said, putting his hands in the air in a gesture of bewilderment. "Who's ever been in a situation like this? How can we have any idea what we ought to do? But I've got a feeling we'd better gather this thing up and take it someplace."

"Where?" Lisa asked.

Bill took her hand. "I wish I could tell you. Someplace where somebody could look at it. Somebody we could trust. Don't ask me who we can trust. I don't know that either. But we've got to see that somebody knows about this thing besides us, that's for damned sure."

"Maybe somebody at a college," Jerry said. "You know, some professor who could look at it and understand what it was, and maybe would know where to go with it. Like to the news people or something."

"That's what I'm thinking too," Bill said. "If we could get somebody to put out a news release, after some experts had looked at the thing, and get the story out, I mean everywhere, before anybody had a chance to grab the evidence and hide it away—"

"Or maybe grab us and hide us away," Jerry said, matter-of-factly.

"Like they say, great minds think alike," Bill replied, trying, not very successfully, to grin. "That's what we've got to do. Get this thing looked at, professionally, and get it in the news. Bigtime."

"Well—" Lisa began, but there was a knock at the front door.

Everyone froze, wide-eyed.

Lisa prayed that the knocking would stop.

It didn't.

30

Truman Lloyd, worrying at the lock to the front door of Paco's Emporium, reflected that as always it was nice, being a member of a privileged governmental caste. One had much better equipment to work with. Like this little pocket device that clamped to the front of a lock, sounded its contours, and electronically simulated a key. Your common burglar, as a private citizen, had to make do with primitive devices, while this—well, this was efficiency in action. He had to wait a few seconds (they were working on a better model, he was given to understand), but soon he heard the telltale click.

"That'll do for openers," he whispered, pleased with himself.

Pocketing the device, he gave a tiny inward push to the door, and the hinges creaked. That would be ironic, to be foiled by something so plebeian. Not that he would have any particular trouble handling the situation if good old Paco Rojas woke up and came downstairs to investigate, but for the moment Lloyd wanted to keep things as uncomplicated as possible, so he fished in his other jacket pocket, extracted a tiny spray can, and gave each hinge a quick squirt. He gave the door a second push, and it swung noiselessly on its hinges. But he took it slow and easy, taking one full minute to open the door wide enough to admit himself, and another minute to close it.

He stood for a moment inside, in the dark, listening.

All was silent.

Gradually his eyes adjusted to the darkness, and objects in the room began to take on dim, hulking shapes, their sharper contours softened by shadows. He looked around and made out the front counter and, farther into the room, the long rows of display shelves receding into blackness. Naturally he had brought a small flashlight, but he preferred not to use it yet. He waited until his eyes had adjusted a little more, then took a cautious step into the room.

The floorboards creaked loudly, and he froze.

Now there was an interesting problem that no one had ever made much progress toward solving: creaking wooden floors.

But all else was quiet, and he put another cautious foot out ahead of him and brought his weight down slowly, slowly. The boards protested faintly, but less than before. He took another such step, and another, and found himself in a part of the room where the floor was apparently less inclined to creak. A few more steps, and he was among the display shelves, whose contents were dim mysteries in the dark, even more enigmatic than when he had seen them in the light. He continued slowly, carefully, until he stood near the back of the store, and paused and listened.

Was that a creak in the boards overhead?

He held his breath, listening. No. Nothing. Maybe the wind. Rojas was asleep up there, he felt sure. He moved on toward the far wall, toward the door.

The door to the cellar.

It was unusual, out here in the desert, for a house or a building to even have a cellar. This was probably one of the very few in the area.

Interesting.

He waited in front of the door to be sure there were no sounds, no indications of anyone's stirring about. Then he placed his hand on the doorknob. It felt cold.

Slowly, slowly, he turned the knob without making a sound, and pulled the door about an inch open, listening.

Good, no creaking hinges this time. He pulled the door toward him again, and it swung silently open, allowing a breath of strange air to be exhaled into the room, from the cellar.

God, what a peculiar odor. He remembered it from before, when he'd been here in daylight, but it was stronger now. Not an unpleasant odor, exactly, just unplaceable, unnameable, strange.

Beyond the door, utter darkness, so complete it seemed almost palpable.

Now he brought his tiny flashlight out and flicked it on, training the beam of light into the doorway. He could just make out a set of rickety-looking old wooden stairs leading sharply down into the dark. He edged through the door, onto the top step, which creaked slightly. He snapped the flashlight off and stood for a moment, listening. No sound from out there, no sound from upstairs. Reaching back and groping with one hand, he pulled the cellar door closed behind him, softly, quietly. Now that the door was closed, he felt around on the adjacent wall and found a light switch, and snapped it.

No light came on.

What lay before him, below him, was a well of darkness.

He turned the little flashlight back on and trained its wan beam down the wooden stairs. The light would be enough to allow him to make his way down, but not enough to see very far down at a time. He took one tentative step down.

The board beneath his foot groaned loudly, and again he froze, listening.

No sounds from out in the store, nor above him. Nothing at all.

Nothing but an undecidable, vague stirring out in the darkness, below, in the depths of the cellar.

The impression was so faint, so unclear, that he might well have imagined it. Aiming the flashlight beam down the stairs, he took another step down. This time the board didn't creak, so he took another step, and another, playing the light ahead of him. He still couldn't see the bottom of the stairs, couldn't see anything really, except more wooden steps dropping down into a maw of blackness. He continued down, slowly, carefully.

At length he could see the edge of a gritty-looking concrete floor below him, at the termination of the wooden steps. The floor simply led off into darkness, and his flashlight beam still failed to show him anything further than a few feet away. It was like looking into the recesses of a cave. Didn't this cellar have any ground-level windows? Come to think of it, he hadn't seen any, outside. It wouldn't have made much difference anyhow, it was so dark outside; the nearest streetlamps out there were some forty or fifty yards away. He took the rest of the way down, and stepped onto the cellar floor.

And stood, listening.

More than listening. Feeling.

That was the only way he could characterize his sensations. It was as if his senses were being required to open up, to do something more than listen or look.

As if he were in the presence of something more demanding than that.

He played the beam of light around, but all he could see was a rusty-looking support beam just to his left, and the vague suggestion of boxes and possibly some old furniture, out in the gloom. Nothing looked quite real in this light.

And nothing seemed quite real with this sensation in his head.

Get hold of yourself, old boy.

He took a few cautious steps into the room, letting the light reach a little farther each time. Still nothing appeared but some dusty-looking packing boxes and, beyond them, the sable edges and contours of some old chairs and nameless bric-a-brac. He stopped.

Because something had moved, slightly, subtly, to his right, in the dark.

He wheeled in that direction, training the flashlight out ahead of him. But it wasn't needed, because another light came on, a lamp of some kind, off in a corner of the cellar.

After the darkness, it took his eyes a few seconds to adjust to the light, which at first seemed almost blinding even though a moment's reflection told him that it wasn't really very bright. The light did indeed emanate from a lamp on a little table in the corner. That whole part of the cellar, illumined suddenly now, was something to behold.

Unlike the rest of the cellar, which evidently was a storage area pretty much uncared-for, this corner was clean, orderly, livable-looking, with diminutive furniture: a little desk, some tiny chairs, a sort of futon for a bed, and the lamp. There were other objects, too, but Lloyd couldn't make out what they were.

Especially as his attention was centered on what stood in the midst of it all.

In the Blue Room at Wright-Patterson, some years before, he'd seen some of the bodies from the Roswell crash, so he should have been prepared. Somehow, nevertheless, he wasn't.

The thing stood perhaps three and a half feet tall, wearing a kind of one-piece jumpsuit of a bluish-gray material that looked almost like cellophane. The creature's grayish-tan head, disproportionately large for the frail-looking little body, nodded on its thin neck, and for a moment he was foolish enough to imagine that it was nodding *to* him, in greeting, before he realized that it was simply part of the creature's inscrutable manner of moving about. The large, almond-shaped eyes regarded him with something that only a fool would have tried to interpret as any understandable kind of expression.

After a moment, Lloyd found his tongue. "So," he said, shocked at the sound of his own voice in the cavernous room that sprawled about him. "So we finally meet."

The creature simply stood and stared at him. Just stood and stared. It was damned unnerving.

"You understand, of course," Lloyd said, "that you'll have to come with me."

The moment in which he uttered this remark might well have been the last time he would ever feel normal in his head, the last time he would ever have the sense that his thoughts, his senses, his emotions, were driven by processes that were essentially sane.

Because the little pear-headed creature took one wobbling step toward him, blinked its dark eyes once, and what hit Lloyd, then, was the—Impression.

That was the only way, at that moment, that he could think of it, to the extent that he could think of it at all.

The Impression was like an instantaneous wave of mental input so vast, so appallingly overwhelming, that it simply swept his consciousness back like a twist of driftwood, helpless. He had the sensation that a huge amount of information had just been impressed upon his mind—information so extensive and so suddenly imparted, however, that for the moment it seemed like no information at all, a kind of mental white light that he could not resolve into its spectrum of component thoughts. What was left to him, then, was an overarching sense of—of what?

Of menace. What else could he think?

His right hand floated indecisively in the air, uncertain as to the wisdom of reaching for his .44 magnum. What was he up against here, in truth? He realized, inconsequentially, that he was still needlessly holding the little flashlight. The alien blinked its black eyes once more and spoke in a reedy-thin voice.

"We shall have to come to some kind of understanding, other than the sort you have intended." As the creature spoke, Lloyd felt as if the words, though audible from the thin slit of a mouth, were also being lightly traced by invisible fingers upon his brain. It was unsettling; terrifying, in fact. He did reach for his .44 now, but somehow seemed to lack the will to draw it out, and stood absurdly with his empty hand in the air, indecisive. All the while, the alien creature just stared at him, its bulbous head nodding slightly. Lloyd couldn't do it, he simply couldn't make a move against the creature.

"I'll—I'll be back," he spluttered, and thought that his words sounded ridiculous when they hit the air. But he *would* be back. That much, by God, everybody could take to the bank. He turned and bolted up the wooden steps, heedless of how much noise he was making. Vaguely, as he sprinted back through the dark interior of the Emporium and reached the front door, he noticed a light coming on somewhere above, at the top of a staircase off to his right. Paco Rojas was waking up, and was coming downstairs. Well, it didn't matter. Lloyd was out of here. No time to stop and chat about idle matters like: what was he doing in the store in the middle of the night? No time for that. He had a mission to see to.

Barely bothering to glance behind him at the man coming down the stairs, Lloyd slipped through the doorway, out into the cool night air, and collided with someone on the sidewalk. Reeling and flailing his arms to regain balance, he saw that the man he had knocked down was old Jefe Sandoval, who, smelling mightily of cheap wine, pushed himself up onto one elbow and blinked in confusion. Then a crafty grin spread across the wrinkled face. "You seen something you didn't bargain on, *amigo*? You ought not to mess with stuff you can't handle."

Lloyd didn't even have time to be angry at the old man's taunting tones, and merely stepped over him. "Stick around, you old fart, we'll see who can handle it." Only passingly aware that Paco Rojas had appeared in the doorway, Lloyd strode away, toward Piñon Street. So far as he could tell, Rojas didn't even call after him to stop.

Rounding the corner onto Piñon and heading for his car, Lloyd thought: it must be one or two o'clock by now, how much time would there be left, before dawn? Passing under a streetlamp, he glanced at his watch.

And recoiled in surprise, enough to make him stop walking.

It was nearly 4:30 in the morning.

Where in God's name had all that time gone?

Back there, back in that cellar beneath Paco's Emporium—back there when he had received what he thought of as the Impression. What exactly had happened to his mind? And how long had it taken? He had of course heard "lost time" stories, with regard to human interaction with aliens, but he'd never thought he would experience it, and it was damned unsettling.

Unsettling, because he wasn't in control, and he hated not being in control.

He broke into a run and made it the rest of the way down the street to his car, starting it up and squealing around the corner to head back to the house.

By the time he got there he had calmed himself and was more than ready to make the call. His mind still held a strange impression, almost a kind of light-headedness, as if that odd bank of unassimilated thoughts were still lodged there, waiting to unfold its details; but he wasn't going to stop to ponder it, he was simply going to make his call, without any further delay; there had been more than enough delay already. Going through the usual security procedures, he soon had Charles Wu's face on the screen. Thank heaven Wu had the graveyard shift tonight. The Asian face broke into a mischievous grin. "Working a little late, are we, Tru? Glad to see you're finally starting to take your job seriously."

"No time to clown around," Lloyd said, "this is Priority One. Pay dirt. I want military surroundment of the town of Chasco. Ground troops on the whole perimeter, air surveillance backup. Get it going right now. And call Madgedale down at Holloman and tell him to get internment facilities ready."

Wu's eyes widened a bit. "Let me be sure I understand you. We're talking relocation of every human being in town?"

"The whole town," Lloyd said. "And not just every human being."

31

It was a heady experience for Jerry Logan, this business of standing late at night in your mother's kitchen in a strange town and listening to that knock at the door, and being eighteen years old and hanging out here with adults who didn't seem to be any more in control of the situation than you were. At least not to judge by their faces. His mom looked petrified, and her boyfriend, if that's what he was, didn't look too overjoyed himself. That nonhuman skeleton still reclined in its osseous placidity on the kitchen table, as if it had just lain down for a little nap, and Bill Weston's words were still hanging in the air, about the necessity of telling someone about this find, and the sooner the better. And then the knocking had started, and kept up.

"We have to answer it," Bill was saying. "Whoever it is, they can tell there's someone in here. They may have been standing out there listening to everything we've said, for all we know. I'll open the door." He started for the door.

"No," Jerry's mom said. "I'll do it." She grasped the doorknob and opened just enough to try to see who was there. Jerry, peering over his mom's shoulder, squinted into the dark, trying to make out who it was. By now, after what Bill had said, he half expected government types, or square-jawed goons in military uniforms. He certainly never expected the sort of person who now stepped, uninvited, into the room.

It was an old Indian woman dressed in foul-looking rags, her face an incredible bewilderment of wrinkles of the sort that one might have expected to see on the withered face of a mummy. But this face, wrinkles notwithstanding, was very much alive, as attested by a pair of eyes that burned like bright little coals from deep in their lizardlike sockets. The old woman nudged the door shut behind her, and moved farther into the room. Jerry glanced at Bill, who was staring open-mouthed at the newcomer. Interestingly enough, the old Indian addressed him first.

"We spoke before, in the park," she said, "and I told you, I know you see things, you understand things."

Bill, despite this description, looked utterly at a loss. "I—I'm not sure I understand much of anything at this point. Why are you here?"

The old woman turned toward the table where the alien bones lay. "Because of him," she said. Jerry, watching her turn, reflected that there was something vaguely disturbing about the way she moved, as if her thin frame swiveled on its bony legs in a way difficult for the mind to follow, moving at strange angles, and in more than one direction at a time. It half reminded him of something, but he couldn't think what.

"I don't understand either," his mom said, moving to one side as if to get a more objective look at the old woman. "Who are you? And what do you know about—that?" She gestured toward the bones.

"People call me Araña," the old woman replied, shifting again in that eerie way she had of moving. It gave Jerry the creeps, watching her. "I have lived in the desert all my life," she was saying, "and I have known many strange things that most people don't know." Her voice was dry, like a desert wind down an arroyo. "Things that are not pleasant to know."

"What things?" Jerry asked. Again, he had the strange sensation of having done a lot of growing up in a hurry, being here tonight like this, confronting a situation that the adults around him were probably no better prepared to handle than he was.

"This poor creature," Araña said, indicating the bones again, "this poor little creature was killed by those who did not understand. It was when the Spanish were exploring these lands for the first time."

"You mean—when Coronado came through here?" Bill asked. He appeared to be doing a quick calculation in his head. "Damn. That was over four hundred years ago. You mean this thing—"

"The Sky-Children came down to my people all those years and years ago," Araña continued, "and they taught us many things. Things you call magic, and sorcery, and shapeshifting. Things I call life. And one of the Spaniards saw my people with the Sky-Children, back there in the arroyo, and killed one of them. The one there on the table."

"*Qué cosa más increible*," Jerry heard his mom whisper. She turned toward Bill. "Do you know what this means? It's not just that we found an alien body. We found an alien body that's been lying there since Coronado. One of his party had an encounter with—creatures from a flying saucer. Don't you see, this is history! This changes everything."

"It changes more than you know," Araña said. Something in the tone of her arid voice suggested, at least to Jerry, that she felt that they were all missing the essential point. "We are all in danger. Not so much me. I can—do things to take care of myself. But you, you are in danger."

"Because of that?" Jerry asked, pointing to the bones on the table. Somehow now they had a sinister look about them. "Because the army or the government or somebody is going to—"

"More than that," Araña said. "Back in the old time, when the Spaniards killed the Sky-Child, an old Indian, a *brujo* like me, put a mighty curse on the place where it happened. I have seen this in a dream-vision."

Jerry's mom looked almost as if it were a relief to hear the problem described only as an Indian curse. "This place?" she asked, pointing toward the area behind the house. "In the arroyo, where we found the bones?"

"Yes," Araña said. "Something lives there, in the arroyo."

"What do you mean, something lives there?" Bill asked.

"Something," Araña replied, "that waits. Something that waits for the stars to come around right. Something that is going to wake up very soon and take its vengeance."

As if to underscore this remark, a thin, spectral cry wavered on the air outside, behind the house. A cry like that of a woman in some unimaginable lamentation. It was eerier than any sound Jerry had ever heard. It was dreadful.

"Something is going to wake up, and *she* knows," Araña said, "and that is why she cries. For the lost Sky-Child, and for fear of what is coming."

32

Truman Lloyd sat by lamplight in his quiet little living room and stared at the blank screen of the comm unit. What was bothering him? Normally, when he switched the unit off, he had always felt a certain sense of missions accomplished, good connections made, jobs well done. Tonight, with the dark screen gaping before him like a blind eye, he felt only a certain confusion, a vague sort of turmoil somewhere deep in his mind. What the hell was it?

He got up, paced the floor a bit, and mixed himself a gin and tonic. Maybe what was bugging him was the realization that it was already nearly five in the morning; it might well take the military a couple of hours to get into place and begin the operation, and by then it would be dawn. He would rather have done this whole thing the way he had lived most of his life: in the dark. The snug and comfortable dark.

But was that really what was on his mind? Downing the last of his drink, he decided to take a bit of a walk to clear his head.

Outside on Chamisa Street the town seemed surreal in the wan light of widely spaced streetlamps, like a stage set fallen idle, the actors and the audience all sensibly home in bed, asleep. He suddenly felt very alone.

Bullshit and nonsense, he thought, snorting. A walk over to Melendez Park would sort things out.

On the way, he began to have the curious sensation that he was about to remember something. Not just something—he was about to remember a great many things, things that right now, unaccountably, were barred to his understanding. But the bars were about to come off, the memory was about to cascade forth. He could feel it, and he didn't know for sure how he felt about it.

He felt a little afraid, in truth.

Crossing the grassy expanse of the park, he sought out a bench not too near the corner streetlamp. And not too far away. He wanted a little light, but not too much. Settling himself on the bench, he tried to empty his mind of extraneous thoughts.

And found that emptying his mind was the last thing in the world he was going to be able to do—because here it came, the veritable avalanche of memory that he had felt approaching. Was it memory, or some unprecedented and less explicable mental activity to which his mind was rising? He couldn't tell. This was a whole new ballgame.

Because what filled his vision, like a daydream, was the placid dark-eyed face of the—the Elder One. How did he know that that was what the creature was called? Lloyd was still dimly aware of his surroundings—the bench, the park, the fountain lurking in shadow off to his right down the path—but what nearly crowded his normal perceptions out was the face. It wasn't physically present, but it was present to his mind, with a force he couldn't remember ever associating with any other awareness. And the face, with a blink of the black almond eyes, nodded once and spoke.

We have never had a proper understanding, the Elder One's voice echoed sonorously in Lloyd's mind, *between your people and mine.*

It was like the feeling he had had back in the cellar, a sort of indeterminate impression of sound accompanied by a fine tracery on his mind, as if by lithe fingers. But this time he knew that the sound was part of the great unfolding of that impulse, that body of information the creature had imparted to him before. He tried to respond, in his mind, but found that he was incapable of doing so. It was not going to be his time to speak; he could only listen. Listen, and watch the ghostly impressions that danced before his eyes.

More than four of your centuries ago, the Elder One went on, *we came down to this desertland to visit and speak with those living here, the ones you call Indians. We came to visit them as we had been coming for thousands of years. At that time, the Spaniards were crossing this land, in exploration. They were encamped some distance north of here, trying to cross the river, which was in flood. We were here, in the arroyo, with the Indians. An old Indian, wise in our ways and his, brought some of the Spaniards here, in the belief that the experience would be a kind of enlightenment for them. But when they beheld our discourse, and when they saw us teaching the Indians how to shapeshift, they grew angry, and one of them killed one of us. The body of the slain one remained in the arroyo, where the Indians buried it in a shallow grave of sand.*

But the old Indian who had brought the Spaniards, enraged by the slaying that had occurred, used his magic to place a curse upon the arroyo. He brought something to life there, something that has hidden, waiting, over the years, for the cosmic cycle to come around right for its awakening. That awakening is about to happen. All are in danger.

You have never understood.

When our ship crashed north of Roswell in the year you call 1947, most of the crew were killed. Your army people found, and took into custody, one survivor, who later died. But there were other survivors, as your government people have recently come to suspect. Some Indians in the desert near the crash site found us, three of us, and took us away in the night before the army people came. Two of the three died soon after. I was the third, and I lived, thanks to the Indians. It was fitting that they found us, for we have long had an affinity, a relationship with the Indians. Their folklore speaks a great deal of truth about us, and their languages are related to our own.

After the rescue, the Indians moved me from place to place for a while, and finally hid me in the cellar of Paco Rojas' store, where you found me. Time does not mean to me what it means to you, and I have not suffered any unhappiness in this concealment. I have in fact come to find great contentment in the human community here. Many people in the town know of me, but have remained silent. Over the years I have fathered children by several women in the town. This has been a mystical experience, for them and for me, this mingling of our genetic codings. You have seen at least one of my children.

Yes, one corner of Lloyd's mind whispered, yes I have seen one. The girl, in the diner. The girl whose mother we—but the thought, at this moment and in these circumstances, filled him with shame.

As if in response, the Elder One's great black eyes blinked ponderously, and the reedy voice resumed speaking. *So great has been your desire to keep secret that which all humankind has a right to know, that your people have killed the woman who bore one of my children. And you would kill them all, all these people, or you would remove them to some prison where they could not tell what they know. Your actions, and your intentions, represent the worst of human qualities. You will not be allowed to prevail.*

Even now a part of Lloyd's mind recoiled, rebelling against this pronouncement. His mind wanted to say: oh yeah, I've made the call, the military is on the way, we'll see who prevails. But he could not project this thought, and it died away in his mind.

You do not understand us. To you, and to your army and government people, we are frail little children who, paradoxically, seem to be a threat to you. You see us as a threat to your nationalism, to your pride, to your mentality.

207

You have used our technology, from the crashed ship at Roswell, to bring yourselves into the computer age, yet you still regard us as an alien menace, and you still regard our existence as a secret to be kept from the rest of your people, a secret to which you, unaccountably, lay exclusive claim. This in spite of the fact that our presence should be common knowledge, and in spite of the fact that we have never done anything that could reasonably be interpreted as a threat to you. You have prodded our dead bodies in autopsy rooms in secret places, you have compiled millions of pages of files on our physiology, but you have never really understood anything important about us.

But you will.

I will teach you.

Your scientists, examining our bodies, have speculated that our sensory apparati may be highly different from yours. This is true, though your people have never appreciated the implications. In particular, our eyes are of vastly different capability. You humans have a visual range from around 400 nanometers, in the violet range, to around 750 nanometers, in the red-brown range. If I may make an analogy with sound, to start at any point in this range and double the wavelength, or halve the frequency, would be to create a change of one octave, but any such doubling, from any point in your visible spectrum, goes beyond the reaches of that spectrum. You cannot see even one octave.

But we can.

Indeed, our visual range extends down through ultraviolet and beyond, and up through infrared and beyond. We can see colors that are an octave apart, and two octaves apart, and far more. We can see nearly seven octaves. And just as sounds that are an octave apart have an emotional relationship for you—just as they "sound the same"—so colors that are an octave apart have an emotional relationship for us. Your scientists have remarked that our faces appear peaceful even in death, and there are reasons for this. We have an aesthetic sense unknown to you. To us, the world of light is a symphony, an eternal cosmic song. We enjoy nuances of emotion that are unimaginable to you, and we have enjoyed them for millions of years.

And we look toward the time, one distant day, when you will evolve to enjoy them too.

Because you are our children.

Abruptly, the vision dimmed. The Elder One's head, in Lloyd's mind, seemed to nod once more, with a last blink of the great dark almond eyes, and the vision simply faded to blackness and silence.

And what welled up to take its place, for Truman Lloyd, was hideous.

He had never imagined, could never have begun to imagine, the depth of sadness, guilt, remorse that surged into the void to fill his mind, his heart, with horror. It was unbearable. Choking, he pitched forward off the bench onto the grass and vomited copiously, and wept.

He sobbed with an insane kind of fury, as if some part of him wanted his heart to stop, because it deserved to. He sobbed with great wracking gulps of breath that filled his lungs with pain. It was the first time in his life he could ever remember having cried.

And by the time he was able to stop, and catch his breath, the sun was beginning to show its first faint intimations of rising, spreading a vague pink aura onto the eastern sky. But it was still fairly dark, and when he sat up, wiping his face and looking around him, he felt disoriented. He had to refocus his eyes to make out the dim outlines of the fountain off to one side, and the shadowy shapes of buildings beyond the park. In another half hour, at the outside, it would be dawn. The military people would be closing in. Already he half thought he could hear a faraway grumble of engines, out in the desert somewhere. And was that the faint burring of a helicopter, or more than one helicopter, off in the distance?

God in heaven, what had he done?

Pushing himself to his feet, he sprinted off across the near corner of the park and crossed Zia Street and ran south along Chamisa. Why in God's name hadn't he driven here? He needed his car. As out of breath as he was, he was far from sure he could make it back to the house on foot. But at length he crossed Old Corona Road and took the porch steps in one leap. Inside, he took only a couple of minutes to get the comm unit back online, and soon he was looking at the face of Charles Wu again. Wu peered at him in evident surprise.

"What the hell happened to you? And what are you doing at the house? Troops will be entering the town within thirty minutes, and you're going to be needed. Major Jenckes from Kirtland will be to reporting to you. He's coming in from the west on Camino del Sol. Four thousand troops will be dispersed in a complete circle around Chasco and relocation will begin by dawn. Now—Christ, Tru, look at you, what's the matter with you, anyway? Here we are about to roll with a major containment operation and you look like you just came in from a three-day pig fuck."

"Listen," Lloyd said, "I've made a terrible mistake. It's all a mistake. The whole thing. You can't send troops into town. Call it off."

Wu's face on the screen was a rictus of horrified amazement. "Call it off? Jesus, Tru, are you nuts?"

"No," Lloyd said, "no, I'm not. I might just be sane for the first time in my life. And I want you to call it off."

"Well, I'll tell you what, Truman," Wu said, "at this point I just don't think that's your decision to make any more." It wasn't lost on Lloyd that Charles Wu had switched from calling him Tru to calling him Truman. Was it going to be "Mr. Lloyd" next?

"What do you mean, not my decision?" Lloyd bellowed. "I'm in charge of this operation."

"At the local level, yes, you're still in charge," Wu replied drily, "but frankly, when I call and wake the President up and have him briefed on a major field operation and then you tell me half an hour later that you want it all called off because of some half-assed idea that it's a mistake—how could it be a mistake? What's got into you?"

"I—I can't explain right now, you're just going to have to take my word for it. It's all wrong. Call it off before it's too late."

Wu stared at him in silence for a moment. "I'm going to call the Pentagon, is what I'm going to do, and I'm probably going to be talking to the President again. I have to tell you, Truman, I don't like the sound of this. I don't like it at all. I've known you for years. I respect you. But in case it has slipped your mind, you can be relieved of your assignment if you keep this shit up. You can be discontinued with Group Epsilon altogether, for that matter. And I think you know what that means."

"Do what you have to do," Lloyd said, and pulled the plug.

He grabbed up a phone book and bolted out the door. Heading uptown, in his car this time, he thought: well, that's it, you're as good as dead. You don't quit working for Group Epsilon unless it's to wear a tag on your toe.

But there were more important things to think about.

Stopping at the corner of Chamisa and Piñon, he propped the phone book up on the steering wheel and took advantage of the light from a streetlamp to thumb through the pages and find the name he was looking for. There it was. The address was 344 Camposanto Road.

When he pulled up at that address and stopped, he saw that the house was a squalid little adobe badly in need of patching, much like the houses around it on both sides. It was a poor northside neighborhood of the sort that he had glanced at, before, in his runnings about town, with scarcely a notice. Thankfully, there was nobody about; it was still early, not quite six, and nobody would be up and on their way to work at this hour.

Well, almost nobody. Waitresses, he suddenly remembered, might well have to get an early start.

Because there she was, coming down the walk as he came up it. There she was, big dark eyes and all: Yolanda Anaya, the girl from the diner. In the middle of the little grass-grown walkway, she stopped and stared at him. He passingly wondered if she lived with roommates, probably a necessity on her income.

"I—" But what could he say to her? What was it even remotely imaginable he could say to her?

"I know about my mother," the girl said simply. The expression on her face was redolent of a refined kind of sadness that had too much character in it to admit of out-and-out anger, though there was a suggestion of that too.

"You know?" Lloyd said impotently, and hated his voice, hated himself. "How——?"

"I should say *we* know," Yolanda said.

"We?"

"My father and I," she said, and in spite of everything, it took Lloyd a moment to realize who the father was. "You forget," the girl said, "we're different. What he wants me to know, I know."

There was something immensely humbling, to Lloyd, in this simple statement. It gave him, anew, a sense of the intelligence he and his kind had been trifling with, all these years. It made him all the more profoundly ashamed, an emotion that was so unfamiliar to him that it felt like a raw wound in his chest. He had to say something to her, nonetheless.

"I can't tell you how sorry I am," he offered lamely.

Yolanda nodded, and the motion was familiar; it reminded him of the father. "I know you can't." And she stepped past him and walked away into the pre-dawn gloom.

33

Bill Weston stood beside the bones of the exhumed creature, and listened to the unearthly wailing from out in the arroyo. He had read it in Lisa's face, and Jerry's—they too found the sound appalling. The old Indian woman's face was simply an expressionless mass of wrinkles, out of which two timeless eyes stared at him, as if gauging his reactions. Somehow the electric light here in the kitchen made everyone's face look a little uncanny, like a scene in some surreal film.

His voice startled even him when he spoke, and he saw Lisa jump a little at it. "Scary." He nodded toward the outside, the crying, the arroyo out in the night. "Scary," he said again, pointlessly.

"Just a squitch," Lisa said, evidently trying for some levity, but her voice sounded shaky.

"I think we ought to go out there," Jerry said, running a hand through his hair and shaking his head as if to say: what else is there to do?

Bill blinked at him. "Go *out* there? Why?"

"I don't know," Jerry said, "I just think we ought to go see."

Lisa clasped her hands in front of her face almost as if she were praying, then gave her head a quick nod. "He's right. We've got to go."

Bill wondered if they were all of them, himself included, losing their minds under the strain of all these bewilderments' coming so close upon one another the past few hours. Why in the world—but maybe they were right, maybe it was useless just to stand around in here and listen to that unearthly wailing. Maybe worse than useless. He turned to Araña. "What do you think?"

The old woman shifted on her feet in that unsettling way she had of seeming to move in several directions at once, her tatters flailing like so many strange cilia. Her voice was a dry croaking when she spoke. "You must follow the path of your heart," she said. "Everyone has a path to follow."

Yeah, Bill thought, and right now I feel like our paths lead straight to the asylum, or the grave.

"Let's go," Lisa said, taking Bill's hand. Bill in turn took Jerry's hand, and Jerry, with one thoughtful-looking glance at the bones on the table, reached and took Araña's ancient hand. For a giddy moment Bill felt as if they had formed a bizarre daisy-chain and were going to skip out to the arroyo that way, like a group of schoolchildren; but everyone dropped hands, and they all simply headed for the door, while the eerie crying from out there in the dark kept up its ululation like some deranged creature, wailing, wailing.

Out in the dark, Jerry cleared his throat and said, "I've got a flashlight in the car." He went for it while everyone waited near the wooden steps, their forms casting long, ghoulish shadows in the porch light. When Jerry came back with the flashlight, they walked toward the arroyo, toward the sound. Lisa took Bill's hand again.

Halfway out to the opening to the arroyo they all stopped and listened. It was unmistakable now, this spectral sound. It was the crying of a woman in torment.

Bill distinctly felt the hair on the back of his neck begin to stand on end. What in God's name was he doing here? What was the woman whose hand he now held doing here? Or Jerry? Only the strange old Indian woman seemed to belong in this scenario. A light wind came up and mingled with the ghostly sound from the arroyo, twirling it aloft, making it fade, then grow, then fade.

Lisa was tugging gently at his hand. *"Vámonos."*

And they all walked toward the arroyo, following the pale beam of Jerry's flashlight as it played over beavertail cactus and clumps of prairie grass and mesquite, making feral-looking shadows that jittered out over the sand like strange dark beasts. As Bill watched, these shadows were overpowered by a larger and more ominous-looking shadow, something seemingly multilegged and spasmodic, like a huge spider. Drawing a sharp breath, Bill turned aside to see that Araña, her tatters whipping in the breeze, had moved in front of Jerry's light beam, sending her own bizarre shadow lurching out over the landscape as her bony form moved in its mind-bending way through the night. She was a disturbing figure to behold, but somehow Bill was glad she was here. He had the feeling, without knowing why, that they were going to need her.

Presently they came to the arroyo, and a shift in the wind brought the keening cry closer, louder. Or had the cry come closer, by itself?

Jerry pointed the beam into the arroyo, but the depths of the wash quickly swallowed up the pallid light, which illumined only vague contours of mesquite and sand. The crying from within sounded almost frantic now, as if the source, the unthinkable mouth that made the sound, sensed their presence and reacted to it. Something in the quality of the sound made Bill feel as if his bowels were filled with ice. Glancing sidelong at Lisa, he saw that she was scared too, but her face, or what he could see of it in the peripheral glow from Jerry's flashlight, suggested something else as well—a kind of dark fascination, a kind of anticipatory awe. Lisa returned his glance, squeezed his hand, and whispered, "Let's go." And they entered the arroyo. Jerry went in first with the light, then Bill and Lisa, and Araña came up behind, her bony feet making odd crisscross scratching sounds in the dry sand. Off in the east, to the right, a faint adumbration of light was beginning to creep into the sky; thank heaven it would fairly soon be dawn.

Gradually, as they all walked on, the low root-entwisted walls of the rivercourse grew higher, until they were too high to see over. The effect, to Bill, at this moment, was distinctly uncomfortable. He had never particularly suffered from any genuine claustrophobia, and he hadn't felt beset by claustrophobic reaction here before, but he felt it now, a constricting sense of being enclosed, trapped. It felt insane to keep going forward, forward, farther into the maze of the arroyo. But forward they all went, stepping around cactus and low mesquite and rattlesnake holes. Somehow Bill would have welcomed so mundane a sight as a rattlesnake, just now. Up ahead, the wailing went on and on, and grew more frenetic. It sounded like someone veritably mad with grief.

And when they came to the wider opening in the riverbed, where the tall canyonlike walls receded into deeper shadow on both sides, there was something moving out there in the near dark.

The sight hit Bill's mind with an impact that was more than just vision, more than light and sound. Araña had said that he knew things, was sensitive to things, and she must have been right, because the vision that danced in the gloom out there across the way, the pale thing that moved there, struck him with a sense of understanding that he found far from welcome. As the figure drew closer, its gossamer form began resolving into the shimmering outlines of a woman, her gown billowing in the wind, her chalky face wide-eyed and full of horror. Somehow, then, the mouth seemed to open wider than the face should have allowed, and the cry that came out was something that one would not want to hear again, ever.

But they were going to hear it again, because the thing drifted closer now, and closer, its pallid face a mask of terror. And when it uttered its dismal cry, time after time, the unbearable understanding, for Bill, was that it wasn't this dreadful woman, it wasn't La Llorona, they had to fear. Her cries themselves were cries of fear, after all. No, it wasn't the wailing woman they had to fear.

What they had to fear was what was coming down the arroyo behind her.

Because something was. He knew. He saw in Araña's ancient face that she knew too, probably better than he. So far he couldn't see anything in the murky dark back there behind the wailing woman, down the farther nighted reaches of the rivercourse, but he knew something was coming. He could feel it. He could feel it in the air, he could feel it in the fear in the woman's cries. It was coming, all right.

He gripped Lisa's hand. "We've got to get out of here."

Lisa turned to look at him, and she was a pale goblin face in the indirect glow of the flashlight. She opened her mouth to speak, but didn't seem to know what to say. But she made no move to retreat. Was she afraid to move? Were they all thunderstruck, paralyzed, like a deer in the headlamps of a car? In the periphery of his vision he could see Jerry, holding the flashlight shakily, but he couldn't make out the expression on his face. And the old Indian woman was just standing, watching inscrutably. If she was afraid, she bore it marvellously well.

Suddenly Bill was aware of another sound mingling with the crying and the wind. Off in the distance somewhere, up on the desert floor above the arroyo, it sounded like the faraway growl of engines. Cars? Trucks? And somewhere high overhead, the whirr of a helicopter?

But now the wailing woman commanded all their attention. The vision of her translucent form seemed to swell larger, closer, until she floated within a few yards of where they stood, and the eyes grew huge, and the tormented mouth gaped to emit one final shriek of horror. She seemed to look behind her, over her shoulder, then back at Bill and Jerry and Lisa and Araña. And then she grew dim, indistinct, and simply popped like a soap bubble, vanishing. And the sky was crowned with light. It was dawn.

But something was wrong. Something was wrong with that.

Bill blinked, shaking his head, trying to get his mind to register what it was that was wrong.

And then he knew.

It was dawn all right, out there, out on the desert floor. But it wasn't dawn up there ahead of them, further up the arroyo.

Because even where timid fingers of incipient light should have been tracing their way down the arroyo's west wall to dispel the shadows there, behind where La Llorona had been, there was in fact only a thick darkness, as dense and murky as the blackest night.

34

Lisa stood transfixed, watching, trying to understand what she was seeing. Even the vision they had just witnessed of La Llorona was mild, compared to this.

Down here in the dry wash, the dawn had at first shown itself only as a faint patina of light creeping down the root-encrusted west wall of the arroyo, but in a surprisingly short time it had spread a soft, gentle illumination around them, changing shapeless mounds of shadow into familiar things: cactus, sage, chamisa, mesquite, rocks, driftings of sand. Suddenly, it was day.

Day here where they stood. Day out on the desert floor.

But not up ahead, further up the arroyo, where the weeping woman had emerged, floated, vanished. Day had not come, had not arrived at all, across the way there.

She and Bill and Jerry and the old Indian woman stood just within the near side of the wide place in the arroyo. The other side, where the watercourse would pinch off narrower again and go on its way northwestward, was perhaps a hundred feet in front of them, maybe a little more. And at that distance, where there should have been light, it was still deep, impenetrable dark. *It was still night there.*

The darkness there looked like a moiling density of shadow, as if the very air had thickened into a kind of palpable black murkiness that might at any moment come pouring down the arroyo like a flood of water. And in fact this blackness, this unnatural well of night, *was* moving closer. Churning, seething like fog, it was coming down the arroyo toward them. It was something that couldn't exist, not in the real world. But it did exist.

Glancing to one side, Lisa saw Bill staring at it too, dumbstruck. On her other side, Jerry too was gaping at the vision before them, his mouth open incredulously, his eyes raw with fear. Beside him, Araña stood with her bony feet planted stoically in the sand, but even in her ancient eyes Lisa could see a kindling of terror. And up the arroyo, the undulating blackness moved slowly, steadily closer, making a low grinding kind of sound as it came on along the arroyo floor and walls, flattening the underbrush as it advanced.

Lisa grabbed Bill's hand and squeezed it as hard as she could, to try to snap him out of it. She wanted to reach out to Jerry too, but he was standing too far away. "Bill! Jerry! Let's get the hell out of here!" Pulling Bill along, she pivoted on one foot and started to make a run for it.

And took only one step before she ran into someone standing there.

It was a man who looked familiar, but in her state of mind just now she wasn't sure at first who he was. Then she remembered. He was the one she had run into out here before, when she first saw La Llorona. What the hell was going on?

"Mr. Lombardy? We've got to—"

The man shook his head, looking oddly apologetic. "My real name is Truman Lloyd."

Lisa gasped. This was incredible. "I don't give a shit if your real name is Pancho Villa! We've got to get the hell out of here right now, *pronto!*" She pointed off up the arroyo, where now the roiling blackness was halfway across the clearing and coming closer every second, ruffling the sand of the riverbed, blotting everything out as it moved toward them.

They all wheeled and ran. At least Lisa's confused senses registered that Jerry was running, and that she herself was pulling Bill along and herding the newly arrived Mr. Lloyd ahead of her with a hand in the middle of his back whenever he didn't move fast enough. Where Araña was, she didn't know. There wasn't time to think about it, because by the time they were all back in the narrower part of the arroyo through which they had come to get here, the churning blackness behind them was all the way across the wide space and squeezing itself like some inky nightmare into the rivercourse behind them, slithering along the arroyo walls, pushing along, snapping the mesquite flat in the sand, surging closer, closer.

What followed was a wild panic of running, running, endless running. Sandy arroyo walls flashed by, cactus and mesquite appeared to block their way everywhere as they ran, dodging, calling incoherently to each other, gasping for breath. Lisa's lungs burned, and she knew, each moment, that she could run no more, no damned more, not another step. Behind, the advancing blackness crunched and crackled its way through the intervening underbrush, slithering along the sand, over clusters of cactus, expunging everything from view as it came on, closing upon them. They weren't going to make it. This she knew. She was going to fall headlong in the sand, and she was going to die, right here, right now. And if anyone stopped to help her, they were going to die too. It was hopeless. They were all going to die.

It was Bill, behind her, who stumbled on a rock and fell headlong, yelping. Finding strength she didn't know she had, she grasped his flailing hand and pulled him to his feet. "Come *on*, damn it!" And they were running full tilt again. But the pitiless thing behind them was so close now, with the time lost in Bill's falling, that it was almost touching them with fingers of black, malevolent fog. It was hopeless, all right. They simply weren't going to make it.

But at length the opening to the arroyo appeared far ahead, and they all plunged toward it, putting more distance between themselves and the lightless horror that bulged and slithered behind them. Jerry and the Truman Lloyd emerged first, with Lisa and Bill close behind. No—unaccountably, Araña had gotten out first, as she was standing off across the open chaparral, watching them. How had she come out ahead of them?

But there was no time to waste thinking about that. Spinning around, Lisa looked back toward the opening to the arroyo, but couldn't see anything out of the ordinary. Whatever it was that was coming down the riverbed, it hadn't reached far enough down to be visible from here, in the angles of the arroyo. But they sure as hell hadn't imagined it, and it couldn't be far behind, the way it had been moving. "Let's go," she said to the others.

"Wait," Bill said, and the others looked at him as if he were insane.

"What do you mean, wait?" Jerry asked.

Bill held up a hand for silence. There was a low breeze among the sage and the chamisa, a whisper of wind, but nothing more.

No sound from the arroyo.

"It's waiting," Bill said.

Lisa reached out and shook him by one shoulder. His eyes were nearly glazed, as if he were the recipient of some bizarre vision. "Waiting? What are you talking about?"

"Just pausing," Bill said. "Gathering itself. Getting ready to move again. And when it does—"

"How do you know all this?" Lisa asked.

Bill looked at her with a pained kind of expression, the kind of look one has when burdened with some awful knowledge that one doesn't know how to share. "I can't tell you, I just feel it."

222

"He's right," a dry voice croaked. It was Araña, from across the way. "He knows. It's still coming."

But these last few words were almost obscured by other sounds, sounds that seemed to be coming from the west or northwest. Sounds of motors, marching feet, imperious voices shouting orders.

Military sounds.

Lisa strained to look out into the desert, beyond the arroyo, and thought she could see a multitude of shapes there. Were those military jeeps, trucks, driving cross-country, bumping through the chaparral, sending up clouds of dust so thick that it was hard to see? Were those lines of men in uniform? Why would the military be coming across the desert, toward town?

But there were other, similar, sounds from *in* town, off to the southeast: engines revving, voices calling out. Just at the limit of her vision, Lisa saw an army-green truck moving east down Piñon Street, full of uniformed troops.

What in God's name was happening?

On some instinct she turned toward Truman Lloyd. "You. You know something about this, don't you?"

He looked stricken. "I—Chasco is being surrounded by the military."

Jerry came up to confront him. "Jesus! Is this about those b—" He caught himself. "Is this about what we found?"

"What you found?" Lloyd said. "What did you find?"

"Never mind that," Bill said. "You said the military is surrounding the town. How do you know that? Just who the hell are you?" Bill made as if to grab him by the collar. "If you don't tell us, right now, what you have to do with—" But Lisa stepped between them.

"Never mind." She pulled Bill and Jerry off to the side, whispering to them. "I don't know what's going on here, but we've got to do something about those bones. We can't let the army people find them. Maybe they're going house to house, searching."

"What bones?" Truman Lloyd asked.

"Not to mention," Bill said, ignoring Lloyd and pointing back toward the dry riverbed, "that whatever chased us out of the arroyo is still there."

"It's Arroyo, that I tried to warn you about," the old Indian woman said, moving up among them with that disorienting spiderlike walk of hers. "I have powers, I may be able to stop it. I don't know. I'll try."

"You'll need help," a voice said.

Something in the timbre of that voice made Lisa's blood go cold, it was so strange. She turned toward the sound.

And what she saw, standing there in the chaparral, changed everything for her. Changed her life. Forever.

It wasn't the old wino Jefe Sandoval that struck her, though he was there, all right, his parched old face solemn with a kind of duty that gave him an odd sort of dignity. No, it wasn't old Jefe who drew Lisa's attention.

It was the little creature that stood next to him.

This wasn't something her brain was ready to accept, wasn't something her eyes were ready to see. It was one thing, looking at a rearticulated collection of bones on your kitchen table. It was another thing altogether, looking at the sort of creature the bones came from, a creature alive, breathing, blinking its huge almond eyes at you in the morning light like a wise little old child, taking your measure, regarding you with an expression of placidity and timeless intelligence.

"God help me understand," she whispered, crossing herself.

Jerry and Bill were regarding the creature with stunned amazement as well. Only Truman Lloyd and the old Indian woman seemed not to be surprised—and Jefe, who stood by the creature's side with a certain proprietary air.

It was Truman Lloyd who spoke up, and when he did, it was to Lisa. "This is the Elder One," he said, giving Lisa the idiotic feeling, for the moment, that she was being introduced to someone at a cocktail party. "Some of the people of Chasco have had him hidden away in a cellar for years," Lloyd said. He directed his next remark to the Elder One: "The troops are closing in. They'll find you."

The alien creature gave Lloyd a blink of the eyes. "We must first concern ourselves with what is coming out of the arroyo," he said.

And when Lisa turned to look back toward the arroyo, she saw how true this was. Where the opening to the rivercourse had been illumined by sunlight before, it was now only a seething blackness, an appalling coal-black fog that boiled out of the opening and onto the desert floor.

"Look!" Jerry said, pointing.

Off on the other side of the arroyo, a mass of green-uniformed troops had gathered, rifles at the ready, and the black thing that filled the dry wash had bubbled up over the arroyo wall toward them. A confused jumble of cries went up, mingled with a fury of rifle shots. But these sounds were choked off as the thing bulged across the intervening space onto the troops, enveloping them. For a moment, strangled cries wafted across the sand, then there was only silence.

"Damn," Bill said. "Damn! It got them."

"Heaven help them," Lisa said.

"Too late for that, and I kind of think we're next," Jerry said, almost emotionlessly.

And then the churning blackness, which had paused in its course, continued to boil up out of the arroyo, and advanced rapidly, remorselessly across the sandy chaparral toward them, coming on with a kind of hunger.

35

Lisa turned toward Bill with no thought but to convey to him the urgency she felt. "We've got to get out of here and take those bones with us. And the live creature. I'll carry him if I have to. Other people have got to know about all this."

Bill, his eyes riveted upon the horror coming from the arroyo, nodded his head and spoke without looking at her. "You'd better believe it. I'm not sure I know what's going on, but I for one am not willing to see it all end here. Let's haul ass!"

They broke into a run for the house, Bill grabbing Jerry by the arm as they passed him. Lisa went for the Elder One, motioning for him and Jefe to come with them. Off to one side, Truman Lloyd was standing at a loss, gaping at the black death that was surging out of the arroyo and crossing the chaparral to meet them. Jerry at first yielded to Bill's grasp and ran a few paces, but then stopped cold and shouted, "Wait!"

Bill looked at him furiously. "Wait, hell! That thing's going to—"

Jerry shook his head. "No, look. There's something happening." He pointed over toward Araña, and toward the little alien creature; he had eluded Lisa and Jefe and was walking toward the old woman, who took his little hand when he reached her. Across in the direction of the arroyo, the unthinkable black nightmare was halfway across the field now, crunching the vegetation down in its path, seething, reaching.

Araña spoke: "The time has come."

"—the walrus said," Bill supplied, laughing mirthlessly. He's losing it, Lisa thought. We're all losing it.

"It is time to end the curse," Araña continued, swiveling her gaunt and angular form on her bony legs and moving in a way that the eye could not quite follow. The Elder One, his hand still in hers, blinked up at her with his ebony eyes. "What has been must be no more," the old woman went on.

With her free hand she fumbled among the rags in which she was clad, and lifted out a leather pouch hanging by a thong around her neck. Fingering it, she brought out what looked like a tiny strip of metallic foil and held it aloft. She released the alien creature's hand now and made cryptic movements with both her arms, finally raising them high to the sky, just as a camouflage-green helicopter buzzed overhead. The chopper nearly drowned out her words, but it sounded as if she said something like "spirits of the dreamtime" and then began chanting in a language that was not English. When the noise from overhead had passed off, Lisa could hear clearly again, but the old woman was still chanting in that other language. At this point Truman Lloyd approached them and spoke to the Elder One.

"Can you forgive me?" he asked, his voice hoarse. "Would that stop whatever is happening?"

The Elder One blinked and nodded at him, and spoke in a thin, reedy voice. "I can forgive you. But to stop what is coming now, requires more. It requires all our power. Mine. Hers. Yours. Those others."

"Help me," Araña said to the Elder One, "help me direct my magic, help me overcome the evil that was done here."

She took his thin little hand again, and he in turn took Truman Lloyd's. Lisa instinctively moved toward them, urging Bill and Jerry and old Jefe along, pleading with her eyes for them to follow her.

They did, and soon all stood in a tight little group facing the horror that was by now only a very few yards away, its miasma of charnel fog blocking their view of the arroyo and the desert beyond. Araña took in a wheezing breath and cast her voice onto the wind, chanting, singing. Bill shook Lisa's arm to get her to look at him.

"He's channeling his power through her," he whispered, "adding his power to hers. I can feel it."

But Lisa didn't need to be told this. She could feel it too. It was like a kind of electric charge, coming through one's feet from the sandy ground, as if the primal Earth Mother herself were pouring her essence up into their bodies. Despite the fact that the black horror from the arroyo was nearly upon them, the feeling of this directed *power* was the most exhiliarating thing she had ever felt; if she died now, right here, with this sensation coursing through her bones, maybe it would be all right.

"Look," Jerry whispered, to no one in particular. He was staring, terrified, not at the horror that had surged up and stood poised to fasten itself upon them, but at Araña herself. Lisa followed his gaze and had no idea how to think about what she saw.

For a moment it wasn't an old woman standing there.

It was the unspeakable arachnid contours of a huge spider, standing on end. A tarantula, as big as Araña herself. It *was*, Lisa realized in a moment of epiphany, Araña herself. The vision passed, and in a moment it was the old Indian woman after all whose shape Lisa saw outlined against the nighted horror from the arroyo, which was now surging across the last few yards remaining.

When it was practically upon Araña it shot tendrils of rotten-smelling fog out to form a sort of cowl about her head, and Lisa knew as surely as she had ever known anything in her life that the thing was going to decapitate the old woman, and worse. Watching with a sick kind of fascination, Lisa only hoped that in the final moment she would be able to close her eyes quickly enough, and not have to see. The thing would take off the woman's head, then would hurl itself instantly across to engulf them all. Too late, too late. Forget about the rest of your life. It was all going to end now. Now. What a terrible word, *now!* And in that moment, when death for them all was inevitable, Araña's chanting voice rose to a shriek, and the little alien creature gave a convulsive jerk, and the black horror swelled to hideous size, and Lisa's mind simply shut down, refused to accept any more input. She took her son's hand, and Bill's, and drew a deep breath and closed her eyes. It was all over.

Maybe the pain would be brief.

But in the next moment she realized that it really *was* all over.

Opening her eyes, she blinked away the tears that she hadn't even known she was shedding, and saw nothing between her and the arroyo but a vast covering, on the sandy ground, of something that looked like jet-black powder. The breeze stirred it, made little swirls in it, and let it lie.

And all was silence.

Araña stood, regal and indomitable, in the morning light, her rags riffling about her. The Elder One stood beside her, expressionless, calm, his great almond eyes regarding the scene with apparent equanimity. Truman Lloyd stood there looking simply stunned, speechless, as did Jerry and Bill. Old Jefe jittered from one foot to the other, muttering incomprehensibly to himself. Lisa herself just felt numb, as if her brain had been overloaded. But it was she who broke the silence.

"It's really gone," she said, not knowing whether it was a statement or a question.

"Yes," Araña said.

"You *did* it," Jerry said.

"Not me," Araña said. "Not alone." She pointed to the Elder One. "Him." She made a gesture taking in the sky, the desert. "Spirit-brothers. The kachinas that walk in the silence. All. All helped."

"I can't believe we're still alive," Bill said, taking Lisa's hand.

Lisa started to say, "I know——" but her voice was drowned out by another, harsher sound.

It was the sound of rifles being readied to fire, and the heavy, uncompromising sound of tramping feet.

Lisa looked up to see a gathering of uniformed men, weapons trained ahead of them, all around. An officer stepped out from their midst. Lisa couldn't remember for sure, but she thought the insignia on his collar meant he was a captain.

"Don't anybody move," the man said, gesturing for his men to close in from behind. "You're all under military arrest."

36

So, Jerry thought: this is how it ends. Here, in a little town in New Mexico, with troops sticking guns in your face, and no way out. Nursing a sick, hopeless feeling in his gut, he had just a moment's reflection that he was only eighteen and not guaranteed by any means to see nineteen, when he realized that it was his mom he should be thinking about. She looked shocked, stricken, defeated, and she sent these looks straight to him, because it was obvious what she was thinking: *What's going to happen to my son?*

Bill was just standing there with his hands half up, half down, as if he was afraid to move. Not a bad idea, this fear, Jerry thought; it could maybe keep you alive a little longer. The old Indian woman looked at the soldiers with her same old unreadable expression; who could tell, in a million years, what she might be thinking? Old Jefe just keep tottering from one foot to the other, mumbling to himself. The man they called Truman Lloyd, looking at the soldiers, had an expression Jerry found hard to fathom, a sort of tired familiarity. And the alien creature himself just stood there on his thin little legs, regarding the scene with perfect imperturbability.

Jerry, his eyes feeling moist, thought: Just when I was about to make it big, putting together that pile of bones, the first alien artifact ever, except for whatever these military and government people have hidden away. Just when we were about to boogie out of here with the most important archaelogical find in history. Just when I was ready to start filling out those college applications. Just when I was going to see how things would work out for Mom, with her new life. And now it all ends here among a cretinous bunch of soldiers. Not fair. Not goddamned fair at all.

The captain, who was tall and thin and whose nametag on his uniform said FENSTER, moved toward them, bringing his men with him. "You people will all have to come with us. Line up right along here." He gestured with his rifle, drawing an imaginary line in the field. "Anybody else in the house there?"

Jerry shot a look at his mom.

"No," she said, her voice sounding shellshocked. "That's my house. There's nobody else, just us."

"Well, if there's anybody hiding in there we'll find out," Captain Fenster said, "when we come back through for the next sweep. Nobody's getting away. Now you people move out, let's go, we don't have all day."

They lined up with Bill in front, then Truman Lloyd, then Jerry and his mom, and the Elder One behind her and Araña behind him, with old Jefe bringing up the rear. The soldiers formed a line parallel to them, to the left, and Captain Fenster motioned for them all to get moving. The whole group began walking toward the road, angling onto the driveway but bypassing the house, and when they got to the end of the drive they continued south down Old Roswell Road toward the intersection with Camposanto. In the early light it was all eerie, unreal, this business of being marched toward the middle of town by a bunch of troops. Jerry felt as if his whole grasp of reality had just been turned inside-out. He thought that some of the soldiers may have felt the same way, for a different reason; they were staring incredulously at the alien creature and muttering among themselves, until the captain silenced them with an icy stare.

But up in front of the line Bill was turning around as he walked, and saying something to Truman Lloyd: "Are you going to tell us now? Are you going to tell us what the hell is going on?"

"Yeah, as a matter of fact I am going to tell you," Lloyd answered wearily.

"No talking," Captain Fenster said, marching alongside them.

"Just for your information, you tinhorn little shit," Lloyd said, "I'm Truman Lloyd with Group Epsilon, I carry a Cosmic Top Secret clearance, and I'm in charge of this operation, and I'm ordering you to stand down. The plan to contain the town is rescinded."

Captain Fenster laughed nastily. "I never heard of you or Group whatever-you-call-it. And for *your* information, mister, I take my orders from Major Jenckes."

"I'm sure you do," Lloyd said, "and he takes his orders from me."

"I told you," Captain Fenster said, "no talking." And he shoved Lloyd with the butt of his rifle. "Just keep it moving."

They marched along through the empty streets, passing Camposanto Road and Piñon Street and heading toward Camino del Sol. To the left and right, off down the sidestreets, Jerry heard sounds of motors, shouting voices, tramping feet, and caught glimpses of military trucks and jeeps and groups of people, some uniformed, some not.

"What exactly did you mean," Bill was saying over his shoulder to Truman Lloyd, "about containing the town?"

The captain shoved Bill flathanded on the shoulder. "I said no talking, you people. I'm not going to tell you again."

"Hasn't it occurred to you," Lloyd asked the captain, "that if I'm who I say I am, and you find out that I'm who I say I am when we meet up in a few minutes with Major Jenckes coming in on Camino del Sol from the west—hasn't it occurred to you that those captain's bars can come off a lot more easily than they went on?"

"Is that a threat, mister?" the captain asked.

"It damned sure is," Lloyd said.

"How do you know," Captain Fenster asked, glaring at Lloyd, "that Major Jenckes is coming in from the west on Camino del Sol?" A military helicopter roared by overhead, nearly drowning him out.

"Because I ordered the whole operation," Lloyd said. "Including those choppers up there, backup air surveillance. The order went out as a Top Secret NOPAL directive. That classification codename itself is classified, by the way. I wouldn't know that if I didn't have a clearance at that level. My clearance is higher than the President's."

"If this is true," the captain said, "and you're divulging classified information in front of people who aren't cleared, you're going to be in a world of shit, mister."

"I already am," Lloyd replied as the line of people continued to trudge forward beside the troops. "But for right now, I am in charge of this operation, by God, and if you give me any more crap about talking to these people here, I'm going to see to it that you're not Major Jenckes's favorite person, so you'd better shut up and leave me the hell alone."

"I'm going to have your ass," the captain said, "you watch and see."

"Fine," Lloyd said. "Meanwhile—" He addressed himself to Bill Weston. "You asked what I meant by containment of the town. It means exactly what it sounds like. The whole town, right now even as we speak, is surrounded by the military. Some are coming cross-country like the ones out at the arroyo, some are coming in on the roads. They have orders to take everybody in town into custody and relocate them to a secret underground installation north of Holloman Air Force Base. An internment site."

Bill, without stopping, turned half around to glare at him. "You mean a fucking concentration camp."

"Well," Lloyd said, "yeah, basically. I hate to call it that."

"Do you?" Bill replied. "Make you feel a little ashamed, does it?"

"That's not the point right now," Lloyd said.

"And if it's not asking too much," Bill said, "can you tell me why the government in its limitless wisdom finds it necessary to corral a whole town full of people and move them to a concentration camp? I presume it's for the great and general good, but silly old me, I just feel like I need to hear a reason why."

"It's because of him," Lloyd said, gesturing back toward the alien creature. "And other things."

"What other things?" Jerry asked. He was a little afraid to talk in front of the soldiers, but he just couldn't keep quiet any longer.

"He—had children by some of the women in the town," Lloyd said, directing his answer to Bill rather than Jerry. "You've seen at least one of them. So have you," he added, looking back toward Jerry. Jerry thought he meant him, but then realized that Lloyd was talking to his mom.

Jerry heard her whisper, behind him: "My God."

"The girl at the diner," Bill said.

"Yes," Lloyd said. "And others. I don't even know how many others. That's why—"

"That's why you're moving everybody to an interment camp," Bill said. "To sort through all the people and find out which ones might be the—and none of us will ever get out, because you people don't want the public to know. We'll be permanent prisoners."

"Now wait a minute," Lloyd said. "You heard me say, to the captain there, that I'm rescinding the order."

"You changed your mind," Jerry said. At first he had felt a little presumptuous, an eighteen-year-old kid talking to someone who was probably one of the most powerful secret operatives in the whole government. Who am I, Jerry asked himself, to talk to this guy? But in the next moment the answer came to him. I have every right, he told himself, to talk to the guy. I'm in this right along with everybody else. I'm going to be taken away to a camp, and I'm probably going to croak there. And by God, that gives me the right to talk to this asshole as an equal. "So why did you? Why did you change your mind?"

Lloyd flashed an expression over his shoulder that astonished Jerry. He expected the man to be cold, indifferent, impersonal. But the look he got was disarmingly like the appeal of one genuine human being to another. "I don't know, son, if I can even explain it. The creature walking back there behind your mother, he's the reason. He—what can I say? Gave me a new vision. He made me understand that I'd made a mistake. He made me see that my whole life has been a mistake."

"This is beginning to sound like a revival meeting," Bill flung back over his shoulder, in a tone of biting sarcasm. "So hallelujah, you seen the light."

"Call it whatever you want," Lloyd said. "I'm not a religious man, but this *was* something like a religious conversion."

"Zen enlightenment," Bill offered, still sarcastically. "A flash of satori."

"You're closer to the truth than you know," Lloyd said. "Anyway, I realized, too late, after I'd already made my call and put out the order, that I can't be part of this thing any more. It's dead wrong."

"Fine time to figure it out," Jerry said.

"Yeah, isn't it?" Lloyd replied. There was something of a profound sadness in his voice, a sadness too deep for tears. He sounded like a man who had just realized he had committed an unpardonable crime, and maybe indeed he had.

But now the group had come to Camino del Sol, where a much larger contingent of troops had gathered on the west side of the intersection. At the limits of vision to the west, roadblocks were up, their lights flashing. Military vehicles were buzzing east along the street, and up and down the cross streets, and the air was alive with voices, some shouting orders, some shrill with protest. Further down Camino del Sol, Jerry could see people being led along in groups, at gunpoint. Evidently the soldiers had taken them right out of their homes.

"Captain Fenster," a voice said, "give me your report."

Jerry turned around to see a red-faced, beefy-looking officer wearing the gold insignia of a major.

Captain Fenster saluted him snappily; the major returned the salute. "First sweep of Sector Seven is complete, sir," the captain said. "Personnel losses are still being evaluated."

Truman Lloyd stepped up to the major, who started to turn away from him and ignore him. But Lloyd followed him. "Major Jenckes, I'm Truman Lloyd. You're to report to me."

The major stared at him in silence for a moment, then spat on the street at Lloyd's feet. "The hell you say." Jerry, watching, reflected that under ordinary circumstances this whole thing would have been pretty funny, like some half-assed corny movie. But these were not ordinary circumstances.

"I'm not going to tolerate any insubordination, major," Lloyd said. "I'm in charge here."

"Not any more," the major said. "My orders are to—never mind what my orders are. You don't have the need to know."

"I'm in charge here," Lloyd reiterated, "and I'm ordering you to stand down. The Top Secret NOPAL directive is rescinded. The operation is cancelled. Cancelled, God damn it!"

"*You're* cancelled," Major Jenckes said, and placed the muzzle of his service revolver square in the middle of Lloyd's forehead.

37

Mother of God, Lisa thought: he's going to shoot him, he's going to pull that trigger and shoot him in the head. It's going to happen right in front of my eyes, right here in the middle of the street, and I can't take it, I can't take seeing anyone killed.

"Major Jenckes," one of the soldiers called out.

The major's eyes cut to one side, without his moving the service revolver off Lloyd's forehead. "What? What do you want, corporal?"

"Where's the old woman who was here with these people?" the soldier asked.

Again the major let his eyes roam without shifting his hand. "How the hell am I supposed to know? If anybody gets away, somebody's going to answer to me. Where's Captain Fenster?"

"Here, sir," the captain said, stepping up closer.

"Check it out, captain," the major said, "and there'd better not be anybody missing. This isn't any goddamn Easter egg hunt we're on here. Report back to me within five minutes, and you'd better have the right answers."

"I'm on it, sir," Captain Fenster said. He turned to look at the rest of his captives. "All right, where did the old woman get off to?"

Lisa watched as Bill and Jerry looked at each other and shrugged. "I didn't see any old woman," Bill said. "Jerry, did you see an old w——"

The captain swung the butt of his rifle up so fast into Bill's midsection that Lisa's eye could barely follow what he had done. Bill let out a terrible-sounding wheeze and doubled over, groaning.

"Leave him alone, you son of a bitch," Jerry said.

"You want some of this, kid?" the captain asked, brandishing the rifle.

Lisa stepped between them. "Sorry, but you're going to have to do me first," she said to the captain. She couldn't believe she was doing this, saying this. But it was true, right down to her bones: she was ready to die before seeing anything happen to her son. Out of the corner of her eye she saw the alien creature standing nearby, watching; she couldn't read any expression whatever on his face. Old Jefe was standing next to him, still jittering back and forth like some spastic puppet.

"Go ahead, captain," Bill said, straightening back up and coughing. "You heard the lady. C'mon. Show us how you can manhandle an unarmed woman for God and country."

"I think you're going to have to kill us all," Lisa said, "if you do anything to any of us, *cabrón.*"

The captain's face reddened with rage. "You spic bitch. If *cabrón* means what I think it does——"

Bill managed to cough again and laugh at the same time. "If my high school Spanish serves me, I think it means something like scum-sucking flatulating dripping-asshole baby-buggering shitface. Of course they don't usually get to words like that till the second semester."

The captain spluttered and fumed. "I can't believe you people are mouthing off to me! Haven't you got the picture yet that we're not kidding here?"

"To hell with this," old Jefe spoke up. "I'm gonna go find a drink." And he started ambling off.

"Hey! Hold it right there, old man," the captain said, swinging his rifle up at the ready.

The old man went shuffling away, muttering.

"I said stop right there," the captain shouted behind him.

"*Me vale tu chingada madre*," Jefe said, and didn't stop.

And it happened. The muzzle of the rifle roared, flamed. Jefe Sandoval staggered once, then dropped in his tracks on the street, and was still.

The captain turned the rifle back toward the rest of them. "I *mean* it, people. Get back in line."

All Lisa could think was: I've never seen anybody die before. Sick with revulsion, she took Jerry and Bill both by the hand, and they lined up near the alien creature, and near where Truman Lloyd was standing. Lloyd seemingly had won a momentary reprieve, as Major Jenckes had backed the revolver off a few inches, pointing it skyward. Lloyd took the opportunity to wipe his brow.

"Fenster, you dumb shit," the major said. "This is supposed to be a simple, clean operation."

"This is supposed to be no operation at all," Lloyd said.

"I thought I made it clear I'm not taking orders from you," the major said, angling the revolver toward Lloyd again. "Captain Fenster, take this man and have him placed under armed guard."

He paused, waiting. Lisa looked at the paving beneath her feet, trying to calm herself.

"Captain, I gave you an order," the major barked. "Now get mov—what the hell!"

Lisa looked up to see the major staring at Captain Fenster. Following the major's gaze, she stared at the captain too, trying to comprehend what she was seeing. At the periphery of her senses she was vaguely aware of rings of faces, sounds of voices, people down the street being herded into the back of a canvas-covered truck—but what captured her attention was what had attached itself to Captain Fenster.

At first glance she thought he had wrapped some sort of brown, furry covering about his upper body, covering himself from mid-chest up to the top of his head. It seemed to cling to him. From beneath it, barely audible, came a muffled cry that could well have been fear, or rage, or surprise, or pain, or any combination of those things. The captain's whole body shuddered once, then he began to sway on his feet. The furry covering dropped off, hitting the pavement with a heavy *plop* and scuttering away on a fiddling confusion of legs. It was a tarantula, but it was the size of a large dog, and it was off between two buildings and out of sight in seconds. When the captain's body collapsed, Lisa could see, all too clearly, that the throat had been chewed away. When the body finished falling, the head ended up resting at an angle that Lisa wouldn't have thought possible. She was going to be sick.

A ruddy-faced Major Jenckes was yelling something, but just then a pair of military helicopters went grinding by, their shadows long and ominous in the rising sun.

"What's *that?*" Jerry shouted as the noise subsided a little.

"Army choppers," Bill shouted back.

"No. *That.*"

Lisa followed Jerry's gaze upward. What indeed *was* that?

Directly overhead, something hung in the sky above the town—far, far above, just visible through a thinning haze of dust and sand left by the choppers. The thing in the sky was silvery, round, distant and tiny at first. But it was growing in apparent size.

Growing fast, because it was dropping straight down, blotting the morning sky out as it came.

38

The object plummeted so precipitantly that Lisa had the giddy sensation that it was simply going to crush them all like insects. At this point she was so weary, so heartsick, that she didn't particularly care one way or the other. But she couldn't take her eyes off the thing coming out of the sky.

Starting off as just a moon-sized disk overhead, it grew in apparent size until it blotted out the whole sky. It dropped to within perhaps two hundred feet of the ground, perhaps less, rotating as it descended. Then it stopped, hanging motionless in the air like a great iron lid over the town, over the desert. Off in the distance, to the north, the two helicopters had swung low to the ground, swerving wildly, trying to avoid the thing from the sky, trying to regain control, but too late—first one, then the other chopper crashed somewhere outside of town, sending billows of black, angry-looking smoke running like fingers of fog along the underside of the object that had arrived.

Lisa still couldn't take her eyes off the thing. A low hum filled the air as it hovered there, but her ears barely registered the sound. This was an experience for the eye.

The underside of the object was a sort of dull silver color, obviously metallic but looking paradoxically soft, almost quilted. There was a complex pattern of intersecting lines, squares, less definable shapes extending all along the bottom of the craft, lines and shapes that seemed to shift and melt together in a way that bewitched the eye, confused the mind. Lisa looked out along the contours of the thing, trying in vain to find any edges; the craft simply stretched out of sight in all directions, blocking out the morning sunlight altogether and substituting a kind of pallid incandescence whose source one couldn't even discern exactly.

In time it would be general knowledge that the object hanging low over the New Mexico desert that morning was roughly the size of Rhode Island.

"Mother ship," Jerry whispered.

"Yes," a reedy-thin voice said. Lisa turned to see the little alien creature regarding the rest of them with his usual placidity of expression.

Incredibly, Major Jenckes pointed his service revolver at the craft overhead and fired a shot.

"Don't be a fucking idiot," Truman Lloyd said.

"Yeah," Lisa said, "don't you know what's happening? Don't you know what this *means*? A ship from another world?" She felt her face break into an ironic grin, and she directed her remarks both to Truman Lloyd and to the major, nodding upward toward the alien craft. "Cover *this* up."

"I'm not in the coverup business any more," Lloyd murmured, nearly too low for her to hear.

The air beneath the hovering object was at first alive with human voices, voices echoing from all over town—amazed voices, frightened voices. But gradually the turmoil died down to an awed silence, and all that was left was the low hum of the craft itself, almost like a bass pedal on a pipe organ. The soldiers stood with mouths open, staring upward. Lisa and Bill, Truman Lloyd and Jerry did the same. What was there to do but stand and stare? You couldn't run away. Wherever you might go, the object from the sky would still be hanging over you.

Everyone waited and watched. Some, no doubt, prayed quietly.

The object hovered, its underside coruscating with shifting patterns of lines, ellipses, squares, diamonds, irregular curves and unnameable shapes, the unthinkable routine of an alien mindset. The bass hum filled the air, echoed through the streets. All else was silence.

And at length something changed.

From a spot on the underside of the great disk, a column of pale orange light came down like a spotlight, illumining the Elder One, whose great black almond-shaped eyes shone almost preternaturally. From somewhere down the sidestreets, people screamed.

The alien creature spoke, and his voice carried as if he were speaking through a microphone, as if speakers were broadcasting the sound. Whatever was magnifying his words, Lisa reflected, was in the beam itself.

"I am speaking to the people of this country," the Elder One said. "You will speak, in turn, to the rest of your world. Be assured that we mean you no harm."

None of this can really be happening, Lisa thought: I've simply gone insane. This is all a fever-dream.

Gradually the babble of human voices died down again, and the alien creature continued speaking, in stilted-sounding but flawless English.

"We have momentarily taken control of your television networks. There is a secret communications center, operated by your government, that will try to block our overriding of your television transmissions; they will be unable to do so. For a brief time, our signal alone will be seen and heard on your stations."

"Neat," Jerry murmured.

"Ssh," Lisa said.

"Momentous things, some good and some bad, have happened here in the New Mexico desert this morning," the Elder One went on. "Four centuries ago, when the explorer

Francisco Vásquez de Coronado and his soldiers were first crossing this land, *we* were here, in an arroyo near this spot, visiting the Native American people who lived here at the time. We had been visiting them for thousands of years, and teaching them things. Things that many of you would call desert magic, things that we simply call power. One of Coronado's captains, a man named Carlos de Moya, witnessed such an exchange between the Indians and our people, and killed one of us. An Indian medicine man put a powerful curse upon the spot. I am aware that many of you do not believe in such curses. You think of them as primitive superstition. Nevertheless, the Indian evocation in the arroyo caused something terrible to come alive there, something that waited, dormant, over the years for the cycles of the stars to come around right for its awakening. This has been coming for some time. Just today, this morning, it fully awoke in the arroyo, and came for its revenge."

"My God," Bill whispered to Lisa. "They *know* all this."

"But for a few courageous people," the Elder One continued, "the horror would have prevailed." He leaned at the edge of the orange beam and took Lisa by the hand and pulled her into the spotlight, and motioned with spidery movements of his hands for the others to come too. Bill and Jerry and Araña stepped into the beam and stood beside Lisa. A diffident Truman Lloyd stood just outside the beam, looking nervous. Under the circumstances, Lisa was only mildly surprised to see Araña among them once again. The orange beam produced an incredibly subtle sort of tingle on Lisa's hands and face; it was not an unpleasant sensation, just unfamiliar.

"Humans alone," the Elder One said, "could not have stopped the curse from unfolding, the horror from coming. I alone could not have stopped it. It was possible to stop it, but only working together. Our power. Your power."

"What would have happened—" Jerry started to ask.

"Jerry!" Lisa said, embarrassed that he would presume to speak up. Good God, according to the alien creature, they were on television all over the country, and there was no reason to suppose that the creature wanted any of *them* to say anything.

"It is all right," the Elder One said.

"What would have happened," Jerry asked, "if we—if it hadn't been stopped?"

The Elder One blinked his great dark eyes. "Quite simply, from its feeding and gathering itself, it would have grown larger, stronger, hungrier, swelling to thousands of times its original size, dividing, multiplying, growing, and it would have killed eveyone for hundreds of miles around. In time, unchecked, it might well have destroyed humankind."

Jerry shuddered, swallowing hard. He looked, suddenly, very young and vulnerable.

At that moment Truman Lloyd stepped into the beam and cleared his throat. "May I say something?"

The Elder One placed a tiny hand on Lloyd's hand, and withdrew. "Yes," he said, "please feel free to speak."

"Are we really on television nationwide?" Lloyd asked.

"Yes," the Elder One said.

"Well then," Lloyd said. "My name is Truman Lloyd. I am—or rather I was, until this morning—a high-level covert government operative working for Group Epsilon, an agency so secret that its existence is unknown even to most members of Congress. I have, or had, a Cosmic Top Secret clearance, several notches higher than that of the President of the United States. Right here and right now, in front of the American people, to whom I owe apologies for numerous things, I am about to violate my security oath."

"I'm warning you, Lloyd," Major Jenckes said from the sidelines, "if you divulge classified information—"

The Elder One turned an expressionless face toward Major Jenckes. "You will not interfere."

The major, standing just outside the orange beam, looked apoplectic. "As an officer in the United States Army, I am sworn to defend, against all enemies—damn. Damn! I can't move my arms!"

"You will not interfere," the Elder One repeated.

"As many of you know," Truman Lloyd went on, "a flying saucer was rumored to have crashed between here and Roswell, New Mexico in 1947, and to have been covered up by the United States government. Those rumors are true. To protect political careers and to preserve what I now understand to be a misplaced nationalism, we covered it all up. President Kennedy was assassinated in 1963 to keep the secret. But the crash really happened. The bodies of the alien crew lie preserved, to this day, at Wright-Patterson Air Force Base near Dayton, Ohio. Technological advances beyond calculation have been derived from the wreckage from that crash—microchips, computers, lasers, fiber optics. And other kinds of knowledge. One notable example. There has been a cure for cancer for the past half century. Because the procedure involves medical sophistication of so advanced a nature, so advanced as to make it obviously nonhuman in origin—because of this, the cure is classified Top Secret. I disclose this to the American people, and to all humankind, with a more profound sense of shame than I have ever imagined possible."

He stopped speaking for a moment, as his voice was breaking up, his eyes moist with tears. Lisa was touched to see the Elder One take his hand. Lloyd cleared his throat again and resumed speaking.

"The government has long suspected that not all the crew of the crashed UFO at Roswell were accounted for by the bodies, and by the one known survivor at the time. Accordingly, Group Epsilon sent me here to continue an ongoing investigation."

Listening to this, Lisa suddenly realized that she must have been under surveillance herself, and Bill too. Even here and now, the realization left her with a smoldering sense of having been somehow—violated, abused. The *nerve* of these people!

"Due to, ah, certain aspects of this investigation," Lloyd was saying, "Group Epsilon, under my directive, had the intention of containing the town of Chasco, New Mexico by military force, and relocating the entire population of the town to a secret internment center in the desert north of Holloman Air Force Base, so that no classified information would circulate. Had we relocated this population—nearly a thousand people—none of them would ever have been at liberty to leave the internment camp again. In point of fact, none of them would have lived."

"Christ," Bill exclaimed, giving Lloyd a hard flat-handed shove on the shoulder. "It wasn't just internment. You were going to have all these people killed!"

"Yes, I was," Lloyd said. "At taxpayers' expense. But I changed my mind. Even a first-class asshole can have a change of heart, believe it or not. I no longer work for Group Epsilon, or for any agency of the United States government. I know it's too late to ask for anyone's forgiveness, but I admit my guilt, and I renounce all that I have ever stood for or worked for. Because of this noble creature"—he indicated the Elder One—"I think I have come, very late in life unfortunately, to understand something of the truth."

The Elder One blinked once, twice, and looked square into Lloyd's face. "It is not only Indians," he said to Lloyd and to them all, "who can shapeshift."

Silence fell upon the group for a few moments. At length the Elder One spoke up again.

"My people have great respect for humankind," he said. "I have lived here among you for many years, due to the kind ministrations of this man and others like him." He reached a little outside the beam and drew Paco Rojas into the light. Lisa hadn't even seen him standing there. "I have had to live in secrecy, of course, but I have learned much, and have been enlightened about many things. My people are millions of years older than yours, but living among you I have been enriched. I qualify our admiration for you, however, in the following way."

Here it comes, Lisa thought.

"Your leaders have chosen to follow policies that do not ennoble your race," the Elder One said. "This is not humankind at its best. You are a young species, and though you have come far, you have yet much to learn. Understand this: with regard to the matters of which we speak here this morning, the age of secrecy is over."

"They'll keep covering it all up somehow," Lloyd said.

"Not any more," the Elder One replied. "Now the American people know. By extension, now everyone will know. Everyone will know everything."

"Agencies like Group Epsilon will simply burrow farther underground," Lloyd said, "and take their information with them."

"This will not be tolerated," the Elder One said simply. "The very fact of this encounter," he added, gesturing with his wiry-thin arms, "makes it impossible, now, to deny the truth that your people have deserved to share, and now *will* share. There will be no more covering-up. We live together in the universe. Everyone has the right to know that."

"What happens now?" Lisa asked, startled by the sound of her own voice. She was still having some trouble comprehending the magnitude of all that was happening.

"I am leaving you now," the Elder One said. "I will return. Others will return. We will have a better understanding, your people and mine, in due time."

Something was happening.

Lisa felt the tingling sensation from the orange beam increasing. It was as if the light thickened, changed. It was all they needed, any of them, to get the idea that it was time to step back out of the beam.

Once they were out, and the Elder One stood alone in the spotlight, he turned to them. "We, my people, live long. When I come back, it may not be you, it may be your grandchildren, or their grandchildren, who come to greet me. Live in peace."

And he simply began to dissolve in the beam, which seemed to swirl him upward as he vanished, into the mother ship.

A moment of astonished silence followed. Then Truman Lloyd stepped back into the orange beam.

"Take me too."

Everyone waited.

Nothing happened.

"Take me!" Lloyd shouted.

Nothing happened.

Then, quite suddenly, the beam thickened again, and the contours of Truman Lloyd grew grainy, dim, and swirled upward, vanishing.

Jerry heaved a sigh. "Can't blame him."

"No," Lisa said. "Not for wanting to go with them. How could he stay here any more?"

"Traitorous bastard," Major Jenckes muttered.

Lisa laughed in his face. "Get a life, major."

Jenckes started to say something to her, but without warning the hum in the air increased, and the craft moved itself, instantly, another four or five hundred feet straight up, hovering there for a moment, then shot upward with such speed that it became a small disk, then a speck, then nothing at all, in a matter of four or five seconds.

The scene on the streets of Chasco, New Mexico was one of stunned silence. Soldiers and civilians alike stood there, at a loss, staring at the sky. What was there to do or say?

But on the periphery of the town, coming in from every direction, was something that was going to change all that.

It wasn't military troops this time, but troops of a different kind.

Quite possibly every news van in the Southwest was converging on Chasco, drivers and passengers yelling and horns honking. In control of their own transmissions again, they were ready to pursue *the* story, the news story of all time.

Even though, essentially, it had already been told.

39

Life went on, after a fashion.

People still got up in the morning, still went to work. The bills still came due, and the weekend still came just in time.

But things would never be quite the same again.

Following the television disclosures about Coronado's party, a scholar of fifteenth-century history at the University of Toledo, in Spain, managed to find, among a boxful of uncatalogued papers at the Biblioteca Nacional in Madrid, a set of letters written in 1547 by Don Carlos de Moya verifying the story of the sidetrip to Arroyo Encantado, at the time when Coronado's men were trying to build a bridge to cross the Pecos River, or the Río Cicuyé as it was then called. Even couched in a language reflecting the overblown piety of the times, these letters made it quite clear that Don Carlos de Moya had indeed been witness to an alien encounter in New Mexico.

This corroboration lent a special significance to the set of diminutive bones newly residing in the Smithsonian, where the crashed Roswell UFO eventually came to rest as well.

And the young man who had rearticulated those bones had little trouble getting into the University of New Mexico in

Albuquerque and winning a hefty scholarship to pursue a degree in biology. Jerry started chasing his dream.

More than one dream, in fact. While staying on in Chasco during those first few months after what has come to be called the Event, Jerry met an intriguing young lady, a dark-eyed part-Hispanic beauty who had been working in Lucinda's Diner. They discovered they were natural soulmates, and now Jerry drives back to Chasco just about every weekend to see Yolanda, who plans to start attending college herself. They intend to get married one day, and Lisa finds herself speculating pleasantly about her no doubt dark-eyed grandchildren.

Lisa herself got that job she had applied for, and has remained in Chasco for the time being anyway. She has bought the house out by Arroyo Encantado, and she walks in the dry wash sometimes, thinking about all that happened there. For a few days, there had been an ash-gray residue scattered over the chaparral nearby and in the arroyo itself, but, in all the excitement, by the time anyone got around to thinking about having the stuff analyzed chemically, it had disappeared altogether, whether dispersed by the desert winds or by other forces. Lisa has a nice life in her house near the arroyo, and has never heard or seen La Llorona again. It's a pity in some ways, because she feels she rather understands the woman.

Not long after the Event, Bill succeeded in getting a position at a newspaper in Santa Rosa, and commutes back and forth between there and Chasco. He and Lisa grow ever closer, and quite possibly they'll get married one of these days. Jerry and Yolanda hope they will. Bill has come to use whatever psychic sensitivities he possesses on more mundane things now, but happier things, like trying to sense what Lisa might like him to buy her for her birthday or for Christmas.

Day-to-day things in general turned out anything but humdrum, though. In the wake of the Event, the political spectacle quickly came to be a fulltime occupation just to watch on television. For most people, it got to be nearly impossible to keep up with the ever-frenzied round of impeachments, resignations, Congressional hearings, trials, federal lawsuits. Scarcely a news broadcast went by without a story of some former secret operative or other government official committing suicide. Constitutional amendments having to do with unreasonable keeping of governmental secrets were on the horizon, and Group Epsilon was no more. Truman Lloyd of course hasn't been seen again, which is probably the way he would want it. Needless to say, the Elder One hasn't been seen again either, and one gathers that Paco Rojas, in his colorful and intriguing Emporium, is a lonely man. He follows the newscasts nonetheless, fascinated with the repercussions.

But beyond all the political turmoil, the world has changed in many other ways. People have simply had to gain a different *vision* of the world now. The truth was sobering when it came: humankind is not alone. Native Americans may have known this for thousands of years, but most other people needed some convincing. But the new vision did come, and in countless subtle ways it changed the way most people thought about just about everything. It had to. And now, even if you weren't one of the tens of millions of people to see the craft descend, the video production of that mother ship hanging over the New Mexico desert just doesn't leave any room to go back to things altogether the way they were; all you have to do is watch that video, listen to those reedy syllables pronounced by a being from another world, and you return to your own routine in your own world with a very different perspective.

Lisa feels, these days, a little surprised—just a squitch—that she hasn't ever seen Araña again. At least she hasn't, so far as she knows. One can look at Araña at times and not know it. Lisa understands this very well. Once when she and Bill were visiting Jefe Sandoval's grave in the old cemetery on Camposanto Road, they thought they saw an uncommonly large tarantula scurry down a hole nearby, but they weren't sure, and anyway, it might really have been only a spider. Bill looked thoughtful at the time, but seemed disinclined to talk about it, and Lisa didn't press the point.

Sometimes, either with Bill or alone, she walks in the arroyo in the evening, when the desert sky is gathering a mystical frosting of stars, and she scuffs the sand and thinks about the tragic little creature who died there, and thinks about the wailing apparition who recently floated and shimmered there, and thinks about the horror that came forth there and very nearly prevailed. And she thinks about what stopped it: desert magic, timeless magic from the icy stars. And she wonders how she could have been witness to all this and still maintain presence of mind.

But then she realizes that the human creature is a much more resilient being than one might think.

We are made, after all, of stardust.

AUTHOR'S NOTE

Living in the desertlands of New Mexico, one sometimes hears rumors to the effect that alien UFO crash survivors have been hidden away by Indians. Frankly, if this should turn out to be true, it wouldn't surprise me in the least. Talk to certain Native Americans, especially among the Hopi, and they will tell you that there are Indians who themselves did not originate on this planet. Who really knows? In any case, as part Native American myself, and someone deeply interested in the whole UFO question, I am vividly aware that Indians have always had very special understandings about extraterrestrial life. In Native American cosmology and spiritual tradition, there is nothing strange about the notion of visitations from other worlds, in an ancient and fathomless universe that is itself a living and connected web of intelligence. We are not alone, and never have been.

——DRB

About the Author

DONALD R. BURLESON's first novel *Flute Song*, about the Roswell UFO crash of 1947, was a finalist for the Bram Stoker Award in 1997. His short fiction has appeared in *Twilight Zone, 2AM, The Magazine of Fantasy and Science Fiction, Deathrealm, Grue, Lore, Terminal Fright, Wicked Mystic, Potpourri,* and many other magazines, as well as in dozens of anthologies, including *Post Mortem, MetaHorror, Best New Horror* (Vol. 1 and 5), *Dark Terrors 4, The New Lovecraft Circle, Made in Goatswood, Return to Lovecraft Country, Singers of Strange Songs, The Cthulhu Cycle, The Azathoth Cycle, 100 Creepy Little Creature Stories, 100 Fiendish Little Frightmares, 100 Ghastly Little Ghost Stories, 100 Tiny Tales of Terror, 100 Vicious Little Vampire Stories,* and *100 Wicked Little Witch Stories.* Burleson's largest collection of short stories is *Beyond the Lamplight.* He and his wife Mollie (herself a writer) moved from Merrimack, New Hampshire to Roswell, New Mexico in 1996.

Photo by Mollie L. Burleson
at the International UFO Museum and Research Center